BENGAL
STATION

BENGAL STATION

ERIC BROWN

Five Star • Waterville, Maine

First Edition
First Printing: July 2004

Published in 2004 in conjunction with
Tekno Books and Ed Gorman.

Set in 11 pt. Plantin.

Printed in the United States on permanent paper.

ISBN 1-59414-212-2 (hc : alk. paper)

*To FINN SINCLAIR,
with all my love.*

ONE

Vaughan stepped from the *Pride of Xerxes* into the sultry, spice-laden night of Bengal Station. For the past hour he'd made his way through the voidship with his security team, scanning the departing passengers for subversives and stowaways. The *Xerxes* had proved clean and his shift was over for another day. Still in scan-mode, he hurried ahead of his six-man cadre, eager to be away from their clamouring thoughts. He'd known them too long, too well, and the contents of their minds—their shallow hopes and desires, their fears and petty prejudices—he found almost unbearable.

The guards boarded a truck and set off for the terminal building: they understood his need for privacy at the end of a shift. As the truck carried them away, their cerebral signatures diminished, melded with the dull mind-hum of the Station's twenty-five million citizens.

He reached up to the back of his head and withdrew his augmentation-pin. He felt the thread of the pin unscrew from its console, the vibration conducted through the bone of his skull. Instantly the mind-hum from the inhabitants of the Station became muted, manageable.

Next to the *Xerxes*, a sleek voidliner squatted in its docking ring. The *Hindustan* had phased in two days ago, but Vaughan's boss, Director Weiss, had pulled him and his team from boarding her. That might not have been so suspicious, were it not for the fact that it was the third ship out of Verkerk's World that Weiss had put into quarantine that week without a word of explanation.

Vaughan looked across the deck of the spaceport. Beyond the perimeter fence and laser cordons, the city that sprawled across the upper-deck was a cultural amalgam of Calcutta and Bangkok: a patchwork of residential apartments, hotels, parks, and gardens, shot through with long roads and crowded pedestrian walkways. The latest polycarbon architecture designed in India and Thailand created a state-of-the-art skyline, while overhead fliers raced along color-coded flight corridors which twisted through the night sky like red and blue streamers. Beneath his feet were twenty levels, each crammed with more than a million citizens. The Station was a vast anvil-shaped hive situated in the Bay of Bengal, midway between India and Myanmar.

He was about to make his way over to the terminal building when he heard a roadster approach from behind him. The open-topped vehicle swerved around the bulk of the *Xerxes* and braked.

Director Weiss sat at the wheel, staring at Vaughan with an expression that appeared habitually aggressive. He was a big man, his athleticism gone to fat, with a full head of silver-gray hair and great fists bedecked with ostentatious rings like gold nuggets.

More disturbingly, Weiss was shielded—a disturbing emptiness where his thoughts should have been—and Vaughan could not get over his suspicion that the Director had something to hide. Especially since his ban on boarding the last three ships from Verkerk's World . . .

"Vaughan." Weiss's manner was always brusque to the point of discourtesy. "All A-OK? Anything to report?"

"The ship's clean." He passed Weiss the screader on which he'd logged his report on the *Xerxes*, then handed over the case containing his augmentation-pin.

Weiss had started coming out to meet Vaughan and take his pin a week ago—as if he didn't trust the telepath to hand in his augmentation to stores at the end of every shift.

Weiss nodded, started his roadster, and drove off. Vaughan smiled to himself: he was on to the bastard. Last week he'd contacted an old acquaintance in the Station Police force and asked him to run a few checks on the Director.

He set off across the deck. His shift finished, he could relax for a few hours. He'd go to Nazruddin's on Chandi Road, grab something to eat, and have a few beers, wind down after another long, stressful night.

Seconds later his handset chimed. He raised the device, which clamped his wrist like a splint, and tapped the receive stud.

A lined Indian face stared up from his metacarpal screen. "Mr. Vaughan?" the old man said. "You do not know me, but I am Dr. Rao."

Vaughan nodded. "I've heard a lot about you, Rao."

"I am calling about Tiger. She is ill. Very ill."

Vaughan's stomach turned. "What's wrong with her?"

"Please, when you get here, I will explain everything. Tiger wants to see you."

"Where are you?" He was aware of his pulse racing.

"Board service elevator 75 from the 'port," Rao instructed. "Drop to level 12. At the exit hatch, there will be someone to guide you the rest of the way. *Namaste*, Mr. Vaughan."

"Rao—"

But the Indian doctor had cut the connection.

Vaughan hurried across the ringing deck towards elevator 75 and dropped to level 12, wondering what the hell had happened to Tiger. Ill, Rao had said. Very ill . . .

The flimsy metal cage carried him into the depths of Bengal Station with a squeal of cables and pulleys. He fell

ERIC BROWN

so fast that the lighted levels flicked by between the dark
bars of the decks like the individual frames of an old film.
He glimpsed frenzied activity on every level. Avenues
stretched into the distance, narrowing with the perspective,
and even at this midnight hour every street was crowded.
Noise strobed as they descended, the collective hubbub of
thousands of citizens going about their business, and along
with the noise came the tidal wave of brain-din. Unaugmented,
he was unable to read individual minds, but he caught
impressions, notes of subtle emotion. He likened the effect
to hearing a hundred individual musical instruments in the
distance, each one playing a different tune so that the
overall effect was a clashing discord.

He'd known Tiger for three years—a skinny, one-legged
street kid with a mind as pure and simple as a Thai folk
song, a mind that filled him with joy at its innocence, and
which at the same time swamped him with regret.

That first night outside Nazruddin's she'd offered him
charo in her high, piping voice, and he'd caught the melody
of her innocent mind. He was hit by a wave of familiarity,
quickly followed by pain. Her cerebral signature reminded
him of Holly's—and he was taken back years, to a time he
would rather have forgotten.

He'd looked down at a girl of about twelve or thirteen.
The first thing that struck him was her seamless Thai face
beneath the universal pudding-bowl haircut: big eyes, snub
nose, lips that seemed swollen beyond sensuality to the
point of pain. She wore a shrunken t-shirt and dirty shorts.

Then Vaughan saw the hatchet job some backstreet surgeon
had made of her amputation. Her right leg terminated
above the knee in an ugly pucker of scar tissue.

He'd bought a gram of charo from the kid, paying over
the odds. He'd used the drug back in Canada in a bid to

10

blot out the emanations of everyone around him. It had worked, though at a cost: he no longer experienced the slightest stirrings of sexual arousal. He considered it a small price to pay for the cessation of the mind-noise that had made his waking hours almost intolerable. He'd had few meaningful relationships in his life before becoming psi-boosted, and the loss of his libido only reinforced his voluntary isolation.

He'd bought her a meal, and between mouthfuls Tiger had asked, "You 'dicted, Mister?"

"Do you care?"

She frowned, shrugged her narrow shoulders.

He said, "I'm not addicted. I just use it from time to time."

"You telepath?"

Vaughan stared at her. "How the hell do you know that?"

She did her best to hide her smile. "Tiger know people who know people. They see you working at the 'port."

"So I'm a telepath." He regarded the girl. "Does it bother you?"

Tiger made a moue with her lips, considering. "Nope. Tiger got nothing to hide."

After that, they ate together two or three times a week for the next three years. He sensed her need of him after the first few months, and for more than just the drug money, but he kept his emotional distance. He met her only at the restaurant, and stayed with her for no more than an hour. He feared giving too much of himself, and receiving too much of her in return; most of all he feared the possibility of becoming so reliant on her as a source of affection that he would only suffer when she left.

Vaughan reached level 12 and stepped through the service hatch. A young boy, a grinning Sinhalese in a brilliant white

11

shirt and a dhoti, waved at him to follow. "This way, Mr. Vaughan. Follow me."

They were in a narrow, ill-lit corridor. The boy opened a hatch in the metal wall and slipped inside. Vaughan squeezed in after him. They climbed down a rusty ladder, finally stepping out into a vast, low chamber that seemed to spread for kilometres in every direction, empty but for a forest of supporting columns. The boy hurried off.

As he gave chase, Vaughan made out shapes on the floor, outlines of what looked like buildings and roadways, like some great, life-sized blueprint of a city never built. On closer inspection he saw that the lines on the floor indicated where metal walls and bulkheads had once stood.

"Where the hell are we?"

Without breaking his hurried stride, the kid said, "Level 12b, between level 12 and 13. Long time ago, this upper-deck. Then they built upwards. Took down all buildings and made this level strong with extra columns."

Vaughan hurried to keep up with the boy. "Hey, do you know Tiger?"

"Tigerji ill. Dr. Rao, he looking after her."

"What's wrong with her?"

"I am not knowing. Tigerji, she say she want to see you."

The boy arrived at a small hatch in a riveted bulkhead. He hauled on a handle and ducked through. Vaughan followed him, and stood up on the other side.

"My God," he said.

They were standing on a catwalk, looking down into a cavernous chamber lit haphazardly by jury-rigged arc lights and halogens that created a mosaic of silver light and yawning shadows. The chamber was festooned with strange plants, a phantasmagoria of anemic horticulture. Great rafts of pale fungus grew from the walls like shelves, and etiolated vines garlanded the struts and spars that criss-crossed the cavern.

Vaughan found the display of sun-starved plant-life amazing enough, but as his eye was drawn to the center of the chamber by the web of spars, like vectors indicating perspective, he was struck by the sight of the voidship. A bulky freighter of antique design, it hung in the center of the web like some imprisoned insect. He sensed the hum of minds emanating from it.

The kid held out a hand. "Home," he said.

He'd heard about the ship that had crash-landed on the Station fifty years ago. Rather than remove the wreckage, the authorities had considered it safer to leave the ship where it was, precariously balanced between decks, and weld it in position with girders.

His guide said, "Ship was carrying seeds from Speedwell. Cargo hold split and seed grew all over. This way."

A bridge fashioned from rope and slats of metal spanned the gulf between the catwalk and the spaceship. Vaughan held onto the rope rail and followed the kid, taking care to place his feet dead center on the precarious walkway.

They passed into the freighter's shadow. Vaughan looked up and saw a dozen urchins perched like observant monkeys on the great curved cowling of an engine nacelle.

The rope-bridge terminated in the entrance hatch of the ship's hold. His guide hurried him across the chamber and down a long corridor. They passed dozens of children sitting on the floor, playing games with stones. Only when Vaughan saw a legless girl propelling herself down the corridor in a wheeled box, did he realise.

He stopped and turned to look back down the corridor. All the children were deformed, paralyzed, or handicapped in some way. Most were missing arms and legs, some were blind, others facially disfigured. He glanced at the boy who had brought him so far. His right hand ended in a white-bandaged stump.

Tiger had told him about Rao, the good doctor who took in homeless street-kids, gave them shelter and food, and set them to work on the streets, begging . . .

"This way, Mr. Vaughan."

They turned right and immediately confronted a Buddhist monk in saffron vestments standing sentry outside a sliding door. His eyes were closed, his lips moving in a silent mantra.

"In here," the boy said, sliding back the door. Vaughan stepped inside. His guide said, "I will go and find Dr. Rao." The door closed behind him and Vaughan found himself alone with Tiger.

She lay on a narrow bunk that almost filled the room. She wore shorts and a shrunken t-shirt, her left foot bare and stained with oil. She was sixteen, but she looked about twelve years old. Tiger had always been slim, but she was skeletal now. The waistband of her shorts hung between the jutting bones of her pelvis. To cool herself, she had pulled up her shirt to expose her concave belly and fleshless ribcage. Her face was gaunt, cheekbones an angry chevron stretching jaundiced, sweat-soaked skin.

The music of her mind was faint, as sweet as ever.

"Jeff . . ." Barely a whisper. It was all she could do to lift her hand a couple of centimeters off the bed and wave her fingers in greeting. "Knew you'd come."

"Tiger . . ." He knelt by the bed and repeated her name, taking her hand and squeezing fingers. She winced, as if in pain, and then managed a smile.

"I've got to get you out of here, to a hospital."

"Dr. Rao looking after Tiger," she whispered.

"What happened?" Vaughan asked.

The words came, soft as her breath: "I was silly."

"Tiger . . ." Something like desperation gripped him. Where the hell was Rao? "What did you do?"

She gathered her strength and said, "There, in bag." She glanced toward the foot of the bed. A canvas bag hung from a hook on the wall. Vaughan took it and pulled out a clear plastic pouch full of crimson powder. He snapped the seal and sniffed. The stench brought tears to his eyes.

"You took this?"

Her lips made a downward curve that signaled assent and a terrible admission that she knew she had done wrong.

"Tiger, you must tell me. What is it? Where did you get this stuff?"

"Kid sold it to Tiger. Tiger took too much. Dr. Rao say I very ill. Feel bad, Jeff."

"Don't worry. I'll get help."

He pushed up his sleeve and punched the surgery code into his handset.

A voice from behind him whispered, "I'm afraid you'd be wasting your time, Mr. Vaughan."

A small, silver-haired Indian, severely upright in a Nehru suit, stood in the doorway. He clutched a walking stick in arthritic fingers.

Vaughan regarded Dr. Rao. He didn't like the sound of the man's mind; it made a noise that he had learned to associate with xenophobia and suspicion through long experience.

He stood and hustled Rao into the corridor. "What the hell do you mean? Why aren't you doing something for her?"

"Mr. Vaughan, please . . . I appreciate your concern. Your desire for the welfare of the girl cannot be greater than mine. But we must face certain realities. Fate conspires to

15

bring down events upon our heads which we must face with fortitude."

"If you don't tell me what's wrong with Tiger . . ." His grip on the little Hindu's upper arm tightened.

"Mr. Vaughan, Tiger overdosed on a drug, colloquially known as rhapsody, a substance imported from one of the colony worlds."

"What's it doing to her?"

Rao stared into his eyes. "I'm sorry. There is no antidote, no cure for a dose as massive as that which Tiger took. The drug is corroding her major organs, heart, liver, even her brain. She was comatose for a day after taking the substance, then wracked by severe internal pains. She is relatively comfortable now. I have treated her with a powerful morphine cocktail."

Vaughan heard himself saying: "How long?"—a ridiculously matter-of-fact statement at odds with the pain he was experiencing,

"I am truly amazed that she is still with us."

Vaughan released his grip on Rao's arm, almost pushing the doctor away from him. He stepped back into the room.

Tiger was smiling, something knowing in her expression. He sat down on the bed beside her.

"Jeff . . ." Her big eyes stared up at him. "You never told me . . ." She paused, marshalling her breath, her strength. Then, after a delay of long seconds: "Never told me about *you* . . . Always so secret."

A sharp pain like laryngitis gripped his throat. He managed: "What do you want to know?"

She said, "Want to know . . . *why?*"

"Why? Why what?"

"Why me?"

Because . . . How could he make her understand his

psychological obsessions? How could he explain that, because of her similarity to someone he had once known, he had been compelled to seek solace from her, and at the same time driven to push her away?

She smiled up at him, something martyred in her expression now. Her eyes were soft-focused with tears. He felt the tune of her mind fading, slipping away.

He held her insubstantial hand while her eyes lost focus and her breath became labored. Her mind drifted away, became almost silent, but for the occasional soft sound, a grace note played far off, and then nothing.

He sat with her for an hour while she slowly died.

He stared at her stilled face. Where before had been life, music, there was now the terrible silence of oblivion.

He closed her eyes, then looked around the room at the pathetic collection of her belongings: a dozen tattered posters of skyball heroes, two faded Calcutta Tigers t-shirts, a pile of 'ball magazines, and an effigy of Siddhartha Gautama.

He saw the bag of rhapsody on the bed and slipped it into the inside pocket of his jacket. Behind him, the door scraped open.

Dr. Rao stood on the threshold, the Buddhist monk behind him. "I'm sorry, Mr. Vaughan," Rao said. "If you would like more time alone . . ."

"I'm fine." He looked back at Tiger, but found that he could not contemplate her face. He stared at her graceful hand, palm up, fingers slightly curled. "I'd like to attend the funeral."

"We had not planned an official ceremony, Mr. Vaughan. The monks are taking her for Contemplation. Perhaps, in a month, a small service might be arranged."

His heartbeat loud in his ears, Vaughan stared up at the

Doctor. He could hardly believe what Rao had just told him. "Contemplation? You've sold Tiger for Contemplation?"

"Not Tiger, Mr. Vaughan. Tiger is no longer with us. Her essence has moved on. I have merely sold her remains."

"No way . . ." Vaughan was shaking his head. "No, you can't—"

"I have the welfare of the children to think of, Mr. Vaughan."

He could not let the monks take Tiger for Contemplation. He imagined Tiger's naked corpse laid out for inspection by the monks, the subject of an exercise in which they contemplated the body and in so doing came closer to understanding their own mortality, the fact of their own place in the passing show called life. The remains would then be taken away, and ten days later brought out again. This time the monks would contemplate not only the fact of death, but the stench and corruption of the flesh.

"I'm sorry, I can't let you do this."

"Mr. Vaughan—"

He stood and pushed Rao and the monk from the room. Rao tried to brace himself in the doorway, but Vaughan took his wrists and twisted. The old man capitulated and backed into the corridor.

"Mr. Vaughan!" Rao whimpered. "You are making a grave mistake. In the name of an ancient and noble religion . . . It is an honor to be the subject of Contemplation in the Buddhist faith."

"Damn you!" He wanted to go on, shout that Rao would know the sham of all religions if he could only look into the human mind as he had, read the fear and the guilt and the universal desire to be saved.

Something in Vaughan's stance caused Rao to back off further, raising his hands in a gesture of self-protection.

"Mr. Vaughan. I am not a violent man . . ."

Vaughan stabbed a finger at the doctor. "You're not violent?" he said. "Are you trying to tell me that what you did to those kids out there—what you did to Tiger . . . do you mean to say that wasn't violent?"

Rao spread his hands. "Mr. Vaughan, I ensure that my children suffer no pain. It is a sacrifice they willingly make. I look after them, take care of all their needs."

Vaughan closed his eyes. He let the seconds build up, fought to control his rage. "I'm sorry. I can't let you go through with this." He paused, contemplating Rao, then said, "How much?"

Rao blinked. "Excuse me?"

"How much is the monk giving you? I'll match it if you'll let me arrange Tiger's funeral."

The monk tipped his head toward Rao's ear, whispered something that Vaughan didn't catch. Rao replied with a whisper of his own. The monk bowed with impeccable serenity, first to Rao and then to Vaughan, and retreated down the corridor.

Dr. Rao said, "I can see that Tiger's funeral means much to you. The monk would have paid me five hundred baht."

Vaughan felt nothing but contempt for the Indian. "I'll match that. I want Tiger taken to level 1 where she can be collected. I'll make all the arrangements."

Rao placed his palms together before his face and performed a servile bow.

Vaughan took out his wallet, counted out five one-hundred-baht notes, and thrust them into Rao's palm.

He turned and stared through the door at Tiger's body laid out on the bed. He wanted to run, to get as far away from here as possible, but something, some absurd notion that to do that would be to show Tiger disrespect, forced

19

him to step into the room and sit down beside the dead girl.

He took her hand, tried to find the words to express what he was feeling. Images of Tiger in life came back to him—and quite naturally he saw in his mind's eye brief flashes of Holly.

At last, in silence, he released Tiger's cooling hand and stepped from the room.

Rao was nowhere to be seen. Vaughan retraced his steps through the ship and found his guide squatting in the entrance. The boy jumped to his feet. "Dr. Rao told me show you out."

"Take me to the nearest inhabited level. I'll find my own way back."

Thirty minutes later he was riding a crowded upchute to the surface, packed between dozens of Indians on their way to work, the unintelligible noise of their minds loud in his head. He left the upchute station and walked into a warm dawn, the wash of brightening crimson sunlight dazzling after the gloom of the lower levels.

He boarded a mono-train heading west and alighted at the edge. There was a quiet park above his apartment where he sometimes went to be alone.

Vaughan sat on a bench overlooking a greensward that sloped toward the edge of the Station. The sky was still dark toward India; the sun was rising behind Vaughan, streaking the shadow of his head and shoulders far out across the grass.

When the morning became too hot he would make his way home and go to bed, first taking a good dose of chora to help him sleep. Later, when he awoke, he would attend to the arrangements of Tiger's funeral.

A voidship rumbled overhead, moving so slowly as to seem improbable. Its shadow took minutes to slide over the greensward; Vaughan looked up and regarded the passage of its great curving underbelly. Through long viewports he made out the tiny figures of the ship's crew, going about their work, oblivious to his presence, to Tiger's death.

In his mind's eye he saw again the image of her tiny body lying on the bed. Like a persistent phrase of remembered music, he recalled the failing, fading melody of her mind.

He told himself that it was over now, that Tiger had confronted the fact of her death and passed on. But he could not banish from his mind the terror Tiger would have experienced upon apprehending the oblivion that awaited her.

His handset chimed. He pushed up his sleeve and accepted the call. Jimmy Chandra's smiling face stared up at him. "Jeff. When can we meet?"

Vaughan said, "You've got something?"

"Something?" the cop said. "I have discovered enough about your Director to cause him severe distress." Vaughan smiled at Chandra's quaint use of English.

"I just got off shift. I need to sleep. How about tonight, around nine? Meet me at Nazruddin's?"

"I'll be there, Jeff."

Vaughan cut the connection and wearily made his way home.

TWO

Jimmy Chandra hunched over a glowing com-screen in his office at the Law Enforcement Headquarters. The room was darkened and insufferably hot, the ceiling fan doing nothing but stirring old air into a slightly more breathable mix.

What Jeff Vaughan had asked him to do was not, strictly speaking, legal—but he owed the telepath a favor and had, a little reluctantly, hacked into the police file core.

And he'd discovered some interesting things about Director Weiss.

He sat back and considered Vaughan. He'd met the telepath four years ago, when he'd worked briefly with the security team at the 'port. Their friendship, such as it had been, had soon dissolved in the acid of Vaughan's caustic world-view. He'd tried to come to some understanding of Vaughan's cynicism, discover the incidents and events in his past that had made him who and what he was. But Vaughan had blocked all his questions, reluctant to let anyone into the locked room that was his earlier life.

"If you were cursed with the ability to read minds," Vaughan had once said in a drunken outburst, "then you wouldn't be blessed with that damned Hindi optimism that I find so sickening."

Chandra had said, "Hindu."

"*What?*"

"*Hindu* optimism," Chandra replied. "Hindi is our language." He had, he realised, been dodging the issue. He had found Vaughan's bitterness so disturbing and difficult to understand that he often refused to be baited, instead side-tracking the argument or ignoring Vaughan altogether.

Perhaps, of course, he feared that Vaughan was right, that humankind was at base evil and self-seeking. Perhaps he feared that Vaughan's ability had given him an insight that he, Chandra, could not possess.

His handset chimed.

"Chandra." Commander Sinton peered up from Chandra's wrist-screen, his ruddy Caucasian features and oiled silver hair bright in the gloom. "Get yourself onto the flier lot right away. Take Lieutenant Vishwanath with you."

"What is it?"

"A respected citizen was reported dead less than twenty minutes ago. Tread carefully, understand? Extend my sympathies to his widow."

"Was he murdered?"

Sinton glared at him. "No, he passed away peacefully in his sleep. What the hell do you think, Chandra? Of course he was murdered. I want a report in my files by dawn."

Sinton cut the connection.

Chandra downloaded the relevant files on Weiss into his handset and left the basement room.

As Vishwanath climbed into the flier beside him, Chandra went through the familiar process of readying himself for what was likely to be a gruesome business. He cleared his mind and slowed his breathing as they rose, banked, and burned away from the Station, inserting themselves into a red fast-lane. He told himself that the deceased was no longer suffering, had passed on to another existence, and that the corpse that would greet him at the scene of the crime, no matter how bloody, was merely the exhausted remains of an incarnation that had reached the end of its tenure in the here and now.

The preparation helped, he knew. But, no matter how well prepared intellectually, he could not prevent his body's visceral reaction to what he was about to experience.

"Details, Vishi."

The young Lieutenant relayed the facts from a screader, his face washed crimson from the light of the fast-lane. "Victim is Rabindranath Bhindra, aged seventy-five, resident of the Sapphire complex, Wellington district, mid-eastside."

"Exclusive." Chandra whistled. "Sinton said he was a VIP."

Vishi looked up from the screader, glanced across at him. "You've never heard of Bhindra?"

"I must work too hard. No time to spend noting celebrities. Screen star?"

Vishi shook his head, smiling. "Politician. But that's not what he was famous for. He was one of the first voidship explorers, fifty years ago."

"Ah, *that* Bhindra . . . Didn't he write a book about his days in space?"

"It was made into a film, theatre drama, virtual-tape, holo-movie."

"I'll remember it the next time I play charades. What was its title?"

"Pass. Had 'stars' in there somewhere, I recall."

Chandra nodded. He gazed down at the lights of the Station's upper-deck as they streamed by below. "How was he killed?"

"Shot through the head with a high velocity projectile."

"Oh, lovely, Vishi. I hope you haven't eaten lately."

"No, sir," Vishi said. "Bhindra was in his apartment at the time. One theory is that the assassin was in a flier."

"So someone just flew by, sighted him, and blew him away?"

"Something like that, sir."

They came to the eastward edge of the Station and Chandra exited the fast-lane, slipped into a blue slow-lane, and turned the flier in a tight, downward loop. The façades of the upper-deck buildings flashed by. The open-ended third level came into view: a spacious, floodlighted plaza surrounded by multi-level gardens and pyramidal apartment buildings. Chandra brought them past the Sapphire complex, reducing airspeed.

"The killer probably came in this close," Vishi said. "All the assassin had to do was lean out of the window, aim, and fire." He pointed to the lighted square of French window, open to a trim lawn on the shoulder of the pyramid. The room was full of officials going about their business of investigation, the efficient machine of law enforcement at work.

"Any witness reports of fliers passing at the time?"

"Unfortunately there was a constant progression of traffic going through this way just before midnight, when the killing occurred. We're looking for witnesses in other fliers, but we've had no luck so far."

Chandra nodded. They landed in the plaza below the Sapphire building. Already reporters and vid-film crews were encamped on the sidewalk beneath the blue and white striped awning. Chandra pushed his way past the melee, ignoring questions. They crossed the foyer to the central elevators and rode to the penthouse level.

"Do you know if Bhindra had any enemies in politics, Vishi? Opponents who wanted him out of the way? Vested interest groups he might have been opposing?"

Vishi shook his head. "He was a well-liked and respected member of the center-left opposition. One of those politicians whose celebrity got them into power, but who then worked hard to justify his position. I think the phrase is that he was a 'man of the people.' " Vishi paused. "Of course, we've yet to conduct a thorough investigation of his affairs. Something might turn up, then. We usually find dirt if we dig deep enough."

Chandra sighed. "You remind me of an old acquaintance of mine."

The elevator doors swept open and Chandra stepped into the corridor. Bhindra's apartment suite was cordoned off by officers. A small crowd of residents, shocked but nevertheless curious, blocked the corridor. Chandra eased his way through, nodded to the salutes of the attending officers, and entered the apartment.

The suite consisted of half a dozen spacious rooms, any two of which would have contained Chandra's own humble dwelling. The lounge beyond the hall was the focus of attention: the troupe of forensic officials, ballistic experts, and photographers engaged in a careful post-mortem choreography around the corpse.

"Go in there and collate whatever information's to hand, Vishi. I'll join you later. I'll just wander about."

Chandra moved from room to room, more to kill the time before the experts packed up and left than to look for crime-related evidence.

The first three rooms were what he expected to find in a residence this exclusive: big, tastefully decorated bedrooms, a bathroom the size of an average lounge. The rooms spoke of wealth without too much ostentation, giving no clues at all to the character of the owner. The study was more personal: the walls were lined with tapes—science and space-exploration, Chandra saw on closer inspection—with photographs and graphics occupying the few available spaces. The visuals showed landscapes of a dozen planets, most with a uniformed figure in the foreground—Bhindra, presumably, in his exploration days. From the ceiling, in a touch at once juvenile and affecting, hung half a dozen model voidships, everything from small three-man exploration vessels of fifty years ago to modern superliners.

The desk was loaded with the mementos of a lifetime: alien rocks, exotic insects encased in solidified resin, holos of extraterrestrial landscapes—and the glove of a spacesuit, mounted on a plinth, like a forlorn wave.

The treasured objects of the dead, collected over years, always spoke to Chandra of their owners' too fond attachment to the physical, which they were now without. The sheer redundancy of the objects themselves made a mockery of man's materialism.

Chandra had long ago learnt to attach no importance to material possessions. He owned nothing other than the necessities of life. Unburdened by objects, unbeguiled by the physical, he told himself that he was closer to the next life—and therefore more accepting of the fact that this life was only temporary.

He was about to leave the study when he saw, on the desk, a solid-looking rectangular object—that increasingly rare artifact, a book. He picked it up, turned the weighty object in his hands. No wonder they had fallen out of favor over the years, superseded by the screaders. Books were heavy, awkward objects—yet at the same time they had a certain . . . authority.

Chandra read the title: *The Stars Beyond*, by Rabindranath Bhindra. The cover showed three explorers in some exotic jungle landscape. On the back, Bhindra's jovial smiling face stared out at the world, a face of wisdom and experience.

Chandra replaced the book and left the study.

The various experts had packed up their equipment and were filing from the lounge. Chandra waited until the last of them had left before venturing a glance at the scene of the murder. He might have prepared himself mentally for the sight, told himself that the body in there was just a vacated shell, but he wished he could have communicated the same logic to his stomach.

The scene was particularly messy.

Chandra joined Vishi in the center of the room, cast a quick glance at the corpse, then looked away and kept his gaze resolutely averted. Bhindra had been sitting in an armchair by the open French windows when the assassin struck. The body had retained in death the position it had last adopted in life: upright, feet crossed at the ankles, hands placed on lap. What made a mockery of the body's posture was the absence of its head. The dark orifice of the windpipe and a notched stub of backbone showed in cross-section. The impact of the projectile had blasted the skull and its contents in a liquidized spray across the room and against the far wall.

"Where's his widow?"

"She was taken to hospital suffering from shock."

"Was she here when it happened?"

Vishi nodded to a vacant armchair. "Right there."

Chandra sighed. "Okay . . . I want you to question her, find out if she noticed anything. Talk to the neighbors. You know the routine. I want a report ready by the next shift. Did the experts come up with anything?"

Vishi passed him a screader. "Everything's in here."

There was a tap at the door. A white-coated Indian poked his head into the room. "The clean-up boys," Chandra said. "I'll leave you to it."

On the way back to headquarters, Chandra put the screader on read-out and listened to the monotonous computer voice as it reeled off the gruesome statistics. In his office, he downloaded the contents of the screen into Sinton's files, added a brief report of his own, and sat at his desk for a minute.

He was about to leave for home when he recalled Vaughan.

He tapped the telepath's code into his handset. It was almost four, and the first light of dawn was making gray rectangles of his office window. If Vaughan kept to his old routine, he should still be up.

He got through to Vaughan. The telepath looked tired beyond words, haggard and desperate—the type of character you would not wish to establish eye contact with in a crowd.

He told Vaughan about Weiss, then signed off, quit his office, and took the flier home. First, he would grab a few hours' sleep, then enjoy a leisurely breakfast. Sumita was due back from the university at noon today, and he'd promised to take her out that afternoon.

As he piloted the flier toward the blood-red dawn, he considered his wife and tried to push the thought of the murder to the back of his mind.

THREE

Vaughan dosed himself on chora before setting out to meet Jimmy Chandra. The drug had its usual effect of dulling his mind to the emanations of the teeming millions around him, and the side effect of damping his melancholia. He found he could think about Tiger without wanting to lash out in rage—as he had done at midday when, unable to sleep despite the chora, he'd paced his apartment, kicking furniture and punching the wall.

He stepped from the upchute station into the light-spangled night of the upper-deck and forced his way through the oncoming tide of humanity toward Nazruddin's. Chandi Road was packed with a solid flow of dark-faced, white-shirted Indians, less a collection of individuals than some great gestalt being, constantly shedding off units of itself and gaining others during its snake-like progression through the sector's canyon-like streets.

Stalls and carts and kiosks lined each side of the street before the lighted shop-fronts, opportunist one-man enterprises selling cooked food, incense, fruit and vegetables, plaster-cast effigies of Hindu gods, juices, and cure-all elixirs. Down the street, channeled by the two-story buildings, a warm wind carried the thousand fragrances of the city, mixing the scent of hair oil, rose-water, joss sticks, and masala paste in a cloying perfume predominantly sweet but occasionally shot through with the pungent reek of air-car fumes and cow dung. The noise was constant—the jangling tinnitus of Indian pop music accompanied by a never-ending hubbub of chatter.

Vaughan had never before experienced crowds like those in the Himachal sector of Bengal Station. Overcrowding had inculcated into the Hindu psyche no concept of the inviolability of personal space. There was no taboo on physical contact, as in the West. Flesh pressed flesh, bodies squirmed against bodies.

He had long since learned how to negotiate the crowds: you had to tread the fine line between being forceful and aggressive. Use of the hands was necessary to part reluctant bodies, as was the judicious employment of the shoulder. Retiring Westerners and colonists new to the dog-eat-dog etiquette of the Station were lost in the flow, like non-swimmers caught and carried off in a riptide. Most visitors chose to travel by exorbitant taxi-flier, or avoid the Indian sectors altogether. The Thai area of the Station, to the north, was a comparative haven of space and civilization, and, as far as Vaughan was concerned, lacked character as a result.

In scan-mode, he would have been unable to face the torrent of minds in the thoroughfare—the overload of so many individual identities invading his own would have obliterated his sense of self. Even unaugmented, the buzz of a thousand minds so close would have affected him like a severe migraine. But with the sedative of the chora damping his senses he felt safe: each mind was a sphere of modulated music, contained within itself.

A gaudy array of neon arrows pulsed in the darkness up ahead, pointing to the entrance of Nazruddin's. Vaughan paused outside the restaurant, watching the street kids. They were a sorry gaggle of waifs and strays, pot-bellied and skinny-limbed—or missing limbs altogether—which Vaughan seemed to see afresh tonight with eyes made observant by loss. Every time a diner approached the open doorway, a couple of kids forced themselves across the side-

walk on crutches with uplifted, outstretched palms. Occasionally they were rewarded with a carelessly tossed confetti
of low-denomination notes, grudgingly given. More often
than not they were ignored. He tried to banish the image of
Tiger from his mind's eye.

He hurried into the restaurant, glanced around the
packed tables for Chandra—but the cop was late.
Nazruddin lifted a meaty hand in greeting from his station
behind the counter and ambled over as Vaughan seated
himself in his booth.

"Mr. Vaughan! Are you dining tonight? Today's
specialty—"

"Just a beer, P.K."

Nazruddin squeezed a wink, a gesture at once servile and
ingratiating. He snapped his fingers and yelled in Hindi. A
thin-legged, teenage waiter hurried over with a bottle of
Blue Mountain lager. Nazruddin made a performance of
drying the condensation from the bottle and pouring a
glass.

"No Tiger, Mr. Vaughan?"

"No," he said. "No, not tonight."

As Nazruddin smiled and sailed away, Vaughan found
himself wishing that Nazruddin had known about Tiger's
death and expressed his condolences. It seemed a sleight to
Tiger's memory that her passing was not universal knowledge—people's ignorance of the fact that she was no longer
around seemed to devalue her existence retrospectively: she
was just another parasitical street kid, after all, and one
fewer would not be missed.

He cursed his muddled introspection. The chora was
wearing off. He pulled the vial from his pocket, tipped a lib-
eral dose into his glass, and drank. He began to feel his
senses dull.

Jimmy Chandra arrived five minutes later.

"Jeff, good to see you. It must be what . . . three, four years?"

Chandra stood uncertainly before the booth, the confidence of his greeting not matched by his expression. He was a short, trim, boyish-faced Indian in the khaki uniform of an Investigator. His smile was the perpetual feature of his round face, but today the smile was uneasy.

"It's okay, Jimmy. I'm not reading. Why don't you sit down? I'll get you a beer." He gestured to the waiter.

"I've got nothing to hide, Jeff. Nothing personal, that is—even if you were in scan-mode. But, you know—investigations . . ."

"Hey, don't mention it."

Jimmy's smile lost its uneasiness, became eager. "So, how are you? It's been a long time. I called by your apartment, but you were always out."

"I work unsocial hours, Jimmy." In fact, Vaughan had always ignored Chandra's odd call. He had nothing against the young cop, but the thought of socializing had never really struck him as that important.

The strange thing was, he liked Jimmy Chandra. He reminded Vaughan of himself ten, twelve years ago, before the operation to make him telepathic had spoilt his illusions. Like Chandra, he'd been idealistic, hopeful for both himself and humanity.

Chandra sipped his beer. His mind emanated a melody of harmonious emotions. Vaughan was unable to read individual thoughts without his augmentation-pin, but he received a general mood of charity and well-being from the young cop. It seemed that Jimmy Chandra had changed little over the years.

Chandra rolled his glass between flattened palms. "Well,

how are you?" he asked for perhaps the third time.

Vaughan shrugged and turned his palm in a *you-know, so-so* gesture. He knew that now, as in the past, Jimmy Chandra found Vaughan's negativity, his laconic cynicism, more than a little discomfiting.

The beer and the chora combined were having an effect. He found himself saying: "Can you remember Tiger? Street kid, one leg?"

"Sure." Jimmy smiled. "Sure I remember her—you helped her out, right?"

Vaughan recalled Jimmy's approval, tinged with just the hint of suspicion, when he'd introduced the cop to Tiger years ago.

"Tiger died early today."

He could not look into Chandra's face when he said this. He waited five seconds, then looked up.

Chandra was not smiling; his mood had darkened: he sensed that Vaughan was baiting him, taunting him with another example of how horrible the world was. Vaughan recalled one drunken meeting when he had, cruelly and cynically, tried to explain to Chandra how terrible the situation was, how corrupt humanity was. It had been here, in this very booth. He recalled that he'd repeated one line over and over—*if you could see what I've seen*—without telling the cop too much about his past: his work with the Toronto police, the minds he'd read . . .

"I'm sorry," Jimmy said now.

Vaughan stared down at his beer. "Strange thing is, I don't know why I'm telling you this."

"Perhaps by talking, sharing the pain, it might make it a little easier."

Vaughan almost smiled. The same idealistic Jimmy as ever. He looked up. "Nothing can make it any easier,

Jimmy. That's bullshit. It might make it easier at the time, briefly. But nothing can take away the grief that corrodes over the years."

Chandra stared at him. "I thought you said Tiger died this morning?"

The cop was fishing, but Vaughan was not taking the bait. There were some things that were beyond discussing.

"Like I said, I don't know why I'm telling you about Tiger." He paused. "She was just another scheming street kid. But she meant something to me." He dried up; he couldn't tell the cop why she meant something to him.

Jimmy said, tentatively, "I remember you saying that no one meant anything to you, or words to that effect. Last time we met—here, at this very table."

Vaughan shrugged. He pushed his glass around the table. "I arranged her funeral earlier today. And guess what?" He forced an ironic laugh. "They're all booked up down at the burning ghats during the day. The only time they've got free is at one in the morning. How about that?"

Jimmy shrugged. "Tough."

"Yeah, tough." Vaughan said. "It'll make a pretty bonfire, though."

The cop cleared his throat, nodded at Vaughan's empty bottle. "Another beer?" He turned and called the waiter.

Vaughan stared at his empty glass. He'd stay here till past midnight, get loaded, then go down to the ghats and attend the funeral ceremony which, now that he'd arranged it, seemed increasingly meaningless. Drunk, he might not be able to recall all the morbid details. Tiger would have understood.

When the beer arrived, Vaughan sat up and looked across at Jimmy. "So much for all that shit, Officer Chandra. You didn't come here to watch me crying into my drink."

Jimmy smiled a *think-nothing-of-it* smile. "I must admit, it was a surprise to hear from you. I'm pleased you got in touch."

Vaughan wondered if the cop was lying. "So you got something on Weiss?" he asked.

Jimmy nodded. "Came up with some interesting facts." He looked at Vaughan. "Can you tell me what you have against this guy?"

"It might be nothing—I might be being paranoid, who knows? What did you find?"

"Well, it appears that his identity card is a forgery, for a start. He has papers to certify he's a citizen of the European Federation, born in Geneva in '35. But I've run checks with Europe and drawn a blank. He just doesn't exist. The persona of Gerhard Weiss is a front. Likewise all his qualification cards and records—all forgeries."

Vaughan nodded, showing a calm he did not feel. He'd had no idea what might be discovered by putting Chandra on the trail of his boss at the 'port, but this was far more than he'd hoped for.

Vaughan considered. "Okay, but this is between you and me . . ." He poured two beers and told Chandra about Weiss and the ships from Verkerk's World.

Chandra looked up from his beer when Vaughan stopped talking. "Could he be smuggling something to Earth?"

"More like *someone*—someone he doesn't want me reading."

"Wouldn't this someone just leave the ship shielded?"

Vaughan shook his head. "I have the authority to take every shielded traveller into custody and demand the removal of their shield. Weiss wouldn't want me doing that."

"Right." Jimmy said. "But why didn't you just read Weiss's mind?"

"Come on, think about it."

"He's shielded, right?"

"As 'port Director it's within his remit to demand that he's shielded at all times. Who knows what sensitive information us teleheads could get our hands on, otherwise . . . Damned convenient for Weiss, though."

Jimmy nodded. He looked eager, the ambitious law enforcement officer faced with palpable injustice. "So we've got this guy going under a false identity running the 'port and letting ships in without the usual checks . . . Where do you go from here?"

Vaughan refilled Jimmy's glass from his own bottle and called for two more. "There's another ship from Verkerk's World due in at midnight tomorrow. I'm on duty. No doubt Weiss will fob me off with some half-baked story. Of course, if he wasn't at the 'port . . ."

"Wouldn't he make sure the ship was manned with guards under orders not to let you near?"

"He might, but I can deal with the guards. It's Weiss I need out of the way, just for a few hours—say, from ten tomorrow evening until two in the morning."

He stared across the table at the cop. "You have enough on him to take him in for questioning, Jimmy. So haul him in, don't make a big deal of it straight away—maybe don't even let him know you know about his false identity. I don't want him spooked yet. I don't want him calling off whatever he's doing here. Make it look routine, so he doesn't suspect we're onto him."

Jimmy was nodding slowly, mulling over Vaughan's words. "I could do that easy enough. I could pull him in on his forged flier license, say we're having a sweep. It's routine, he won't suspect a thing. I'll book him for driving with invalid papers and let him go at dawn."

"I'll do my best to get aboard the ship. I'll let you know if I find anything."

They shared another beer, but Vaughan's silence must have spooked the cop. He quickly drained his glass and said he'd be in touch.

Vaughan watched Chandra hurry from the restaurant, then watched the minute counter on his handset approach the time he should be setting off for the ghats.

He made the edge in five minutes and shared a downchute cage with a dozen Taipusan cultists, a Hindu sect that practiced self-mortification as a means of purifying the soul. They were naked and emaciated, old men with stick-limbs and long hair matted into stiffened hanks. They had anointed their limbs and torsos with gray ash, and painted their foreheads with Hindi script. Six of the group had arms or legs missing. One saddhu, reposing in a plastic tray on castors, was a limbless torso, his huge member slung across his abdomen. They were making their way to the burning ghats to eat the flesh of the Hindu dead.

Vaughan turned his back on them and stared through the mesh gate as the cage descended. He was aware of their minds behind him. The collected energy of their thoughts hummed at a low threshold, a deep, vibrant note sustained serenely without fluctuation.

Through the mesh gate, which cut the scene into a grid pattern, he watched the ghats come into sight. The dark margin of the stepped platform, raised above sea level, encircled the Station like a plinth. Countless fires burned on the broad upper step, a succession of roseate beacons diminishing into the distance. Each pyre illuminated a knot of mourners, dark figures washed in the ruddy glow of the flames. Vaughan counted fifty individual pyres before they merged into one long, unbroken line of fire.

The cage clanked to a halt and Vaughan hauled open the gate. The saddhus filed past him, pushing their limbless compatriot in his cart and murmuring an eerie, monotone chant as they stepped out onto the holy ground. A crowd of hawkers and beggars swarmed outside the cage. They allowed the holy men through without hassle, then surged at Vaughan, thrusting everything they had to offer—joss sticks, images of Buddha and Kali, holy relics, and amputated stumps—into his face. He pushed through the crowd, ignoring their cries, swatting away the more persistent hands that tugged at his jacket.

The fires extended in either direction, north and south, each pyre located in a long, narrow strip cordoned off from the next by a length of white tape. On the sheer, polycarbon façade of the Station bold black numbers were painted on circular white backgrounds. Vaughan stood before a massive numeral Sixty-Seven. For a period of perhaps thirty seconds, disoriented by the unfamiliarity of the place, drink, and chora, he searched his memory for the number the funeral director had given him over his handset. It was something in the forties. The ghats numbered from one to fifty were Buddhist, he realised; from fifty-one to one hundred, Hindu. He set off at a hurried walk along the crowded ghats. It was almost one o'clock.

His progress was impeded by the passage of mourners crossing his path from the many funeral parlors set into the wall of the Station. On biers they carried their dead, swaddled in crimson, white, or saffron winding sheets, to the waiting pyres beside the sea. From the cremations already in progress came the stench of petrol fumes and burning meat, the ululating cries of prayer. The heat from the fires swept the ghats like a desert wind.

He paused before the great painted number Forty-Five. The parlor beneath was deserted but for a tiny, orange-wrapped figure laid out on a trestle table. Slowly, his steps retarded as if he were walking through mud, Vaughan approached the cut-price catafalque. The tightly wound material robbed Tiger's body of individuality, reduced her to just another anonymous corpse-shape.

An old woman in funeral whites appeared from the shadows of the parlor and prattled at him in Thai.

"I'm sorry . . ."

She switched to English: "You here at last. Come to collect . . ." She rattled off a Thai name of many consonants. Vaughan was nonplussed for a few seconds. Tiger had told him her name, years ago, but he had always known her as Tiger.

"Take her." The woman waved meanly. "Monk waiting." She scurried back into the parlor to prepare the next corpse.

Vaughan reached out, removed the cloth from Tiger's face, and gazed at the sleeping girl. Her expression was composed, serene. Her eyes were closed, her lips parted in the hint of a smile. Her dark skin held a waxy sheen, where fuel had been injected to accelerate the combustion of the corpse. Leaving her face uncovered, Vaughan bent forward and slipped his hands beneath shoulders and thighs. She was so light that, when he lifted her, he almost fell backwards. He turned with her in his arms and stared across the deck. The funerary area between him and the sea was deserted but for the Buddhist monk standing beside the stacked pyre.

He was conscious of his isolation as he carried Tiger's body across to the pyre and laid her atop the stack of wood-substitute. The monk surrounded the body with a barricade of the material, obscuring the saffron sheet and her clean profile from sight.

40

Vaughan backed off as the monk pressed a touchpad with his sandaled foot, and the pyre ignited with a roar like a jet engine. The heat beat Vaughan further back and he stood with his forearm protecting his face, squinting to see the dark outline of the body in the orange heart of the leaping flames as the monk intoned a monotonous chant. Vaughan sat cross-legged, hung his head, and closed his eyes.

Seconds later he became aware of sad mind-emanations. He opened his eyes. Gathered around the pyre were perhaps ten young boys and girls, quietly watching Tiger's body burn in the raging flames.

Dr. Rao, Vaughan noted, was not present. As if he'd really expected the rapacious Doctor to pay his last respects . . .

From time to time the monk added fuel, and the pyre exploded as if in anger. The sound of the flames, the cracking and popping of bones, lulled Vaughan to the edge of sleep.

He awoke suddenly, jerking upright, disoriented for a second. He was the last mourner at this funeral: the children had departed. To the east, the sky was gradually lightening: hours had elapsed; it was almost dawn. Before him, the monk was sweeping the remains of the pyre into the sea with serene, measured strokes of his broom. Only a dark, oval stain remained on the deck to mark the position of Tiger's pyre.

Vaughan climbed uneasily to his feet, hung-over, his head throbbing. The monk called to him in Thai, waved at him not to leave. The old man hurried over to Vaughan and pressed something into his palm, patting Vaughan's fingers shut around the gift like a magnanimous uncle. Vaughan watched the monk scurry across to the funeral parlor, and only when the holy man passed from sight did he open his hand.

A small vial, containing a portion of Tiger's ashes . . .

Vaughan moved toward the edge of the ghats and climbed down the deep steps until he was standing before the slow green swell of the ocean.

He unscrewed the lid, then scattered the gray ashes into the sea. When it was empty, he tossed the vial in after them. He stood and watched the ashes turn the color of the brine and disappear, and then he climbed the steps and crossed to the upchute.

He rose to the third level and walked the rest of the way to his apartment. Ten minutes later he opened the door, closed it behind him, and locked out the world.

He pushed his armchair into position before the window that comprised the entire out-facing wall, then slumped into the chair and stared out at the two-tone view, the blue of the sea and the lighter blue of the dawn sky.

He reached out, and from the table took the bag of red powder, the rhapsody, that had killed Tiger. He opened the bag and stirred the contents with a finger. It would be so easy to take the drugs in a glass of beer and end it all, to go the way of Tiger.

Then he considered what Jimmy Chandra had discovered, and what Weiss might be doing, and as ever he postponed the decision to terminate his existence. He had a sudden flash vision of the minds he'd read back in Canada, and the truth that experience had given him. Anything but *that,* he thought to himself. He could get lower, he knew from experience, much lower than this. He was in the situation he was in now through his own stupid mistakes. He should never have allowed Tiger to get close to him—he should never have allowed *himself* to get close to *her.*

But it would never happen again. He told himself that he would allow no one to penetrate his defenses from now on.

Vaughan returned the rhapsody to the table, lay down on his bed without undressing, and slept.

FOUR

Another Bangkok night . . .

Sukara's day started at eight in the evening. Her ancient Mickey Mouse alarm clock detonated on the table beside her bunk, drilling its din into her dream-filled sleep. Half awake, she swung her legs out of bed, searching for her sandals with her toes. She smacked the clock silent and hung her head between her knees. All the alcohol she'd consumed last night had not made her drunk, but she had a throbbing headache and her mouth was dry and sore. She reached out and opened the door of her cooler, dragged out a bulb of orange juice, and drank.

Her room was just a little bigger than the thin bunk it contained; from the bed, she could reach everything she needed: cooler, cooker, vid-screen, the spirit-house in the corner and the shelves that held her clothes, the knick-knacks and ornaments her customers had bought her over the years. She'd rented the room six months ago, paying a thousand baht for the year's lease. Before that she'd lived with three other girls in a damp room over the Siren Bar, but every other night she'd fallen out with the girls and sometimes they'd put things in her bed: a live toad, a dead rat, a mirror, and, once—this was what had finally driven her out—a small, perfectly curled human turd, which Sukara had nearly poked with her toes as she was climbing into bed. She'd hurried downstairs to Fat Cheng, the Chinese owner of the bar, and yelled at him in pain and frustration.

Fat Cheng had heard her out, then said in English: "You

43

good girl, little Monkey. I tell other girls they no good. Any more, they go." He shook his head. "First this, then that."

"Other girls, they no like little Monkey! It no good you just tell them. I go, find own place!"

And she'd taken her belongings and tramped the streets for two days before she found a room for rent on the other side of the city. Its size, when she had finally dragged all her possessions up the five flights of stairs, had almost made her weep. But she'd made shelves and stacked things on top of other things and covered the walls with graphics of alien worlds, and in a couple of days the room was comfortable and cozy and somewhere she could call home.

No more bitchiness from the other girls, no more unpleasant things in her bed, no whispers from the other side of the room when she undressed and they saw the strange, sucker-shaped markings on her torso . . .

Not that this room was a palace. The electricity stopped just when she needed it, and the noise from the traffic in the street below at dusk and dawn was deafening, and it took her two hours to get across the city to the Siren Bar, and that was travelling on the metro. But it was her own place she could come back to in the morning after a hard night, and fall asleep watching films on the vid-screen.

All in all, for a working girl just turned twenty-one, she had done well for herself.

She pulled a basin of water from under the bunk and splashed her face, took off her t-shirt, and washed beneath her arms. She turned on the vid and listened to the news while she dried her legs and feet—just to get the grime off her body. She'd get a proper shower when she got to work.

"Victim Six!" the announcer almost shouted in Thai. "The sixth victim of the Bangkok slayer was found in a city klong at dawn today. Like all the other girls, the victim was a child, blonde and foreign. She has not yet been identified. Police are mystified . . ." Sukara looked up at the screen. The pix of six little blonde girls, all very much alike, stared down at her. *All dead,* she thought; *they were alive when those pix were taken, and now they are dead.* She quickly turned off the screen. The six pix were replaced by her own reflection, and she turned her head away and closed her eyes, gasping. There were no mirrors in her room. She had thrown out her mirror three years ago, after the madman had attacked her with a knife. He had shouted he wanted to cut her open from the top of her head right down to her crotch, like a mango, but he had only got part of the way. She had been so close to being dead. She wondered if her picture would have been on the vid-news. "Working girl Sukarapatam sliced from top to bottom like a ripe fruit!"

Fat Cheng had been good about it. He'd had her rushed to a people's hospital, and had paid half the bills—the other half he'd taken from Sukara's wages. He'd even come to see her in the hospital. He'd grabbed her chin, turning her face this way and that. "Damage goods, little monkey. Who pay for you now? Always in trouble, this and that."

"You pay top surgeon, he mend face. Make beautiful."

And Fat Cheng had roared with laughter. "Beautiful! Wise man says, 'Can't turn frog into songbird.' You too dark, have monkey face, little Monkey. Now you scarred good."

"You throw me out, Fat Cheng?"

He'd turned her head painfully, right and left, scowling. "You do, little Monkey. Some men, they like damage goods."

Sukara pulled on a short black skirt, a clean red t-shirt. She flicked on her lighter, opened the glass door of the spirit-house, and lit a candle, placing a piece of banana beside it as an offering. She tipped her head forward and murmured a short prayer. "No violence today, no bad things. Spirits guide me, I promise to be good."

She found her mask, to keep out the filthy city air, and slipped it over her head. She preferred the type that fitted over her nose and mouth, covering more of her scar than just the mouth-masks. With her long hair falling over the rest of the face, she hoped that most people wouldn't notice.

She turned off the light in the room, locked the door behind her, and hurried down the dark stairs. The street was a solid caravan of cars and trucks, fumes hanging low. Advertising lights were coming on in the dusk. Overhead, fliers screamed like wronged spirits, taillights blurred in the pollution.

She made it in good time to the station and caught the trans-Bangkok express to the station closest to the Chao Phraya River. Sukara hung on a strap, squashed between two fat men. The trip took just over two hours and she wished she'd brought along a comic to pass the time. Instead she closed her eyes and thought about her sister, and invented a fantastic future for her in which she met a handsome rich man who took her to a colony planet and they had lots of children and were happy . . . She ran this fantasy almost every day, with variations, and the variation she played today was that her sister visited Earth and found Sukara and said, "Come back and live with us." She smiled to herself, both at how wonderful that would be, and also how unlikely. She told herself that she should not think of herself in these fantasies—they were fantasies for her sister, and if she wished too hard for things to happen for herself, then they might not come true for her sister.

And then the train reached the Chao Phraya, and Sukara struggled out and up the escalator to the street.

Lights advertised bars and strip clubs and brothels. The

street was full of strolling men, the occasional working girl in heels and strip rags and little else. No one glanced twice at Sukara as she hurried down the street, and she felt safe, anonymous. These were the times when she was glad she wasn't beautiful, when her beauty would have attracted the eyes of the cruising *farang* men.

She came to the entrance of the Siren Bar and climbed the rickety wooden stairs. The bar and dance floor and the other rooms, the mirrored rooms and the cubicles and the pool rooms, were built out over the river. Sometimes, in the early hours when business was bad and the music stopped, she could hear the scummy water of the river sloshing about under the floorboards, and Sukara would play the fantasy that she was aboard a boat sailing downriver into the bay of Bangkok.

Fat Cheng was in his usual seat at the bar. He swiveled when he saw her, great bulges of white-shirted fat pressed through the chromium struts of the barstool. She wondered how his slit eyes could see through so much fat.

"Little Monkey, you late, girl."

She pulled off her mask. "Train slow, Fat Cheng."

"Hokay. You go get shower, customer waiting."

Sukara felt a quick disappointment that she would have no time to herself, then a surge of curiosity. "Who, Fat Cheng? You know him?"

"Regular, little Monkey. Ee-tee."

"Which Ee-tee?"

"I don't know which Ee-tee. I didn't ask name. Now you go get shower, hurry up."

She ran through the bar. One of the girls, the tall, beautiful, sophisticated women who chatted to businessmen and politicians about world affairs—then ended up flat on their backs like every other working girl—saw Sukara and hissed in imitation of some leering extraterrestrial.

Sukara ignored her and hurried to the showers.

While she soaped herself, luxuriating beneath the pounding needles of hot water, she remembered the stand-pipe under which she and her sister had washed when they were little girls. Stripped down to their knickers and sharing a cracked sliver of soap between them, they had laughed and played under the great surging column of cold water. Those had been good times, life in a small village on the border with Cambodia, and she wondered how it had come to this. So many things might have happened to make things different. Their mother had died when Sukara was five, and she had looked after her sister while their father worked in the fields. She took Pakara to school with her in the mornings, a little sleeping bundle strapped to her back, and then worked in the fields with her father in the after-noons. Later, when Sukara was twelve, she worked in a small factory in a neighboring town, sewing dresses for the city while Pakara worked with her father. She wished that she could have worked in the fields instead of the factory, but her father said that they needed the money. Sukara re-sented her sister the privilege of being with her father in the afternoons, and grew jealous of the close relationship that had developed between her father and Pakara over the years. Her little sister was the pretty one, lighter skinned than Sukara and with big, round eyes, unlike Sukara's Chi-nese eyes. She was her father's favorite, that much was ob-vious. He said that she reminded him of her mother. Sukara told herself that it was not her sister's fault, and that she should not feel jealous because of it.

She would never forget the day a farm laborer rushed into the factory and told her that her father was dead— killed in the blades of a tractor's plough. She remembered her reaction—a sadness, yes, but at the same time a stomach-churning apprehension about what would happen next.

Her father owed money to the landowner he had worked for, gambling debts he had never told his daughters about. Sukara sold their hut, but *still* they owed money. Her wages were taken from her every week, and her sister was forced to work in the fields all day. They lived in a communal hut on the farm, ate two meager meals a day. Pakara was often beaten for not working hard enough, and Sukara set off to work before dawn and did not get home until after dark. For years and years she hardly saw the sun.

It was Pakara's idea to run away. One night, after watching a film on the communal vid-screen, about a young boy who worked his way up from being a beggar to owning a factory in Bangkok, Pakara had said to Sukara: "We must leave here. Tomorrow night we take the train to Trat. Then we take another train to Bangkok. I know times, okay? Don't worry." Sukara had agreed, nodded her head in wordless wonder at her sister's audacity.

She was sixteen when she saw Bangkok for the first time, Pakara just ten. The films had not prepared her for the noise and the smell and the crowds of the city. Pakara had managed to steal fifty baht from the commune kitty, but even eating just one meal a day it soon ran out. They walked the streets in the tourist area of Patphong, begging for money and food. For two nights they slept in alleys, growing hungrier as the hours passed. There were other street kids begging too, and others who went with rich *farangs*. Her sister watched them, then dragged Sukara to the bar where the street kids worked. Her little sister talked to the owner, and then miraculously they were given a meal and a hot shower, and told to sit at a table in the bar. Men

49

came and talked to them, bought them drinks, strange bitter tasting stuff that made Sukara laugh, and then be sick. Late that night an old Westerner took Pakara's hand and led her from the bar. Pakara gestured for Sukara to follow, and whispered to the *farang*, who glanced at Sukara and didn't seem pleased that she was coming too. He took them to a hotel room and, while Sukara watched, he undressed her sister and made her do things to him that Sukara could not believe that anyone would want done to them, or that her sister knew how to do.

Later, out on the street with a fat roll of baht between them, Sukara had stared from the money to Pakara. "How could you?" she asked.

"He was okay. He was gentle, like daddy."

And Sukara had felt shocked, and then envious of the strange affection that their father had shown Pakara.

Now Sukara stood beneath the drier and combed her hair. She slipped back into her skirt and t-shirt and found her sandals. On her way to the room she used with the Ee-tees, she stopped at the bar and picked up a wrap of yahd from Fat Cheng. Hurrying down the corridor, feeling a tingle of anticipation at who the Ee-tee might be, she rubbed the yahd into her gums. The drug gave her a pleasant dislocated feeling and also helped her stay sober. Some of the Ee-tees could not drink Terran alcohol, and Sukara amazed them by drinking bottle after bottle of ice-cold beer and still being able to touch her nose with her fingertip.

She knocked on the door, then opened it and peeked through. Her heart was hammering with the effects of the drug. The Ee-tee was sitting on the chair near the window, looking out at the rippling play of lights on the water. From this angle she could not tell who it was—just that it was an alien, for which she was grateful. Sukara preferred going with aliens—they were kinder and more gentle than human men, never beat her up or treated her roughly—but some of them were disgusting, strange shapes and stranger textures, creatures she had to force herself to go with.

"Hi there!" she said with forced gaiety as she stepped into the room.

The Ee-tee turned. "Su . . . Su, so pleased. Together after one Terran month. Much has happened. Let me tell you . . . So pleased."

She hesitated. "Dervan? Is it . . . Dervan?"

"Of course. Dervan. So pleased."

Sukara smiled. Dervan looked like a human being might look if they lived for three hundred years. His skin hung in pink wrinkled folds, and he was completely hairless; his nose was almost non-existent, his mouth a mere slit, and his eyes pink like those of an albino. Sukara forgot where he came from—she was never any good at remembering details—but she did know that he was an important member of a voidship crew that landed at Bengal Station three times a year. Two years ago he had visited Bangkok on leave, and had found himself in the Siren Bar. None of the other girls had gone near him, and Sukara had felt sorry for the fat, ancient-looking alien. She had joined him, and soon found herself in fascinating conversation with the weird Ee-tee. He had told her of far planets, distant suns, and Sukara had listened wide-eyed. "But there is another way I can show you these wonders . . ."

He had taken her back to the room and made love to her, but a love unlike any Sukara had experienced before. For the first time in years it had made her feel wanted and appreciated.

"Su . . . so little time, this time. Two hours. A flier waits to take me back to the Station."

51

"Oh . . . I'm sorry. I'm sorry I was late."

He arranged the folds of his robe across his lap, patting his knees with a pink hand more like a webbed claw. Sukara kicked off her sandals and climbed on to his soft, wide lap, leaning her head back against his chest. She felt herself sink in. His arms enfolded her. From beneath his robe, she felt the gentle movement of his ancillary arms, his pseudopods. She closed her eyes. She found the experience pleasurable, but the sight of the 'pods, the first time, had made her a little queasy.

She felt something warm and soft slide across her belly, worm its way beneath the waistband of her skirt. She opened her legs to accommodate the tentacle, felt it squirm into her. At the same time, others slipped beneath her t-shirt, wrapped themselves around her torso. Finally a pseudopod snaked up between her shoulder blades and attached itself to the back of her neck. Sukara felt herself drifting off, but not actually losing consciousness. She had had dreams like this in the past, on the edge of sleep—lucid dreams, they were called—but never any as vivid as these. Dervan knew exactly what she wanted, and gave her fantasies to make her forget her circumstances.

She was free and walking through tall blue grass on an alien world, with multiple moons in the sky, and structures like castles floating in the air. Someone was with her— Dervan in essence, but in human form—and Sukara trusted and felt affection for this someone, and the feeling was blissful.

And then she was swimming in the effervescent sea of a vast waterworld, nosed gently by creatures like dolphins who communicated by touch. Again, someone was with her, a Dervan-someone. Again, the experience was a delight.

Dervan had told her, after their first union two years

ago, that this was how people on his planet made love. The male lulled the female with mind dreams that stimulated his mate's egg-producing glands, which the male then inseminated with a thick, green substance like jelly. The jelly bit was the only part of the experience Sukara had not enjoyed, when she had overcome the shock of the pseudopods—but after the first few times she had become accustomed to wiping the goo from her thighs.

It had been one of her first experiences with an alien, and she had rushed out to tell the other girls how wonderful it had been. But their reaction had hurt and upset her. They did not listen, and turned their backs on her when she tried to explain. They told her they did not wish to associate with a girl who worked with monsters. And she had tried to explain that, although they might look like monsters, in fact they were gentle and caring. Only later did she come to understand the reason for the other girls' reaction to her.

Now the dreams came to an end, leaving her feeling dozy and relaxed. She opened her eyes to find herself lying on the bed. Dervan was sitting by her feet, stroking her leg. Something like a smile crinkled his wrinkled features. "So pleased, Su. Until the next time."

It was all Sukara could do to lift her arm and wave her fingers as he stood and eased his bulk from the room. Her eyes fluttered and she fell into a deep, dreamless slumber.

Later she got up and showered, scraping the jelly-stuff from between her legs and examining the strange, circular sucker marks, like painless blue and yellow bruises, that dotted her belly and chest.

She returned to the bar, hoisted herself onto a high stool, and sent a kid out to fetch her breakfast. She ate noodles and chicken with a refreshing cold beer. It was after midnight and the bar was filling up. Couples moved on the dance floor, jerking around beneath the multicolored flashing lights. Girls drifted from table to table, chatting to customers; others sat at the bar, waiting for trade and ignoring Sukara, which suited her fine. She thought of Pakara, and wondered what she was doing now.

She finished her meal and tossed the tray behind the bar. The yahd had taken effect, making her feel as though only her body was in the here and now. Mentally she was somewhere else, viewing this reality as though on a vid-screen.

With luck, she would have only two or three more customers before dawn, when she could go home. If her luck was even better, those customers would be Ee-tees.

At times like this, having seen Dervan and experienced the dreams, and with the drug performing its special magic, she told herself that she could do a lot worse for herself. For instance, she could still be working for the first bar owner Pakara had approached—or she could be dead.

They had lasted one year at the first bar.

There were many times during that year when Sukara wished she were back in the village, working at the factory. From time to time she spoke to Pakara about going back, but her sister had looked at her with a wisdom beyond her years and told her that there was no going back. "We go back, they punish us for running away. We okay here."

Pakara might have been okay. She had regular customers attracted to her youth and beauty, men who treated her well. She even told Sukara that she loved one or two of them. Sukara didn't know whether to believe her, didn't know whether Pakara was putting a brave face on the situation she was responsible for getting them into. Also, she didn't know how Pakara could bear what some of the men did to her. If, that was, they did the same things to Pakara that they did to her . . . Perhaps because Sukara was older and not pretty, she attracted the type of men who abused her, treated her badly. She desperately wanted to meet a man who would show her genuine affection, someone she could say that she loved.

Then five years ago, a year after arriving in Bangkok, Pakara told Sukara that she was leaving.

"I had enough of work here, Su. We go, okay?"

She had it all planned. Pakara would slip away from the bar at the end of her shift at three in the morning. Su, being older, worked until dawn. At six, Su would leave the bar and meet Pakara at the bus station across town. She told Su that she had been talking to someone who said that for two hundred baht they could buy a raft on the coast of the Indian Ocean and sail away to start a new life. They would do this. They had three hundred baht saved between them.

"But a raft on the ocean? You'll drown, or shark will get you!"

"You rather stay here?"

"No. But there must be better places to go."

"I decided! A bus leaves for the coast at seven. See you at the station, Su. Okay?"

That night, at three, Pakara had found Sukara and hugged her farewell.

Later, as dawn was lightening the sky outside the bar, Sukara had packed her belongings and slipped though the window of her bedroom, climbing down the fire escape and heading through the crowded streets to the bus station. She lost her way once, found herself in a square she didn't recognize, and realised with panic that she had only ten minutes to reach the station before seven o'clock. She climbed aboard a taxi, waving baht in the driver's face, but the traffic was so congested that she was quicker on foot. She jumped out and ran, following the driver's directions, and didn't stop until she arrived at the glass-covered terminus, the air blue with exhaust fumes, and looked up at the big clock to see that it was five minutes past seven. She tramped from bay to bay, hoping that Pakara had waited for her. But there was no sign of her sister, and Sukara sat on her pack, too devastated to cry, and wondered what to do now. Should she get the next bus to the coast? But the coast was long, and dozens of buses headed for the coast each day, and she knew that Pakara was lost.

Only slowly did it come to her that she might never see her sister again, and then she did begin to cry.

An old woman approached and spoke to Sukara, offered her a bed for the night. She looked like she could be trusted, and as Sukara had nowhere else to go she followed the old woman through the streets to the river. "Be good and trust in benevolent spirits," the woman had counseled, "and you will be safe."

They walked down a side alley, and into the storeroom of a building which Sukara guessed, from the stacked crates of Singha beer and the throbbing music, was a bar. Then a big, fat man waddled into the storeroom and smiled at Sukara, and although she knew, knew where she was and what the fat man was, she trusted his smile, and anyway she was too tired to start running again. He spoke with the old woman, and his big face folded into a mask of compassion. He reached out and took Sukara's hand. "Come, little Monkey, you will be safe with Fat Cheng."

And, for the past five years, she had been.

She often looked back at that fateful day and was overcome with many emotions, the worst one being sadness at the loss of her sister.

Sometimes, Sukara woke up in the middle of the night, sobbing with loneliness.

Sometimes, she woke in the night from a dream of alien meadows and floating castles.

FIVE

Vaughan stood on the windswept deck of the spaceport, his stomach knotted with apprehension as he waited for the freighter to complete its transfer from the void.

It was all very well planning to board the ship in the comfortable safety of Nazruddin's, but the fact of what he was about to do—the danger he might face aboard the ship—only became real as the time to act approached.

As he watched, the *Pride of Vanderlaan* appeared briefly to the south of the 'port, a gray ghost in the darkness, and then disappeared. For fifteen seconds it flickered like an image on ancient film, before it mastered the slippage and appeared finally, solid and substantial, in this reality. The ship engaged auxiliary burners and moved in slowly across the sea, a stylized wedge of gunmetal gray carapace, company colors excoriated by the void.

Across the 'port the loudspeaker system relayed orders, the bored woman's voice duplicated in Vaughan's earpiece. "Okay . . . twenty-three hundred hours. This one's ahead of schedule. Coming in due south, estimated docking: four minutes. Berth twelve prepare lines. Hauliers at the ready. Emergency services on stand-by. Class-3 freighter out of Verkerk's World, Riga, terminates at the Station. It's all yours, boys and girls. Out." The drawl clicked off abruptly, the silence immediately replaced by the dull drone of the freighter's engines.

Vaughan stood beyond berth twelve, an oval crater of raised steel flanges. Fuel lines, colored cables and leads, turned the berth into a snake pit. The freighter swung in over the superstructure of the terminal building, its stanchion legs braced akimbo, landing lights sequencing along its sleek flank. Behind lighted lozenges of viewscreens, crewmembers could be seen chatting casually around tables or leaning against the rails and staring out with the relaxed postures of travellers at journey's end.

Around the berth, one by one, 'port authority vehicles drew up: a fire truck, an ambulance, a tanker to siphon off unused fuel, and three or four other specialist juggernauts. Their personnel climbed down, stood around in bored cliques, chatting and mopping their faces in the relentlessly humid night. Vaughan could not help but read their thoughts, just as he would have overheard music played loud. Without concentrating, he caught only fragments of verbalized cognition from a nearby engineer: >>>*Last one this shift, thank Allah. Home . . . Parveen . . .* Then non-verbal thoughts of security, warmth, sex, and accompanying mental images.

His handset chimed. He accessed the call. "Jimmy?"

Chandra's smiling face looked up at him. "Mission accomplished."

"You took your time."

"Weiss was a bastard. He kicked up a fuss when I hauled his flier down and demanded to see his papers. Called the odds—you know these big shots. He nearly gave me an excuse to arrest him for abusive behavior to a police officer. He's in interrogation now and demanding a solicitor. He's here for a good three, four hours. Hope that gives you long enough. Catch you later." The screen blanked.

Vaughan felt a weight of responsibility fall on his shoulders. The first job would be to assess the level of security around the ship, and then put his plan into action. He doubted that Weiss would have overlooked the possibility that he would not always be on hand to shunt his telepaths to other duties; he would have posted guards.

The *Vanderlaan* came in over the berth and turned slowly on its axis, lowering itself gradually to the deck. Muscular, ramrod stanchions took the impact and the ship dipped a quick, hydraulic curtsy.

Minutes later the ramp came down, hitting the deck with a clang like a bell tolling the hour. Two big Sikhs in the light blue uniforms of a private security firm ascended the ramp and positioned themselves on either side of the exit.

Vaughan scanned. The men had been hired by Weiss and instructed to let not a living soul aboard the freighter. Weiss had used some vivid language to get his message across, and the guards had taken notice. They were tensed-up and vigilant, as if expecting a terrorist strike at any second.

He strolled casually around the freighter. From the minds of the 'port workers gathered in the berth beneath the ship he detected not the slightest flicker of suspicion at his presence. He paused on the lip of the berth, staring down at a group of three engineers as they accessed the emergency exit cover.

One engineer was consulting a screader, reading off a reference number to his deputy. Vaughan scanned.

>>>*Twenty minutes should see this through—small ship, no maintenance work reported. Where's that damned code . . ?*

The engineer found it on his screader, and Vaughan memorized the code for future use. He would wait until the ground crew had finished their work and departed, and the ship's crew disembarked, then enter the freighter through the emergency exit.

A roadster veered around the ship and headed toward

Vaughan. He felt the power of the driver's mind, the thoughts strengthening as the car drew up alongside him. >>>*Fuck Weiss having me do his running about. What the hell's he doing . . . should be here by now. Don't like these damned sneaking teleheads . . . unnatural. Don't trust the bastards.*

The security officer leaned through the roadster's open window, an olive-skinned southern European. "Vaughan— just got word from Director Weiss. Don't bother with this ship—just cargo, anyway. He wants you to go over some files at Terminal Three."

>>>*If the bastard's reading me . . .* Followed by nebulous images of violence.

"Fine. I'll make my way over now."

"Look, don't ask me why . . . Weiss told me to make sure I delivered you there." >>>*Don't know what you done wrong, telehead, but Weiss doesn't trust you.* Thoughts of uneasiness, the desire to be elsewhere. >>>*Can't say I blame him . . .*

Vaughan climbed into the roadster, doing his best to ignore the miasma of unease leaking from the driver, the irrational urge to do him violence because of what he was. As the car set off, he leaned forward and disengaged the augmentation-pin. He had no desire to be corrupted by the thug's primitive mind-set.

"Relax," he said. "I'm no longer scanning."

The officer glanced across at him, smiled uneasily. "Hey, no sweat. I can handle the idea of 'heads. Just doing your job, after all."

Vaughan smiled. He recalled the words of a fellow psi-positive at the Ottawa Institute ten years ago: "Prepare yourself for a lonely life, bud. No one likes a telepath."

The officer dropped him off at terminal three. Vaughan climbed from the car and began walking toward the building, and the officer watched him all the way. Just carrying out orders.

He entered the office and, ignoring the three clerks busy at their screens, crossed to the bank of terminals ranked beneath the windows overlooking the deck. He accessed the report files he'd been completing over the past week and feigned diligence. From time to time he glanced over the screen and watched the activity in the glare of halogen lights around the Rigan freighter.

The numerous service teams performed their duties and departed; the bowser finished first, sucking the excess fuel from the tanks and then trundling off across the 'port, lights flashing. Teams of engineers came and went, disappearing beneath the underbelly of the freighter to perform their routine checks. Technicians swarmed over the carapace of the ship, expertly utilizing the purpose-built footholds in the sloping flanks.

As he watched, a shuttle beetled out from the terminal building beneath him and zipped across the deck, pulling up before the ramp and waiting patiently. Minutes later the crew disembarked, ten men and women in the stylish black and silver uniforms of the Riga Line. They boarded the shuttle and it looped around the ship and headed back toward the terminal.

Vaughan stood and stretched, then casually left the office.

He strolled across the deck, heading away from the Rigan freighter. To his right, the officer's roadster was parked outside the security wing of the terminal building. Vaughan increased his pace, putting the bulk of a voidliner between him and the terminal.

He turned left, making his way toward the freighter. As he walked through the humid night, he slipped his pin from its case and inserted it into his skull console. Although he often strolled around the deck between jobs, and his presence here tonight would not be considered amiss, he nevertheless felt self-conscious—as if the few engineers and security guards he passed were aware of his intentions. Swift scans told him that their thoughts were as banal as ever.

He approached the freighter, becalmed now in the aftermath of its landing. He made sure that he went unobserved—it was not within his duty remit to board ships through their emergency exits . . . The coast was clear. There was no one in the vicinity, other than a team of engineers busy working on a nearby ship, and they were too engrossed in their work to notice him.

He hurried to the lip of the berth and descended a ladder into the shadowy pit beneath the belly of the freighter. He paused, regaining his breath and his composure. That was the first stage of the operation successfully completed . . . all that remained was to board the ship. He scanned, probing behind the sleek curved lines of the freighter. He detected a single mind, too high up in the ship to be read with any clarity.

He found the emergency exit cover and tapped the entry-code into the lock. The cover sighed open, extruding steps.

He climbed into a small, darkened compartment. At his presence, sensors activated and a hatch above him slid open. Low lighting came on, illuminating a corridor. He hauled himself into the ship and stood. He was in the working end of the freighter: the corridor was spartan, uncarpeted. He set off in the direction of where he judged the cargo hold to be. First, he would inspect whatever goods the ship was hauling; later he would investigate the source of the distant mind-noise in the crew-cabins high above.

The cargo holds were situated on either side of the corridor. He pressed the sensor panel on the hatch to his left, and the hatch eased open to reveal a small, dimly-lit hold, empty but for hauling trolleys and lifting equipment. He closed the hatch and crossed the corridor, palming the sensor on the opposite hatch. The dull steel cover slid open and Vaughan saw that this hold was occupied.

He stepped into the vaulted chamber, poorly illuminated by sporadic strip-fluorescents. A bulky, oval case stood in the center of the bare steel floor. The case was the approximate size of a flier, shoulder high at the rear, sloping to around waist high where Vaughan stood. It seemed to be constructed of some brass or copper-like material, engraved with an intricate pattern of spiral and curlicue striations. He walked around the case; the random design of whorls was repeated on every facet, and nowhere could he make out a seal, lid, or hatch.

The most remarkable aspect of the casing, however, was the fact that it was shielded. When he scanned, he detected the strange emptiness—an *absence*—that denoted a powerful mind-shield. He touched the cold surface of the case, lay his cheek against the inscribed patterning surface. He scanned again, read nothing.

He backed off a pace, contemplating the case and wondering what it contained . . . If Weiss was transporting illegal immigrants to Earth from Riga, why do so like this? Why not just have them travel as foot passengers? Weiss would have called off his telepaths anyway, so there would have been no threat of discovery.

Animals, then . . . was Weiss smuggling some proscribed species of fauna to Earth—and, if so, why?

There had been two earlier freighters Weiss had warned him off. Vaughan wondered how many shielded containers Weiss had successfully smuggled into the Station.

He recalled the mind situated high above him. As he hurried from the cargo hold and took the elevator to the upper-decks, it occurred to him that he should have felt pleased that he had uncovered the illegal operation—satisfied that a hunch had hit the jackpot. Instead, Vaughan experienced a subtle uneasiness at his discovery and its ramifications.

As the elevator climbed, the contents of the mind above him came into focus. He realised that it was the mind of a child, a young girl, and that she was distressed.

The lift door opened onto the third floor. A red tiled corridor dwindled into the distance, archways opening onto other passages at regular intervals. He set off at a jog along the main corridor. The cerebral signature became louder as he ran, then modulated almost imperceptibly: he had passed the turning down which the kid was located. He retraced his steps, took the turning. The mind cried out.

>>>*Help—someone please help!*

Even as he moved toward the girl, something told him to ignore the cry and leave the ship now. He tried to analyze the desire. The cry was human, in need of help, and yet his initial impulse was to run.

He arrived at an archway leading into a bedchamber. The girl was in the room, hiding in a storage unit.

Vaughan stepped into the room, crossed to the stack of units. He touched the control panel on the unit, and the door whirred open. A young girl, perhaps ten, hugged her shins and stared at him. She had blonde, curly hair, blue eyes . . . Her resemblance to Holly struck him like a blow.

He probed and found her name: Elly Jenson.

He knelt before her, trying to block her sudden surge of fright, and held out a hand. "Please . . . don't be frightened. I can help . . ."

She whispered: "Who are you?"

"Don't worry. I'll get you out of here. Please, trust me . . ."

He probed, and her mind entered his in a kaleidoscopic whirl of fragmented images. He sorted through them, discarding extraneous thoughts and memories, picking out only what he needed to know. He shared her fear, her memories of life on Verkerk's World. He identified the image of her father, and read her incomprehension at why he had allowed her to be taken away. He relived the day two strangers came to her father's house and took her, and shared with the girl her bewilderment when her father tried to explain that she had been Chosen, and must go . . .

He reached out for the girl's hand. She flinched at his touch, but did not pull away. She watched him with wide eyes, wanting to trust him and yet fearing to do so.

"I'm not with the people who took you," he said. He sensed that part of her confusion was that she did not know where she was. She had been told that she was going to Earth, but her young mind had been unable to encompass the idea.

He said, "You're on Earth now. You came through the void from your world. I want to help you."

"Please, take me home. Can you take me home?" The words were clean and sharp with the ice of Scandinavian intonation. "Please, take me away from here!"

He thought through the situation, considered his options. He could always take her from the ship, back through the emergency exit, then contact Chandra and deliver her into the care of the police.

He wondered if the presence of the shielded container and Elly Jenson aboard the freighter was anything more than a coincidence.

He scanned her again, tried to read the whereabouts of

the people who had escorted her to Earth. He read a name—Freidrickson—caught the image of a man in the black and silver uniform of the Riga Company.

He took Elly's hand and pulled her to her feet. "It's okay, Elly. You're safe now—"

Something in her wide-eyed expression of surprise alerted him. Vaughan tried to turn, to follow the direction of her gaze, but the neural incapacitator hit him before he caught sight of his assailant. He arched as voltage stabbed him in the back and coursed through his body. In the fraction of a second before he lost consciousness, he scanned but read nothing.

He seemed to come to his senses almost immediately, but even as he struggled to his feet, his body protesting with spasms of pain, he knew that minutes at least had elapsed.

Elly Jenson was no longer in the unit.

He staggered to the entrance of the chamber and sent out a probe. There was no sign of the girl's harried cerebral signature—but he did pick up, approaching him at speed, the minds of the Sikh security guards. Whoever had attacked him—Freidrickson?—had alerted them to his presence.

He ran down the corridor in the opposite direction. The guards were ascending in the main elevator. He made his way to the auxiliary shaft at the back of the ship, his muscles jarring with every step.

He read the guards as they emerged from the elevator and ran along the corridor to the chamber he'd just left. He slammed a palm against the lift sensor, willing the doors to open. He scanned the guards. They were in the bed-chamber, searching for him, their minds loud with anger. Three seconds was all it took for them to ascertain that he was no longer there. They exited and split up to search the ship. One headed away from him; the other ran down the corridor toward him.

He prepared himself for a fight, knew the futility of the idea. The Sikh was a matter of metres away, about to turn the corner and discover him, when the elevator doors sighed open. He dived inside, thumbed the sensor panel. The doors whirred shut and the lift carried him down into the belly of the ship.

A minute later he dropped through the emergency hatch into the hot night. He climbed from the berth, made sure his way was clear, and jogged from the shadow of the Rigan freighter. He scanned the deck for Elly Jenson in vain. Beyond the terminal building, fliers took off and banked into the red and blue airlanes above the Station. He realised, with a sudden, plummeting despair, that the girl and her captor might be aboard any one of them.

He slipped the augmentation-pin from his skull console. If taken beyond the boundaries of the spaceport, the pin activated an alarm back at stores, detailing the device's precise position: augmentation-pins were valuable commodities, dangerous in the hands of the wrong people. He would have to waste precious seconds and return it to stores: the last thing he wanted was for Weiss's henchmen to find him now.

He was running across the deck when his handset chimed. He halted and quickly pressed the caller code—if it was Weiss, he would not answer.

The code was Jimmy Chandra's. Vaughan accepted the call.

Chandra stared up at him. "Jeff. Can you get over here?"

"Sure. I need to see you, too. I found something aboard the ship."

Jimmy looked grim-faced. "Later."

"What's wrong?"

The cop shook his head. "Not now. I'll tell you when you get here, okay?"

Vaughan handed his pin to the clerk in stores and hurried to the flier rank.

The Law Enforcement Headquarters was a centrally located ziggurat of stressed polycarbon rising high above the surrounding buildings like a Teflon-coated Aztec temple. As the taxi-flier banked toward the third-level landing strip, Vaughan gazed out at the long windows that fronted the offices, interrogation rooms, and corridors, illuminated with a soft green light like so many tropical aquaria.

The flier landed on the broad margin of the step before the entrance. Vaughan paid the driver and climbed out. A young Indian officer was awaiting him. "Mr. Vaughan? Investigator Chandra is expecting you. This way, please."

Vaughan followed the officer into the building. Despite its sumptuous exterior appearance, the headquarters was a warren of shabby corridors and cramped offices. The low lighting failed to conceal the scuffed floor-tiling and mildew-patched walls. Khaki-clad officers hurried back and forth like the soldiers of an army beset on every side by an invisible foe. Even unaugmented, Vaughan caught the mental miasma of a tense and harried workforce.

They arrived at an open area of desks loaded with computer terminals. The operations room was filled with the aroma of strong coffee and a head-height layer of floating cigarette smoke like captured cirrus. Across the room, Vaughan made out Jimmy Chandra, talking to a uniformed woman. Chandra saw him, dismissed the woman, and threaded his way through the desks.

"What's happening?" Vaughan asked.

"What isn't happening? It's just another busy night at HQ. The usual murders, robberies, drug busts . . ."

"You didn't call me in to tell me about your workload."

"No, of course not. Come with me."

They left the operations room and walked down an ill-lit corridor stinking of stale sweat. The walls were lined with benches, and dozens of weary men and women, Indians and Thais, either stared into space or tried to sleep.

Vaughan looked at Chandra. "Petty criminals waiting to be processed," the cop explained.

They turned down an empty corridor. "As I said earlier, I took Weiss in for questioning. Routine stuff. I told him I was running tests on his flying license. He demanded a solicitor—an unusual request for a minor misdemeanor. We're allowed to keep suspects for up to four hours before granting legal representation. I checked the other papers he was carrying. When I told him that I was taking his other ID to run checks on as well, he didn't like it. So I relented. I didn't want him to guess we were onto him so soon. I thought if you discovered anything aboard the ship, we might be wise to put a trace on Weiss, follow him about, watch his every movement until we found out what he was up to." Chandra paused. "Well, he must have guessed something. He didn't give us the chance to find out . . ."

They came to the green door of an interrogation room. Chandra leaned through, exchanged a few words with someone inside. Through the gap, Vaughan could see two men and a woman busy attending to someone seated in a black leather swivel-chair. That someone had his head tilted back, staring at the ceiling with unseeing eyes.

Vaughan was aware of Chandra's mind beside him, and those of the officers within the room. But the seated, silver-haired figure no longer emanated the mind-noise of the living, and the silence was shocking.

He stared into the room at the familiar, overweight form of Gerhard Weiss, deceased.

"What happened, Jimmy?"

"I left the room for a coffee. There was an officer in attendance. Weiss asked if he could smoke one of his own cigarettes, and reached into the inside pocket of his jacket. He came out with a device and clamped it to his neck, here—" Chandra slapped his hand over his carotid artery. "He was dead within seconds. Forensic are trying to find out what it was."

"He knew you were onto him," Vaughan said. "He didn't want you discovering his true identity or what he was up to at the 'port."

"You found something in the ship?"

"Yeah, I found something."

Chandra's next question was interrupted by the forensic team as they left the room. "He's all yours," the woman said. "We'll be back with the test results as soon as they're through."

Chandra gestured Vaughan through the door. "It's not exactly pretty, Jeff."

They passed into the tiny room, empty but for two chairs, a desk, and the corpse.

Weiss had been a big, florid faced man in his fifties, and his face was even more florid now. Veins had broken under the surface of his skin, suffusing his flesh with the mottled crimson blush of a blood orange. His nose had bled in the seconds before his death, the stream of blood dividing at his thick top lip and spreading around his mouth like a macabre, cosmetic moustache.

Vaughan glanced at Chandra. "Do you ever use a mind-shield?"

Chandra nodded. "When questioning suspects, of course."

"But you don't have one for personal use?"

Chandra shook his head. Vaughan reached into the

inside pocket of Weiss's jacket, but the pocket was empty. He tried the breast pocket and found what he was looking for. He produced a flattened, silver oval and held it out to Chandra on his palm.

"It's yours."

Chandra looked wary. "I'm not sure if I should . . ."

"Take the damned thing, Jimmy. It'll come in useful. He'll hardly miss it."

"Don't you need one?"

Vaughan shook his head. "I'm fitted with a shield built into my console. I can't be read."

Chandra still seemed reluctant.

"Take it, for chrissake," Vaughan said. "Look, this bastard was up to something on a big scale, and he wasn't alone. I want you to wear this thing all the time, understood? You'll be investigating him and you'll no doubt run into his partners. If they have a telepath working for them, then I don't want him reading what you know. Okay?"

Chandra took the shield and slipped it into his pocket. Instantly his insistent, low-level thoughts ceased. "So . . . what did you find aboard the ship?" the cop asked.

Vaughan described the container he'd discovered in the hold.

"It was definitely shielded?"

"I know when I'm scanning a shield."

"But why would Weiss have shielded people brought to Earth like that?"

"He wouldn't. Illegal immigrants would just walk off the ship. I was supposed to be out of the way, remember?"

Chandra stared at the dead man in the chair. "So . . . what was he transporting?"

"I don't know . . . how about animals, a species banned on Earth?"

71

Chandra gave him a dubious look.

Vaughan hesitated. "There was something else. I don't know if it's connected. When I was aboard the ship I found a young girl. She'd been given away by her father on Verkerk's World, taken and brought to Earth by someone called Freidrickson."

"Where is she now?"

"I wish I knew . . ." He told Chandra about the attack.

"I'll get a team over to the 'port immediately, see what we can find. Can you give me the details of the ship?"

A minute later Chandra was talking to a dispatch team on his handset. He cut the connection and nodded to Vaughan. "They're on their way."

"What now?"

"How about a ride over to Weiss's villa? He had a wife and kid. Someone has to break the news . . . I'd like to question her while I'm at it."

They took a lift to the police flier compound and requisitioned a vehicle. As Chandra engaged vertical thrust and they rose high above the ziggurat, Vaughan watched the streets recede beneath him, losing definition and becoming no more than vectors of blurred illumination in the darkness. The hum of mental activity fell away too, so that soon Vaughan enjoyed the rare luxury of being alone with his own thoughts.

They banked and joined a crimson air corridor, heading south toward the conurbation of exclusive residences reserved for politicians and the higher administrators of the Station.

The Weiss villa occupied a prime lot in New Mumbai, on the very edge of the upper-deck. A split-level ranch-style dwelling, it overlooked a sloping lawn and the ocean beyond. Spotlights illuminated the villa front and back, but there was no sign of lights from within the residence. Chandra brought the flier down on the lawn with a roar of thrusters loud enough to wake the neighborhood. They climbed out and walked up the lawn toward the villa.

Chandra pressed a chime panel and stood back, admiring the sloping glass and carbon façade. Vaughan sensed spheres of mind-noise in the neighboring villas, but none from this building.

"No one home, Jimmy."

"No? That's odd. Weiss asked to phone home to tell his wife that he'd be late back."

Chandra took a card from his belt, ran it through the door lock. The door swung open and they stepped inside and moved through the open-plan house. Lights came on automatically as if the pair were being ushered through the rooms by a ghostly guide. Vaughan gazed about him, amazed by an Aladdin's cave of rich carpets, furnishings, works of art: free-standing sculptures occupied strategic positions throughout the ground-floor, and paintings—both old oils and more modern plasma graphics—decorated the walls.

"Genevieve Weiss is an artist," Chandra told him. "She specializes in com-gen 'painting,' according to the files I accessed earlier. Apparently she's very highly regarded. Her pieces fetch millions on the interplanetary market."

The two men walked from room to room like children in wonderland. Vaughan had never experienced such space between four walls since arriving on the Station. He whistled. "You could get agoraphobia just walking to the john."

He detoured down a short, carpeted corridor, came to what was obviously a child's bedroom: a shadowy platoon of teddy bears and clowns lined the far wall. As Vaughan strayed across the threshold, the sensors activated a soft bedside light.

On the bed a single sheet outlined the form of a child, blonde hair showing on the pillow.

"Jimmy," he called. "Here."

Chandra appeared down the corridor. He peered past Vaughan at the child. "I thought you said there was no one home?"

Vaughan nodded. "There isn't."

He crossed to the bed and pulled back the sheet to reveal the little boy's face, still and pale. He felt for a pulse at wrist and throat, found none. "He's been dead for a couple of hours."

Chandra unfastened the boy's pajamas, checked the thin torso. He found the puncture marks on the inside of the arm. "Hypo-ject. I think you'll find that whatever killed him was administered through the vein."

The two men exchanged a glance and hurried from the room.

They found Genevieve Weiss sprawled on a chesterfield in the lounge, her scarlet gown flowing to the floor as if arranged at the second of her death for maximum aesthetic impact. Her head was thrown back over the arm of the chesterfield, long black hair hanging in a sheer fall. Her throat, a beautiful exposed arch of cream flesh, was marred by the ugly bruise of a hypo-ject entry point. The gun had fallen from her limp fingers and skittered across the chess-board tiles.

"You said that Weiss called his wife?" Vaughan said.

Chandra nodded. "Around three hours ago."

"Did you hear what he said?"

"Of course, I was in the same room." Chandra shrugged. "He told her he'd been delayed and wouldn't be home till dawn."

Vaughan thought about it. "It might have been a prearranged signal, warning Genevieve that he'd been rumbled."

"Maybe." Chandra shrugged. "But why? That's what I don't understand. Why would she kill her son and take her own life, just because her husband's fake identity is about to be discovered?"

Vaughan regarded the dead woman, thinking of the cold oblivion that had taken Genevieve Weiss. Some intimation of that oblivion, recalled from all those years ago, sent a shiver through him.

Chandra glanced at him. "She's in a better place now," he murmured. "They both are."

Vaughan turned a withering look on the cop. "Are you quite sure about that, Jimmy? Are you sure they're not both stone cold dead and gone?"

Chandra opened his mouth to reply, then though better of it. He turned his back on Vaughan and spoke into his handset.

Vaughan moved across the room, pausing before an archway leading to an unlighted room. He passed into the room, and concealed lighting obligingly illuminated Genevieve Weiss's studio. Compared to the rest of the house, this room was spartan: a big com array stood on a desk in the center of a polished parquet floor and a dozen plasma graphics adorned the walls.

Vaughan crossed to the computer and seated himself before the screen. He activated the machine, accessed files, and for the next ten minutes scrolled through the portfolio of Genevieve Weiss's collected work.

He spent a second or two with each graphic, not sure what he was looking for—some clue, some visual link to anything that had gone before.

He was almost ready to give up when he struck gold.

The girl stared out of the screen, the expression on her beautiful face caught between ecstasy and agony. She seemed to be floating, bare feet trailing, arms outstretched in the approximation of a crucifix.

Vaughan stared at her face. He commanded the computer to create a print of the graphic.

Chandra appeared beneath the arch. "I've just spoken to the head of the dispatch team at the 'port. They've been through the ship from top to bottom."

"And?"

"It's empty. Apparently an outside team of hauliers came for the container an hour ago. The security guards had voice-code authority from Weiss himself, so they let the hauliers through."

"I'll scan the guards when I get to the 'port," Vaughan said, "read the hauliers' faces. I might come up with something."

"Weiss must have thought of that. The hauliers were Zen cultists, wearing the masks of Denied Identity—or rather they were disguised as cultists. The case could be anywhere by now, even off the Station."

"Great." Vaughan tore the graphic from the printer and held it up to Chandra. "It's the girl I found in the freighter, Jimmy. Elly Jenson. She's the subject of a Weiss graphic called *Adoration of the Chosen One.*"

Chandra's handset chimed. He took the call and spoke rapidly in Hindi. He nodded, his expression serious, and cut the connection.

"That was forensic. They know what killed Weiss—a drug called rhapsody." He looked at Vaughan. "Probably what killed Genevieve and her son, too."

"The same stuff that Tiger took . . ." Vaughan began.

Chandra went on: "They've traced its point of origin,

too. I'll give you three guesses."

"Not Verkerk's World?"

"Right first time," Chandra said. "How about this: quite apart from whatever Weiss was bringing shielded to Earth, he was also smuggling rhapsody?"

"It's possible, I suppose." Vaughan shrugged. "I wonder where the Jenson kid fits in?"

"You tell me. I've got alerts out for her. And we're trying to trace dealers in rhapsody."

When the Scene of Crime team arrived minutes later, Vaughan and Chandra left the villa and boarded the flier. The cop ferried him to an eastside dropchute station, and Vaughan pushed his way through the noisy crowd as the flier took off and climbed into the dawn sky. Clutching the scrolled graphic of the Chosen One, he dropped to level 3 and walked the kilometre home through the still-busy streets, the concentrated mind-noise drumming in his head like a migraine.

Fifteen minutes later he let himself into his apartment. He sat before the window without turning on the light, reached out, and fumbled on the table for the vial of chora. He washed it down with a swig of stale beer from a bottle he found wedged down the cushion of the chair.

Quickly the drug took effect, reducing the mind-hum and allowing him to relax. As the sun rose on the other side of the Station, the night turned from navy to gray and pale light flooded the apartment.

He stood up and found half a dozen magnets in a storage unit. He clamped the graphic of Elly onto the wall, then slumped back into his chair and stared at *Adoration of the Chosen One*.

Common sense told him to drop the case. Forget about the Chosen One and whatever Weiss had been up to . . .

Then he remembered the kid's terror back at the ship.

He wouldn't let the bastards win.

He had a couple of weeks' leave due—he'd contact the 'port and tell them he wasn't coming in for a while. Then he'd concentrate on the Elly Jenson case.

He tapped Dr. Rao's code into his handset, got through to the Indian, and arranged to meet him at nine that evening.

SIX

It was two in the morning and the Siren Bar was filling up.

The dance floor was a mass of bodies, writhing to the rhythmic thump of the latest pop hit. Fat foreign men sat at tables, half-naked girls squirming on their laps. The girls sucked on bottles of beer, feigning interest and animation, but achieving only a look of boredom.

From time to time couples left the bar and passed Sukara on their way to the cubicles. The girls smirked at her as they clung to their rich customers. Sukara tried to ignore them, but felt herself blush beneath the gaze of the men. She drank her beer, lining up the bottles on the bar before her. Fat Cheng had once told her that she drank too much. "Beer okay, Fat Cheng," she had replied. "I take plenty yahd."

He'd shaken his big head. "Not you drunk I worry about, little Monkey. Beer no good for your insides, your liver."

Sukara had just shrugged. She had more to concern her than what beer might be doing to her insides.

A drunken Indian laborer was arguing with two tall escort girls further along the bar. He kept pawing at their breasts, trying to run a hand up inside their thighs. One girl backed off, screeching at the Indian in machine-gun rapid Thai. The guy pulled out his wallet, staggering with the effort, and waved baht in the face of the first girl. She hissed at him, turning her face away contemptuously. The second girl whispered to the Indian and pointed along the bar at

Sukara. He looked up, squinted, then staggered toward her. Behind him, Sukara saw that the girls were laughing.

He slurred something at her in Hindi, waving the cash, a measly fifty-baht note.

Sukara turned away, ignoring him. Her lurched towards her and pincered her arm in a painful grip.

"Let go!"

"I said, come with me!"

For a split second, she considered telling him where to go—but something nasty in his eyes told her that that would not be wise. The alternative was to go with him, and pray that the bastard wouldn't turn violent.

Quickly Sukara grabbed the note, stuffed it into her waistband, and slipped off her stool.

She led the Indian to one of the tiny cubicles, not the room she used for the Ee-tees; she didn't want the memory of what she did with the Indian tainting her special room. He collapsed against the door, staring at her and unfastening his trousers. Sukara slipped the baht under the mattress and pulled down her skirt, leaving her t-shirt on: she did not like going with human men, and tried to keep as much of herself covered as possible.

She knelt on the edge of the bed and held onto the rail on the wall, letting him have her from behind. She heard him belch, smelled the beery fumes in the air. She felt him thrusting between her legs, his first few attempts missing and sliding up and across her back. She felt his fingers forcing apart her legs, felt him try again, this time entering her brutally. He was so big that she feared he might tear her. She closed her eyes and cried out in pain as he thrust repeatedly. She pulled forward so that he slid out before he came, and her relief was immediate.

The first blow struck her across the back of her head, so

painful that she thought he must have picked something up, or pulled a cosh from somewhere. The blow rang through her skull. She fell face down on the bed, protecting her head from his punches. She would not cry out, would not give him the satisfaction of knowing that he was hurting her. She curled into a ball, covering her face with her forearms. He pulled her toward him, prized her arms away from her face, and backhanded her across the jaw. Now she knew why his blows hurt so much: his fingers were studded with big, square-faced, imitation-gold rings. Behind his flailing hands, Sukara stared at the ludicrous sight of his huge cock bobbing up and down in time to the blows. She leapt forward, snatched at his scrotum, and twisted with all her strength. He yelled out in rage and pain and fell to the floor, curled protectively around his injury. Sukara grabbed her skirt and skittered from the cubicle down the corridor and into her Ee-tee room. She locked the door behind her and collapsed onto the bed.

Minutes later she heard the Indian barge from the cubicle and hurry out into the bar, cursing. If he complained to Fat Cheng, then Sukara would tell him that he had hit her, and Fat Cheng would throw the bastard out.

She sat up and felt her head for bumps, then tested the tender area around her chin. As the pain receded, she smiled in pained satisfaction at the thought of the expression on his face when she'd grabbed his balls. It was the last thing they expected, men who hit working girls—that the girls might turn and fight back.

She went with men only rarely now; Ee-tees paid Fat Cheng well for her, and he allowed her to turn down men when she wanted. She wished she hadn't been so greedy tonight, and had told the Indian to get lost.

Three years ago, before the attack that left her scarred,

aliens came rarely to the Siren Bar. Then, she had gone with humans; some men had treated her well, were gentle and considerate, but they were rare. Most men were rough and selfish, others brutal. She could count on a beating every other night. She became accustomed to the rough treatment in time, might even have accepted it if not for the fact that always, at the back of her mind, was the fear that the aggression would turn to something more: again and again she'd heard of customers killing girls in the supposed safety of bars and clubs.

Then she had been attacked, and as she lay in the pool of her blood she thought that this must be the end. In fact, it had turned out to be the beginning of a new phase of her life.

Fat Cheng had taken her back, and for a couple of months she had gone with strange men fascinated with her scar, many of whom did nothing but caress the puckered ridge that bisected her face.

In time the interest in her scarred face fell away—the perverts no longer visited her; perhaps they had found other, more mutilated girls—and the regular customers preferred the beautiful, unscarred girls. For many days, Sukara had attracted no customers, and she feared then that Fat Cheng might tell her to go.

Then he arrived at the bar one night in the company of a tall, thin man—obviously alien—and introduced him, or it, to his prettiest escort girls. They had simpered to the alien, tried all the tricks. Sukara, watching, had felt a surge of jealousy. She'd heard from working girls at other clubs that aliens were gentle lovers and paid well.

The alien had whispered something to Fat Cheng, and Cheng had dismissed the beautiful girls and waved forward others, Sukara among them. She had sat beside the alien on

a high stool, while the other girls fawned over the elon-
gated, blue-skinned being from Barnard's Star.

He had spoken to each of the girls in turn, asking them
personal questions with a formality at once novel and disturbing. Trivial small talk was not the alien's way—he
wanted to know the age of each girl, something of her background. Some of the girls tapped their temples and drifted
away; others, intrigued, stayed and tried to win the Ee-tee's
patronage.

Then he had turned to Sukara. "You are quiet," he said
in his strangely modulated English. His eyes, slit vertically,
stared at her. "What is the marking on your face, Sukara—a
sign of beauty with your people?"

And for the first time she had realised how truly alien
aliens were.

When she explained how she had received the injury,
and that far from being a sign of beauty it was just the opposite, the Ee-tee became fascinated. For the first time in
years, Sukara talked with a potential customer about something other than how far she would go for the least possible
payment.

The Ee-tee had taken her to a cubicle and made love to
her in the way of his people, with her seated face-to-face on
his lap, his many-tentacled member tickling her vagina
while his hands caressed her neck and face. He had not hurt
her; in fact, the experience had been almost enjoyable. He
had even paid her well.

Two days later, another Ee-tee turned up, an alien from
another distant star, and he too had chosen to go with
Sukara. Within a week, she had two or three customers a
night from all points of the galaxy. Fat Cheng had even
given her a room in which to entertain her guests. When the
other girls, jealous of her newfound popularity, had started

taunting her, Fat Cheng had called them into his office before work one evening. Listening at the door, Sukara heard Fat Cheng say: "Sukara, she bring in many baht—more than you, Koruna, or you, Suki. No more bad tricks, okay? I see you treat her badly, you go, quick smart."

After that, the taunts and cruel tricks had been carefully concealed from Fat Cheng—but were all the more cruel because of that—and no one had admitted to putting things in her bed.

Fat Cheng had taken her to one side. "You no listen to other girls, little Monkey, you hear me? They only jealous. You know why Ee-tees like you, little Monkey? They like what in here—" and he had tapped her head. "To aliens, matters more what in here than what you look like, okay?"

Now Sukara opened the door of the cubicle and peered out. There was no sign of the drunken Indian. She ran down the corridor to the other cubicle, slipped inside, and lifted the mattress. She felt underneath, then stared in disbelief.

The Indian had taken her money.

Sukara showered, easing her battered head in the hot jet of water. While she was drying herself, she accidentally caught a glimpse of her face in the mirror. She was surprised, as ever, by the extent that the scar ridge divided her face into two equal halves, each as plain as the other. Her most remarkable feature, she had to admit, was the scar.

She fingered the swelling on her chin, where the flesh was becoming discolored.

She dressed and returned to the bar, sat on a stool, and drank another cold beer. In the half-light, no one noticed her bruised jaw.

It was almost four and the Siren Bar was emptying. Even the flashing lights and the beat of the music had slowed. Fat

Cheng had vacated his stool and dragged himself to his hammock in his office. A few desultory couples still traipsed around the dance floor, supporting each other more in drunkenness than through any desire to dance. Girls sat around the tables, their bare legs crossed, smoking cigarettes and staring blankly into space. Sukara had two hours to kill before she could go home. In that time, if approached by a human, she would flatly refuse him, even if he offered two hundred baht, three hundred . . . If an Ee-tee turned up, she would go with it.

She finished her beer and counted the empty bottles. Eight. She signaled for another from the yawning barman. The yahd was beginning to wear off, the alcohol taking its chance to affect her. She felt tired, and found herself clock-watching, which was always a mistake. The minutes seemed to last forever.

A handsome human man in a sharp suit walked in, ordered a beer. He stood by the bar, turning to take in the girls with an intensity that suggested he was looking for someone. A girl moved from her table, swaying across the room toward him. She placed a hand on his sleeve, stood on tiptoe to whisper into his ear.

It was then, with the girl trying her best, that Sukara noticed that the man was staring at her.

There was something disconcerting in his gaze, almost as if he recognised her, was surprised at finding her here. She looked away, flustered, and raised her bottle to her mouth. When she looked back at him, the man was brushing aside the startled escort girl and making his way along the bar.

She had decided to tell him to fuck off when she saw the look in his eyes. He had warm, brown eyes that smiled at her. They were not the eyes of someone who could hurt her, she told herself. The man was Western, perhaps forty, with dark receding hair and a wide, pleasant smile. Everything about him said that she should trust him, and yet the very fact that he had approached her, instead of one of the many other working girls still in the bar, told her to be careful.

"Can I get you a . . ." he began, then saw the row of bottles before her. He smiled. "Silly question." He hitched himself onto a high stool beside her. "Don't tell me," he went on, gesturing to the regiment of bottles, "yahd, right?"

She looked at him, suspicious. "How you know, mister?"

He shrugged and smiled easily. "Calculated guess. You don't look drunk. Yet eight bottles of beer would be enough to put you under the table. Ergo: yahd."

She smiled despite herself. Some of his phrases didn't make sense to her, though she understood his general meaning. She glanced quickly at him. He wore an expensive-looking pendant on a chain around his neck, a golden oval that glinted in the light from the overhead fluorescent.

"Where you come from, mister? You European?"

"Canadian."

"You here on big business?"

"You could say that. I move about, here and there . . ." He mentioned a few of the cities he'd visited recently.

She noticed that, when he thought she wasn't watching him, his gaze would linger on her face, not her body—and specifically on her eyes, as if trying to see inside her. He made a brilliant show of not noticing her scar.

"What you do? What your job, mister?"

He smiled, a modest hitch of the lips, and it was enchanting. "Oh . . . I work for my country's government, buying and selling."

Sukara giggled. It was like a game. "Buying and selling what? No! Don't tell me. I guess. Ah . . ." She put on a thinking frown, pushing out her lips. "Okay, you buy and sell fruit, no? Mangoes and durian?"

He laughed. "No, not quite. Machinery. Production equipment . . . you know, robots."

"Robots? Like this?" She stiffened her arms and rocked from side to side on her stool. "I robot!"

He laughed again. The other girls had noticed how well they were getting on. Sukara felt buoyant with the alcohol.

"No—production line robots, machines that build fliers and voidships."

She nodded, lifted her beer and drank. "So, mister, what your name?"

"Osborne. And yours?"

"Guess." She folded her tongue and poked it into the neck of the bottle, staring at him.

"Okay. Let me see . . . You look like a . . . a Su."

Sukara blinked, sat bolt upright on her stool. "Hey, how you know that?"

Osborne smiled, shrugged casually. "I guessed, how else?"

She squinted at him, suspicious. "You guessed right. But millions of names. Lucky guess, mister. You always that lucky?"

He shrugged again, finished his beer, and ordered another. He paid from a thick wad of baht. While he was busy with the barman, Sukara took in his clothing: the expensive suit, the stylish silk shirt.

He swiveled his stool to face her, drinking from his new beer.

"So, Mr. Osborne, you want come with me?"

He frowned in playful consideration, shook his head. "No. I'm fine here. I'm enjoying our little chat."

He reached out, lay a hand on her knee, and squeezed. The touch affected her like an electric jolt. She ran a ridiculous fantasy—this man was different: not a customer, but someone who wanted her for what she was, not for how good she was in bed.

Then she stopped herself. There was only one reason he was talking to her now. He wanted to use her. Perhaps he was another scar freak.

They chatted about cities of the Earth, and then some of the colony worlds he'd visited. Sukara sat open-mouthed at the descriptions of the cities he'd seen, the natural wonders of the Expansion.

When she next looked at the clock behind the bar, it was almost six. Strange thing was, she no longer felt like going home. She could have sat and talked to Osborne all day.

He must have noticed her glance. He tapped her knee again. "Like I said, nice talking to you, Su."

She was momentarily tongue-tied. She wanted to beg him to stay, to talk to her more.

He pulled a baht note from his wallet, slipped it into her fingers. "See you around, okay?"

"Yeah, sure. See you around." She tried to make it sound like she wouldn't be bothered if she never saw him again.

Osborne eased himself from his stool and strolled, casual to the last, from the bar. Sukara watched him go, her heart sinking. She told herself not to be such a little fool. Then she lifted her hand and stared at the note. Two hundred baht . . . The sight of the bright orange note gave her a kick, and she told herself that she should be thankful.

At six, she jumped down from her stool and made her way unsteadily from the bar. She picked her mask up from reception, slipped it over her head, and hurried through the polluted dawn to the metro station.

The express was almost empty at this hour, heading out of the city, and she arrived home in record time. She locked the door behind her, switched on the vid-screen, and cooked egg noodles on her tiny stove. She ate them while watching an adventure movie set on Mars, then turned down the sound and prepared herself for bed.

As she lay on her back and stared at the ceiling a meter above her head, she thought over the past few hours. She considered the drunken Indian, then Osborne. She should have felt pleased that he had talked to her in preference to the other girls, pleased that he'd given her the two-hundred-baht note.

But, she could not help asking herself, why? Why her? She wanted to hate him for leading her on like that, giving her false hope. Then she recalled the charm of his smile, and how it had made her feel, and she could not bring herself to hate him.

She let her mind wander, and soon she was considering her little sister, wondering what she might be doing now . . .

She reached under the pillow and pulled out a silk scarf and unrolled it, smoothing her fingers along the embroidered message.

Last week a plastic-wrapped package had arrived at the Siren Bar, brought in by a girl who worked at a nearby club. The parcel was addressed to Chintara Sukarapatam, Working Girl, Bangkok, Thailand—and miraculously it had found her, though the postmark indicated that it had been mailed over a year ago.

She had torn away the plastic with trembling fingers. She knew only one person who could have sent the parcel. She had unrolled the scarf, wondering at such a present, and it was a minute before she saw the message stitched in Thai beneath the procession of red dragons:

Dear Sister, I am on Bengal Station, keeping well and

working. I think of you every day. When you have money, come to the Station. I will be outside Nazruddin's Restaurant, Chandi Road, Himachal sector. I am well and hope you are. Love, Pakara.

And, stitched in smaller letters in the very corner of the scarf, was a P.S.

My friends now call me Tiger.

It had been the best present Sukara had ever received— proof, after so long, that her little sister was alive and well. She kept the scarf safe beneath her pillow and dreamed of one day meeting Pakara again outside Nazruddin's.

SEVEN

So this was how the super-rich lived . . . and died.

Perhaps a hundred mourners were gathered on the sloping lawns of the Sylvan Gardens that afternoon, preparatory to the ceremony that would see Gerhard Weiss, his wife Genevieve, and son Toby interred beneath the expensive sod of Bengal Station's only cemetery.

Vaughan stood in the shade of a silver birch, nursing a glass of white wine and examining the mourners. So far as he could make out, they comprised three distinct sub-groups. He recognised Weiss's managerial colleagues from the 'port, sober men and women in traditional black, doing a good job of feigning an appropriate response to the loss of someone they had never really liked. Then there were the artist friends of Genevieve Weiss, agents, rich patrons, and the usual social parasites of the art world. A group of Toby's school-friends and their parents formed a smaller clique. All told, it was the kind of elite soiree that Vaughan would rather have avoided. A greater contrast to Tiger's funeral he could not imagine.

Unaugmented, he nevertheless felt the tone of varied emotions from the minds of the mourners, and grief was not uppermost.

He spotted a waiter bearing a loaded tray, eased through a press of chattering artists, and captured another glass. He wandered through the gathering, less self-conscious while on the move.

"Jeff. I didn't think you'd bother turning up." Chandra

appeared beside him. "Not that I'd ever accuse you of lacking compassion."

"Of course you'd never do that, Jimmy." Vaughan raised his glass in an ironic salute. "Actually, I'm not here to shed tears."

"I thought not, somehow. How about shedding a compassionate thought for innocent victims?"

Sometimes, just sometimes, Vaughan felt like pushing a fist in Jimmy Chandra's smug, smiling little Indian face. "Bullshit. I don't feel anything for anyone they're planting here today. To tell you the truth, I think it's a waste of space."

"Why are you here, then?"

"I suspect for the same reason that you are, if you're honest."

Chandra considered that. "So, what do you hope to find?"

"I don't know. I don't even know what I'm looking for."

"Another piece of the enigmatic puzzle?"

"Yeah, right."

"For what it's worth. I've been doing a bit of work on the case."

"What is it worth?" Vaughan asked.

"Precious little, to be honest. I've contacted the police authorities on Verkerk's World, inquired about the Jenson family."

"And?"

"We won't hear back for a few days. I also asked about the trade in endangered or proscribed animal species."

Vaughan nodded. "Do you know anything about Verkerk's World?"

"The planet was explored, developed, and settled by the Verkerk-Scherring company, fifty years ago. It's a bit of a

92

backwater, no big cities or heavy industries. The same governing council ran the place until recently. A couple of weeks ago the government was ousted in a peaceful coup."

A tasteful loudspeaker announcement informed the guests that the ceremony was about to take place in the burial glade. Mourners close to the family began to move from the lawn, while other guests waited respectfully.

"I've talked to all the known drug dealers, Jeff. They're either lying, or they know nothing about rhapsody. There's nothing to suggest that Weiss was smuggling the drug to Earth. Then again, there's nothing to suggest that he wasn't." Chandra smiled up at Vaughan, a sliver of gold glinting between incisors. "Did I tell you, Jeff? I don't like puzzles."

"Me neither."

"I'm going to circulate. I'll be in touch. Contact me if you come up with anything interesting, okay?"

Chandra strolled off through the crowd. Vaughan joined the sedate procession of mourners from the lawn and into the glade of silver birch that was Sylvan Gardens proper.

Three coffins stood on a raised platform for all to see, the child's tiny and pathetic between those of his parents. In a touch at once novel and macabre, the material of the caskets was transparent. As Vaughan filed past with the other mourners, he saw that the morticians had done a good job on Gerhard Weiss's blood-suffused face: his death mask was unnaturally pale. His wife was as beautiful in death as in life, an imperious ice queen garbed in black velvet and surrounded by red roses, as if, artist to the very last, she had had a posthumous hand in the aesthetics of her send-off.

As the coffins were lowered into three precisely excavated rectangular graves, a choir of a dozen female sopranos

93

warbled an aria, and a silver haired man in a white suit—combining practiced *gravitas* with avuncular hospitality—welcomed everyone to this sad yet joyous occasion, the celebration of the lives of the family Weiss.

"Gerhard Weiss was a loved and respected member of the community, as admired among his loyal staff as he was by his friends. Genevieve, as we all know, was a world-renowned artist who never let her fame interfere with her work or her regard of the many people close to her . . ."

Spare me, Vaughan thought. As tactfully as possible, he eased his way to the rear of the gathering. He was waiting for a suitable opportunity to make his exit when he sensed someone beside him.

"I take it that you are not an artist?"

He looked up. "I consider that a compliment."

The woman was of African origin—the skin of her severely angled face as black as graphite—and tall. Vaughan was six-four, and the woman stood a good head above him, her height emphasized by the attenuated quality of her limbs and the fact that she wore a tight, white suit.

"I'm Dolores Yandoah." She held out a limp hand. The glow of her mind suggested someone blitzed to a Zen-state acceptance of *everything* by expensive designer pharmaceuticals.

He nodded, ignored the proffered hand. "Vaughan." He returned his attention to the eulogy.

"What do you think, Vaughan?"

He looked at the woman. She was serenely staring over the heads of the guests, watching the ceremony. "Of this? To be honest, I think it's a hypocritical farce. And tacky."

"Oh, do you? I think that, as funerals go, this one is rather good. Aesthetically satisfying, and yet cathartic to those here to mourn."

94

"Perhaps that's the reason I can't share your appreciation," Vaughan said. "I have no aesthetic sensibility, and I'm not mourning."

"I was right," she murmured, more to herself. "You're not an artist. I've been watching you. You look at everything as if you hate everything. You have a rather negative view of reality, Vaughan."

He laughed. "Is this reality?"

"It's just as much reality as anything you would care to offer up as such," Dolores drawled. "But then you're the kind of person who would sneer at your own reality, even."

Vaughan glanced up at the woman. "What are you, some kind of psychologist?"

Dolores smiled, her mouth expanding to reveal a wide corncob of teeth. "I'm an artist, Vaughan. Tell me, what are you doing here if you're not mourning?"

"I've come to sneer," he said.

Dolores laughed, as if in perverse delight. "You are one sad bastard, Vaughan."

Their sparring was interrupted by the arrival of a small woman in a black suit. Her pale, pretty face, diminutive stature, and flighty, bird-like movements were the complete antithesis to Dolores's attenuated, ebony hauteur.

The new arrival, barely half the size of the African, linked an arm around the top of Dolores's right thigh. "Lola, darling. What have you found? Do share!"

"An interesting specimen," Dolores wisecracked. She bent and whispered something to her friend.

"Don't mind Lola," the young woman laughed. "She's highly temperamental. Carmine, by the way. Carmine Villefranche."

He nodded. "Jeff Vaughan."

"Now let me see. This is exciting!" Carmine tapped her

lips with a straight finger. "From what Lola has mentioned, I'd guess you're an atheist, right? But not a humanist—am I warm?"

"Boiling."

"How wonderful! I do so enjoy the vicarious thrill of despair one gains from dialogue with a nihilist. Lola, darling, do you mind if I steal Vaughan for a little while? I might even be able to convert him."

"You're welcome to him, darling. But do treat him gently." Dolores leaned over, bending herself into a stark, white-suited right angle, and kissed the young woman on the forehead. "Till later, *ma chérie.*"

Carmine, her mind bright with love and delight at life, took Vaughan by the hand and tugged him away from the gathering. "Would you care for a drink, Vaughan? I bet you drink scotch neat, am I right?"

Vaughan shook his head. "Beer. Blue Mountain," he said. "Did you know the Weiss's well?"

Carmine twisted her lips into a thoughtful *moue* as they crossed the lawn. "Not *that* well, Vaughan. They were fellow believers. I met them at the Church—"

"The Church . . . ?"

"The Church of the Adoration of the Chosen One," Carmine said.

Vaughan almost halted in his tracks. He said, "Tell me about your religion."

"Gosh!" Carmine cried theatrically. She mimed speaking into a Dictaphone. "Subject indicates latent interest in abstract philosophies," she whispered, but there was a smile in her eyes acknowledging the game.

They found an *al fresco* bar on the lawn overlooking the ocean and ordered drinks. As Carmine made her selection, a daiquiri with ice, Vaughan felt that for some reason—no

doubt Carmine would have a suitably cutting psychological
hypothesis—he could not equate the young woman sitting
opposite him with anything to do with the kidnapping of
Elly Jenson.

"How long have you been a member of the Church?"

Carmine sipped her drink, watching him over the rim.
"Why the sudden interest, Vaughan?"

He shrugged. "Religions fascinate me."

She positioned her glass on the table. "What do you
think of the dominant religion here? Hinduism?" she asked.

Vaughan shrugged. "I don't hold with it myself. But I
can understand how millions of Hindus believe—"

"You sound like you condone such superstition."

"I understand how historical and social conditions create
the climate for the growth of belief systems," Vaughan said,
watching the girl. "I don't condone, I try to comprehend.
Anyway, you have your own belief system. Who are you to
call someone else's religion a superstition? Isn't yours?"

Her gaze hardened. "No. No, it isn't, Vaughan." She
paused there, watching him, seeming to consider her words.
"I was like you a year or so ago. I had no belief, no hope. I
could see nothing good in anything around me."

Vaughan took a swallow of beer. "What happened?"

"What happened? I found the Church, that's what happened. I met Dolores. I fell head first and we shared everything. She had her belief, her Church. I was skeptical at
first. Like, it wasn't 'on' to believe in anything but the lib-
eral ideal of no-holds-barred free expression, right? So I
went along, expecting to hate the whole thing."

"And you were converted."

"You know something, you're so ugly when you sneer."

"I'm sorry." He tried not to smile. "But you were
converted?"

She waited, nodded finally. "I found the truth. I found I belonged. I was no longer alone, adrift. You know—even when you have someone, you're still alone. Inside. We all need something more than just someone."

"So what was it you found?"

"I told you. The truth. Cosmic awareness. Suddenly, I understood."

"I'm trying not to sneer, okay?" He pointed to his woodenly straight face. "But please tell me—you know, I'd really like to know: what is the truth, Carmine? I'm really eager to know."

"You *bastard.*"

"Okay, so I'm a bastard. I don't believe a damned word. So convince me. Tell me: what is this Truth of yours?"

She spoke deliberately, each word as hard as steel. "I took communion. I ate the wafer and for the next thirty minutes or more, I was no longer Carmine Villefranche. I was . . . unified. I shared cosmic awareness. I saw the place of humanity in the universe, the small part we are of the much vaster sentient organism in which we exist and share." She stopped there, eyes wide, as if she were reliving the experience.

Casually, aware of the sweat breaking out on his forehead, Vaughan said, "Who is the Chosen One?"

"She is the very center of our Church."

Vaughan reached into his jacket pocket. Earlier that day he'd had the Genevieve Weiss's graphic copied to the size of a snapshot. He passed it across to Carmine. "Is she the Chosen One?"

"Hey—how come you have this?" She looked at him, suspicious.

"Like I said, I'm interested in religions."

Carmine gazed at the pix, and Vaughan could not mistake the look of awe in her eyes. "Every two years, the God-head chooses anew. She is the present Chosen One."

Attempting to keep his voice even, he said, "Have you looked upon this Chosen One?"

She blinked. "Why, of course. Just last night."

"Where? Where did you see her?"

"In church, where else?"

Vaughan nodded. He took a swallow of beer. He had to be careful, very careful. He could not be seen to be concentrating his interest on the girl to the exclusion of Carmine's religion, the focus of his original inquiry.

"Tell me about your religion. Its history, origins."

Carmine finished her drink, gestured to the waiter, and ordered another daiquiri.

"It started perhaps thirty years ago on my homeplanet, Verkerk's World," she said, and Vaughan tried not to show any reaction to the mention of the colony.

Verkerk's World, again . . .

Carmine went on: "A young girl was granted a vision one day while walking alone in the mountains. She was granted communion, and told to spread the word. She told colony leaders, those in authority, about a drug that would bring humanity together, eliminate the division caused by greed, put an end to national pettiness, aggression, and warfare."

"This drug . . . what's it called?"

Carmine smiled. "We call it rhapsody," she said.

He nodded. "I've heard of it. It's very dangerous. It kills."

"Alcohol kills, Vaughan. One must not abuse substances, or they abuse you—"

"You should have told that to Genevieve Weiss and her family."

Carmine looked at him with surprise. "But Genevieve knew what she was doing, Vaughan. It wasn't just your regular everyday suicide. The Weiss family decided that they wished to make the ultimate sacrifice, the sacrifice of the self to the all. She is in a much better place, now. She and her loved ones have been absorbed into the infinite."

Vaughan nodded, withholding the impulse to laugh.

"Over the years," Carmine went on, "the religion grew on Verkerk's World. A few years ago it spread to Earth. It will gain hold, slowly. How can it hope to succeed *immediately*, when competing against so many ancient, entrenched belief systems, however simplistic they are? But the Truth will overcome, in time."

"It sounds . . . interesting."

Her expression showed feigned surprise. She spoke into her imaginary Dictaphone: "From mocking skepticism, subject exhibits first signs of curiosity."

Vaughan played along. "How regular are the services, the acts of communion?"

"Daily—that is, nightly. We congregate every midnight for the communion with the Chosen One."

"Are the merely curious welcome?"

"We're always recruiting new members, Vaughan. But if you came along, you would have to take communion."

"Sounds like quite an experience. Where's the church?"

She gave him an address in the Thai district of Tavoy, eastside, level 5. "Be there just before midnight, Vaughan, or you'll miss out on all the fun."

Over in Sylvan Gardens, the ceremony was coming to an end, the mourners drifting away from the lawns to the exit. The sun was going down in the west, over the bulk of the Station behind them. Vaughan glanced at his watch.

"You have to go so soon?" Carmine asked.

"Afraid so. I must meet someone."

"Pity. I thought maybe you and me—"

He looked at her. "I thought you and Dolores were . . . ?"

She raised her eyes to the sky. "You *straights!* Hey, I'm my own person. I'm adaptable, okay? Why don't we . . . ?"

"I'm sorry."

"You have someone, right? So, what does it matter? *Enjoy* yourself." She glared at him with barely concealed loathing. "Hell, and I thought I was living in the permissive age!"

"I've enjoyed our talk, okay . . . ?" Vaughan muttered. "I'm sorry."

"Hey, don't apologize. *I'm* okay. You're missing the party, buddy."

He wondered if, were it not for the side effects of the chora, he might have found Carmine Villefranche sexually attractive. He sincerely hoped not.

"I must go. Perhaps I'll see you tonight. Midnight, right?"

"Yeah, sure. Midnight. Hey, and if you change your mind . . ."

As he walked away, she raised her fist to her mouth and said, "Subject declines offer of sexual union, but evinces interest in transcendental communion. Perhaps there's hope for him yet."

The sun was setting by the time the train carried Vaughan into Chandi Road Station. He forced his way through the press of humanity on the platform and was carried along the crowded street toward Nazruddin's. Legless beggars in wheeled carts beseeched him with pitiful eyes and outthrust palms, the more able attempting to keep pace with him. He could not imagine a much greater contrast to the affluent citizens of the northern sector.

Outside Nazruddin's he bought a vial of chora from a street kid and entered the restaurant. He slipped into his booth and checked the time; he was not due to meet Dr. Rao for another thirty minutes. He typed Jimmy Chandra's code into his handset.

As he waited for Chandra to answer, he mimed drinking beer and Nazruddin obligingly ferried over an ice-cold bottle, self-mockingly holding it label upwards for inspection like a wine waiter. Vaughan gave the thumbs up as the restaurateur toweled off the condensation and placed the bottle on the table with a glass.

His handset flared into life. Jimmy Chandra smiled up at him. "Jeff. How was the afternoon—stay till the end?"

"Till the very death," Vaughan smiled. "How's the search for the Jenson girl going?"

"Need you ask?"

"It's just that I learnt one or two things this afternoon. I thought you might be interested."

Jimmy leaned out of shot to conduct a brief exchange with someone. He reappeared. "Sorry, what was that?"

"I said, I know where Elly Jenson is—or rather where she'll be at midnight."

A silence greeted his words as Jimmy Chandra just stared. "If this is some kind of joke . . ."

"Have you ever known me to joke?" Vaughan recounted his meeting with Villefranche, told him what the woman had said. He repeated the church's address.

Chandra leaned back, typing on a terminal keyboard. "Okay, I've got that." He looked up. "And she said that the Chosen One would be at the church tonight?"

"At midnight, for communion."

"We're talking about the same Chosen One?"

"I showed her the Weiss graphic."

"I mean the girl you saw in the freighter, Elly Jenson . . . Is she definitely the Chosen One?"

"I know what I saw, Jimmy. And anyway, it all ties in. The Church of the Adoration of the Chosen One was founded on Verkerk's World. The communicants use rhapsody to gain this so called 'cosmic unity.' "

"But why would this Villefranche character tell you all this?"

"Because she's a member of the congregation who wants to spread the word."

"Okay, okay . . . I'm trying to think." Chandra typed at the off-screen keyboard again. "Okay, this is what we'll do. You go along as planned. I'll have the place staked. We'll come in, round up the congregation, and get the Jenson girl. Try to get to the kid so they don't spirit her away. Not that I plan to let that happen. We'll have the exits covered. Hey, Jeff, if you ever feel like joining the force . . ."

"Yeah, I'll know who to apply to. See you later."

Vaughan took a long drink of beer, ordered a masala dosa, and snacked before his meeting with Rao.

The little doctor arrived punctually at nine.

Dressed like a million Indians of his age and caste in a Nehru suit—a faded ochre evening jacket and tight white leggings—Rao had the appearance of a frail and inoffensive grandfather. Vaughan sensed, behind the ancient wire-rimmed spectacles, a mind primed with self-importance constantly on the lookout for the next break.

The doctor bowed and placed his palms together before his face. "*Namaste*, Mr. Vaughan. I received your summons."

"Glad you could make it, Rao. Take a seat."

"I am always interested in hearing about a business proposition," Rao said. "Especially from sources as reliable as yourself." He knocked his walking stick on the floor, his arthritic fingers knotted around its handle like broken cheroots.

He ordered a lassi and Vaughan refilled his own glass. He sipped the beer, considering his words. "I've heard that you're the man to approach if something is required . . . some device that the authorities don't like private citizens owning?"

Rao spread his hands. "Your information is correct."

"I need an augmentation-pin."

Rao looked puzzled for a second. "Ah, you mean a telepathic enhancer."

"I mean an augmentation-pin. You can call them what you like. I've heard that bootleg pins can be bought, if you know the right people."

Rao fingered his tikka spot, a splash of crimson paint on the middle of his forehead, stuck with three grains of rice. "An augmentation-pin. Ah-cha. Very bothersome. A very difficult commission, Mr. Vaughan."

"Can you do it?"

Rao was theatrical with his repertoire of frowns and grimaces. "Well, let me see. I suppose . . . perhaps. Yes, it could be done. The price will be high, very high, I must warn you at the outset. And also the quality of the bootleg will not be of the quality of the precision engineered variety."

"As long as it will enhance my present ability."

Rao nodded. "Yes, I understand. Of course, I cannot obtain this device immediately. I must make contacts, delicate communications involving characters with whom I would rather not deal. Do you understand my meaning, Mr. Vaughan?"

"How much?"

"A very tricky question. A conundrum, sir." He unhooked his spectacles and proceeded to knead his tired eyes. "One year ago, if my memory serves me, I recall a pin changing hands for something in the region of . . . five thousand."

"Rupees, of course?"

Rao made a sad face. "Baht, Mr. Vaughan."

Vaughan whistled.

"That was one year ago, and of course taking into account inflation . . ."

"Of course."

"I am confident that I can furnish you with an augmentation-pin for six thousand baht."

"If you can get me a pin before tomorrow midnight, I'll give you four thousand baht."

"Mr. Vaughan . . . I have my children to cherish. Would you be so churlish as to deprive my starvelings?"

"Four thousand or nothing, Dr. Rao."

"Four and a half thousand if I supply you with the pin before six tomorrow, Mr. Vaughan. You can ask no fairer."

Vaughan extended his hand across the table. "Deal, Dr. Rao. Four and a half before six. After six, and I'll give you four."

He gave Rao his handset code, and the doctor inscribed the number in a tiny notebook with an ancient ink pen. "Until tomorrow, Mr. Vaughan. *Namaste.*"

"Ah-cha, Rao. See you tomorrow."

Vaughan finished his beer and watched the charlatan hobble from the restaurant. He ordered another bottle, accessed his handset, and called up the map of the Station's rail and dropchute routes. For the next thirty minutes he worked out how to get across to Tavoy on the fifth level, eastside.

He set off at ten-thirty, to give himself plenty of time.

The upper-deck rail network was busy at all hours, so Vaughan walked to the closest dropchute station and descended to the next rail system on the seventh level. A rattling carriage ferried him through the industrial heart of Bengal Station, the journey passing for the most part through darkened tunnels. Occasionally they emerged into the bright photon illumination of a platform populated, at this time during factory work-shifts, by lone travellers, beggars, and bored station cleaners. Now and again the bulkheads on either side of the train, the walls of the factories themselves, were emblazoned with photon tubes or ancient neons spelling out the names of companies and corporations: Tata, Boeing, Hindustan Inc. . . . There was something almost despairing about such advertising, like cries in the dark.

He alighted at the eastside terminal and walked through the busy street corridors of a food market district, following ceiling arrows in red to the nearest upchute station. He shared a cage with half a dozen mendicant Thai monks, fists clenched inside bronze meal bowls like boxing gloves. At level 5, they stepped out and he followed them from the station. Across the street—more a wide, enclosed corridor illuminated by artificial daylight—a sign displayed the district's name, Tavoy, in English, Hindi, and Thai.

Vaughan consulted his handset's street map and set off west. The area was predominantly Thai and gave the appearance of affluence: the two-story polycarbon façades were bright with photon advertisements, and hi-tech gimmickry worked its magic in the air—advertisements exploded like harmless fireworks before the eye, and holograms of naked men and women beckoned passers-by into emporiums selling everything from sex to the latest pharmaceutical concoctions.

He moved away from the commercial heart of the district, passing down street-corridors flanked with restaurants and food-carts. The carts, wreathed in steam, tendered delicacies as varied as roast hog, dog, and kebabs strung with rats and toads. The aroma of cooking meat filled the air, along with the piping cacophony of Thai pop music.

The eating establishments gave way to an avenue devoted to visual entertainments: old-time cinemas, dramavilles, and hologram palaces, the façades on either side of the street an honor guard of exotic, larger than life images—walls of copulating couples, fighting soldiers, speeding fliers . . .

Vaughan came to the address Villefranche had given him. He found himself outside not a church but yet another dramadrome—this one advertising itself as the Holosseum. He consulted his handset to ensure he wasn't mistaken, checked the stenciled numerals above the arched, neon entrance: it was the same address. He backed off across the street, allowing the crowds to flow past him, and looked right and left for an establishment more in keeping with a place of worship. He was beginning to wonder whether Villefranche had tricked him when he heard a shrill summons from across the street-corridor. "Hey, Tarzan—here!"

She stood in the entrance to the Holosseum, reaching up on tiptoe and waving. He pushed through the crowds. "What's a tarzan?"

Carmine made her eyes massive. "You're *so* uncultured, Vaughan!" she cried. "Tarzan—popular cultural icon of the twentieth century, a primitive heroic ape-man."

"You're so complimentary." He looked around at the façade of the Holosseum. "Is this the place?"

"This is it. It's almost midnight. Let's get inside."

He followed the woman into the plush foyer of the Holosseum, still more like a theater than a church. As they passed down a darkened corridor, Carmine took his hand

and led him through swing doors into an even darker area. They came to a halt.

"Where are we?" he asked, apprehensive.

Before she could reply, the darkness was banished: a fanfare announced the sudden, celestial arrival of light. Around him, he heard gasps of delight. He blinked. He was standing in a crowd of perhaps a hundred citizens, Europeans, Indians, and Thais, and he was no longer in a building. As he watched, the crowd moved away around the tiers of a vast amphitheater of stone and sat down beneath a cloudless blue sky. The illusion was remarkable. A warm wind blew, birds sang, and the scent of blossoms hung in the air.

Carmine tugged his hand. "Come on." She drew him into the bowl of the amphitheater, down a central aisle. She was about to move to a stone seat five rows from the front, but Vaughan suggested the very front row. They sat before the level performance area, Vaughan still marveling at the fidelity of the illusion. He turned and looked behind him, up the rising sweep of the amphitheater; the church was rapidly filling.

"What is this?" he whispered.

She reciprocated with a conspiratorial whisper of her own: "The Holosseum, Batang Road, Tavoy."

"Very funny. I meant, which planet?"

"Verkerk's World. Where else?"

Where else, indeed? He should have known. Beyond the semi-circle of the amphitheater, foothills rose to a distant mountain range, spectacular in its clarity. The occasional bird, long-beaked and silver-winged, darted from trees as twisted and tortured as specimens of overgrown bonsai.

After his initial rush of amazement, Vaughan began to detect the reality behind the illusion. He touched the "stone" seat beside him, and instead of feeling the rough-napped texture of chiseled stone, his fingers encountered what was obviously a wooden bench embroidered with a fine network of holo-capillaries. He watched his fingertips disappear, eerily overlaid with the surface of the stone.

Oddly, knowledge of the deception did nothing to lessen the visual impact of the scene. A part of his mind still believed he was out in the open air of a colony planet light years from Earth.

"It's about to start!" Carmine whispered, squeezing his arm.

Seconds later, to a spontaneous outburst of applause, a tall figure strode from behind a stand of trees and stood behind a dais in the performance area.

Vaughan stared. The Master of Ceremonies wore a white cloak that flowed from shoulder to foot, and a black mask that was no more than a featureless oval. There was something nevertheless familiar about the figure, something at once imperious and languid.

"Welcome, communicants," said a deep, dark voice.

Vaughan turned to Carmine. "Dolores!"

Carmine was staring, rapt. She nodded. "Dolores is the High Priestess of our Church. Now, shhh!"

Dolores was saying: "After the sharing of wisdom, the meditation, we will participate in the Communion of Unification. Today as ever we are blessed by the Godhead incarnate, the vessel through which the ultimate union can be achieved. Let us give thanks!"

As one, the congregation bowed their heads and murmured a prayer led by Dolores. "Let us give thanks for the munificence of the Godhead, the holy ultimate through which we all find enlightenment. For many years we have struggled to bring the true word to the uninitiated, but now that struggle has entered upon a new and wondrous stage. Let us pray for the salvation of all those unfortunates who have not yet found the Truth, but who with the guidance of the Godhead soon will, and let us look forward to the day when enlightenment will be universal. Amen."

"Amen!"

Vaughan glanced at his watch. It was fifteen minutes after midnight. He wondered when the Chosen One would make her appearance.

"Communicants, the sermon today is the Parable of the Lost."

The sermon was a repetition of platitudes and high-flown oratory, the moral being that only when the world became, like everyone present, true believers, would humankind be saved. Vaughan found the whole thing simplistic in the extreme.

He glanced around at the congregation. He wondered when Chandra's men would make their entrance.

"And now, fellow true believers, the act of communion." Dolores turned, spread a long hand. Onto the performance area from beyond a green hillock strode the tiny, upright figure of Elly Jenson, as pretty as an angel in a long white dress.

"Communicants," said Dolores. "The Chosen One!"

Vaughan drew a breath. There was no mistaking the perfection of features, the gemstone brilliant eyes. Her hair was a perfect halo of radiant curls. The expression on her face was one of stoic determination to give a flawless performance.

He recalled her terror in the freighter, and tried to detect some indication that the girl was drugged, was doing this against her will. But all he sensed was her contentment.

She carried a small wicker basket before her, and when she reached a second, smaller dais she placed the basket upon it. She knelt, staring at the gathered congregation. Her expression was focused, serious.

Dolores said, "Will the first communicants step forward?" She moved from the performance area, so that all attention now was focused upon the Chosen One.

A man and woman, further along the front row, stood and walked toward the dais behind which Elly Jenson waited. First the woman knelt, bowed her head, then looked into the eyes of the Chosen One. Elly reached into the basket, took a small crimson wafer, and slipped it into the woman's open mouth. The girl murmured something; the woman stood and left the stage as if in a trance. The man knelt and the procedure was repeated.

Beside Vaughan, Carmine sat tense with excitement.

He gripped her arm. "I'm not sure I want to go through with this."

"Don't be ridiculous!" Carmine hissed. "How can you forego communion?"

"I don't even believe!"

She turned to him. "Then soon you *will!*"

The man returned to his seat. Carmine stood and hurried forward. With reluctance, Vaughan followed her. As he stepped onto the performance area, sand crunching realistically underfoot, he told himself that he could not become addicted from just one dose of rhapsody.

Carmine knelt, closed her eyes, and opened her mouth. Elly Jenson placed a wafer upon her tongue, repeating soft words. Carmine stood, her expression ecstatic, and drifted back to her seat. Her mind fizzed with sudden euphoria. Vaughan looked about him. Other than himself and the girl, the stage was empty. He stepped forward, knelt, and stared into Elly Jenson's bright blue eyes.

He was greeted with not the vaguest flicker of recognition.

He sensed a pacific, calm mind—a far cry from the frightened signature she had emanated at their first encounter.

She reached into the wicker basket. Vaughan murmured: "Elly—don't worry. It'll soon be over."

She stared at him, as if his words had meant nothing. She slipped a wafer past his lips and said, "Glory with the One. Peace be with you." And before he thought to spit out the wafer, it dissolved, tingling on his tongue, into nothing.

Numbed, Vaughan stood and returned to the front row. Carmine was sprawled out across the stone bench, arms dangling like some melodramatic prima donna playing a death scene. He sat down heavily, the rhapsody beginning to take effect. He felt light-headed, slightly nauseous. He had to lie down. His last coherent thought, before he too sprawled out across the front row, was to wonder at the power of the drug to act so fast.

Then he lost all sense of self as a physical being. He was a mind afloat, and gradually even his sense of individual identity began to leave him. Soon he was just a sentient entity with no memories of past, of self, just an all-encompassing awareness that the light he was travelling toward was his goal.

He crashed into the light, and on impact it was as if his soul was satisfied at last, as if this was what he had been venturing toward all his life without knowing it. He felt a sensation of unification course through his being . . . but unification with what he was unsure.

The sensation was inexplicable, and later he was to think back to Carmine Villefranche's inarticulate attempts to describe the sense of unity, of oneness, experienced in communion. It was a feeling of fulfilment and affirmation unlike anything he had experienced before, and the entity that had been Vaughan could only marvel.

He knew that he was safe; he knew that he belonged; he knew that he was loved. All these things, and more. At the very edge of his perception, for a fleeting moment, he sensed the entity responsible for what was happening to him, the Godhead . . .

Then he was withdrawing from that light, returning to himself. He felt his senses return one by one, his sense of personal identity, his memories, and his pain.

Slowly, he sat up. The rest of the congregation, having taken the drug after him, were still experiencing its effects. He held his head in his hands, trying to come to terms with what had happened to him.

The miasmic ecstasy of awed minds filled the amphitheater.

It was, he told himself, nothing other than the hallucinogenic side-effect of a very powerful drug—a pleasant and alluring side-effect, without question, but a side-effect nevertheless. It could be nothing more, he told himself. But it was understandable why people thought otherwise, and entirely understandable why people became addicted . . .

He glanced at the watch set into his handset. He had been under the influence of the drug for just thirty minutes.

Behind him, the other communicants were stirring. Elly Jenson knelt behind her dais, staring into space, the bowl empty. Carmine stretched and smiled at him dreamily. "Well, Tarzan. Was it worth it?"

Vaughan heard a sound from the rear of the amphitheater: the crack of a door being forcibly opened, then a shout. Instantly he was on his feet and diving across the stage. He was only peripherally aware of the tall figure of Dolores, running from the performance area. As he knocked away the dais and picked up the girl, the illusion of the amphitheater, the surrounding mountains, flickered and disappeared.

He felt a nexus of what seemed to be wires around the girl's body, but for seconds he was oblivious of what this meant.

He was standing in an old warehouse, a grandstand of cheap wooden seats rising before him, garlanded with deactivated holo-capillaries, and the sudden transition from the idyllic amphitheater to this bleak chamber was startling. The congregation, dazed with the after-effects of the drug, sat in stunned confusion at the disappearance of the colony world.

In seconds, the performance area was invaded by a dozen khaki-clad police. Others ran down the aisles, rousing the communicants to their feet and arresting those able to stand.

Across what had been the performance area, Vaughan saw the cloaked figure of Dolores slump to the floor. Crying out, Carmine pushed herself from her seat and knelt beside her lover, imploring someone to do something. Dolores stared blindly into space, her face as inanimate as her discarded mask.

A cop knelt, examining the body. He stood and crossed to Jimmy Chandra. "She's dead, sir. Something self-administered."

"Take her away, round them all up, and take them in for questioning. Have the medics examine them for any side-effects of the drug."

A cop appeared and eased a sobbing Carmine to her feet and away from the performance area.

Vaughan clutched the Chosen One to his chest and could not let go, even though he knew that the raid had failed—could never have succeeded.

Chandra turned to Vaughan. "Jeff . . . Jeff, you can let her go, now."

Slowly, reluctantly, Vaughan lowered the child to the ground and released his hold on her. She was no longer Elly Jenson, but a jet-haired little Thai girl. She wore only shorts and a t-shirt, her limbs and torso, head and face, enwrapped with the fine black mesh of holo-capillaries. She raised her arms as an officer knelt beside her and began gently unwinding the capillaries from around her body.

Chandra said, "Dolores Yandoah killed herself like Gerhard and Genevieve Weiss before her. My guess is she knew more than she wanted us to know." He looked around the warehouse. "As soon as we get near them, they have no qualms about killing themselves. In a way, you know, I admire their faith."

Vaughan looked at the corpse. If he had his augmentation-pin, he would be able to dive into the dying mind, learn all her secrets . . . If he dared.

Chandra glanced at Vaughan. "We'll find the Jenson kid eventually, okay?" Then he looked away, embarrassed by the platitude.

Vaughan left the Holosseum with Chandra, declined a ride home, and took the train to the Himachal sector. One hour later he entered his apartment and slumped into his armchair.

He stared at the graphic of Elly Jenson on the wall, mesmerized by her radiant face, her blue eyes. He remembered her fear in the freighter, his failure to save her. He wondered what they were doing with the girl, the true, real life Chosen One—he wondered who *they* were.

He pushed himself from the chair and rummaged through the contents of a drawer in his desk, found the bag of rhapsody he had taken from Tiger's room. He opened it and stared for a long time at the crimson powder. He recalled the sensation of communion he had experienced in the Holosseum, the affirmation of existence, and although he knew it to be a lie—yet another lie—he laid down a line of the powder and rolled a ten-baht note. Perhaps, with the drug, he might exorcise the ever-present specter of oblivion that had haunted him for so many years . . .

He snorted the line and felt the powder pinch his adenoids.

He staggered over to the bed and sprawled out. He waited for the euphoric rush, the journey to the rhapsodic light. He waited for the union, that sense of vital affirmation.

This time, though, it never came.

For an hour all he felt was a certain remove, a distance. Then the effects of the drug wore off, and reality returned, and with it the pain.

He turned off the lights and lay awake in the darkness for a long time, waiting for sleep.

EIGHT

Vaughan was in Nazruddin's, nursing a beer and watching the crowds surge down Chandi Road, when Dr. Rao entered and approached the booth. He lofted his walking stick in greeting.

"*Namaste,* Mr. Vaughan. I have good news for you. I have procured the implement which you were desiring."

"Take a pew."

Dr. Rao seated himself primly and ordered a lassi. "You cannot begin to imagine the degree of difficulty I experienced in endeavoring to guarantee the delivery of the augmentation-pin. My resources were stretched almost beyond their limits. It was only through my innumerable contacts in very high places, and the esteem with which I am regarded in these quarters, that I succeeded at last in making the purchase."

"I'm glad to hear that."

Rao dug into the pocket of his Nehru jacket and pulled out a battered, black velvet container the size of a pen case. He slid the container across the tabletop.

Vaughan lifted the hinged lid, took out the pin, and held it up between forefinger and thumb. It was a three-inch long needle, with a threaded barrel opposite the pointed end. It looked to Vaughan like a ten-year-old model, and the needle which would interface with the circuitry in his cerebellum was tarnished. But he'd worked with older and more beat-up models before, and he saw no reason why the pin should not have the desired effect.

"And now, if you are satisfied, perhaps you might see

your way to reimbursing—"

"It *looks* okay," Vaughan interrupted. "But that doesn't mean it'll work, does it?"

"But surely you do not mistrust the word of a loyal and trusted servant?"

"I'll just test it first, if you've no objections."

"In here? Won't the mass of minds interfere . . . ?"

"Surely you have nothing to hide from me?"

Rao spread his hands in a gesture of benign candor. "Mr. Vaughan, my conscience is as clear and pure as my mind."

Vaughan nodded. "Good to hear that, Rao . . ." He reached behind his head with the pin, inserted it into his console, and felt it pull away from his fingers and screw into position.

Instantly, what had been a general background hum became a clamorous din. Stray thought fragments entered his head from the surrounding diners. He tuned out much of the noise, allowed only the mind across the table to impinge upon his consciousness.

The bootleg pin was not as efficient as the one he'd been equipped with at the 'port, which would have brought Rao's thoughts into his head with three or four times the clarity of this device—but Vaughan had no complaints. The notion of being any more privy to Rao's secrets disturbed him.

>>>*He's a foreigner and not to be trusted! Untouchable! I should be wary in future! Deal only with Brahmin fellows . . .*

And below this sanctimonious mind-babble, Vaughan detected a self-importance based on Rao's knowledge of himself as a Brahmin, as the recipient of karma gained in previous incarnations.

Vaughan delved further, swam through the depths of the doctor's memories, and looked upon scenes and images from Rao's past that piqued his curiosity.

He discovered the image of Tiger at the age of eleven, and the sight of her, small and helpless and wholly reliant on Rao's charity, fuelled Vaughan's grief.

He shared in Rao's earliest memory of the girl.

She had been brought to Rao's voidship kingdom by a gaggle of his street kids. She'd been found wandering the lowest level of the Station, lost and in tears. Gradually, Rao had prised from her the events that had brought her to Bengal Station. She had fled Thailand aboard a raft with a dozen other street kids, heading for who knew where, and fetched up on the Station ten days later, starving and dehydrated. She had begged food and water, largely unsuccessfully, until a scavenging gang of Rao's kids had spotted her and tempted her to come with them, with tales of shelter, food, and warmth.

Vaughan relived the scene as if it were his own memory. Rao had questioned her about her past, her life in Thailand. Grudgingly, shyly, Tiger had told Rao that she had worked for a man who gave her a bed and food, in return for what she did for other men.

Vaughan was privy to Rao's excitement as she told him this, his thoughts as to the possibilities offered by such a pretty and experienced little thing . . .

He had said, "Would you like to continue that life here, on the Station, working for me? I would ensure you safety, and guarantee that you would come to no harm."

Tiger had just hung her head.

"Or, perhaps . . ." Rao had considered selling her to an acquaintance who made films and holo-vids, but then rejected the idea. He had heard bad stories from children who had fled from the pornographer.

"Of course, there is always begging. Look at my children. Go and talk to them. See how happy they are . . ."

And Tiger had lifted her head, considered the gallery of pinched faces of the children watching her.

Tiger had whispered, so softly that Rao could hardly make out the words, that she did not wish to go with men again, that she would rather beg.

And a week later Dr. Rao had amputated her right leg.

Vaughan ejected the pin. He could not look up, across the table, into the eyes of Dr. Rao.

"I trust that all is satisfactory?" Rao said.

Vaughan nodded. He pulled his wallet from his jacket and counted out the agreed four thousand five hundred baht.

Rao smiled. "My children will be most grateful, Mr. Vaughan," he said, pocketing the notes and rising to leave. "Thank you."

As Vaughan watched Rao hurry from the restaurant, he could not banish from his mind the fact that, for all the man's mean-spirited greed and arrogance, for all his deeds that many would consider barbarous, in his heart of hearts he did feel something for the children in his charge. He had, after all, given Tiger a home.

His handset chimed. It was Jimmy Chandra, his boyish face filling the tiny screen. Vaughan unstrapped his handset and propped it against the bottle of beer while he scooped rice into his mouth.

"Jeff, I'm having a party at my place later tonight. Why don't you come along? There'll be a few interesting people, a few single women."

Vaughan smiled. "Think I'll take a rain check, Jimmy."

"Well, if you change your mind . . . I've been telling Sumita about you. She'd really like to talk to you."

Vaughan cringed inwardly. Chandra's wife was a psycho-therapist.

Chandra was peering up at him. "You don't look too

well, Jeff. I hope you don't mind my saying."

"I'm okay." He told Chandra about his purchase of the augmentation-pin and his plans to follow up the few leads he had so far.

"Jeff, you don't think you're overdoing it a bit? I'm as eager to find this kid as you are—"

"Are you?" Vaughan said. "You don't even know for sure that she exists. You've only got my word for it."

"I believe you, Jeff." Chandra hesitated. "I just thought . . . maybe you should leave me and my team to sort it out. We'll come across the girl eventually. Look, I don't want you to become obsessed."

Vaughan paused, halted a handful of rice before his mouth. "What do you mean, obsessed?"

"I didn't mean it like that. It's just that, so soon after Tiger's death . . ." Chandra paused, choosing his words. "Look at it this way, Elly Jenson's the focal point of their Church. I'm sure she won't come to any harm."

"I don't know . . . Hell, I just want to get to the bottom of this, get the kid home."

"And then you can get on with your life?"

Vaughan sensed something censorious in Chandra's tone. "What do you mean?"

Chandra sighed. "I mean . . . So we solve the case, get the girl home, find out what Weiss was doing with those illegal shipments . . . what then? What sort of life are you going to go back to?" He paused, then said, "You look like you could do with a year in a sanatorium to get your system scoured."

Vaughan took a long draught of beer. "What makes you think—?"

"You're on a police register of users, Jeff. Okay, so it's only chora. No big deal. But prolonged use of the stuff does nasty things to the system."

Vaughan stared at the vial of blue powder on the table before him. "Do you know why I take it?"

"I've read up on psi-related problems, yes. Look, I'm not censuring you. I'd probably take the first thing that came along if I read what you read every day." Chandra paused, his lips forming a dissatisfied frown. "What I'm trying to say is, get yourself sorted out, okay? When all this is over, go for a long holiday. Have you ever thought of getting rid of the implant?"

From time to time it had crossed Vaughan's mind to have the console removed, to rid himself of the chattering demons that rode in his backbrain. But fear had prevented him from turning the thought into positive action. He might not have liked what he learnt when delving into the minds of his fellow men, but to be without his ability, to be without that supplementary sense which over the years he had grown reliant upon . . . Even unaugmented, he knew he used his ability to judge moods, assess character.

Perhaps, he admitted, he used his psi-ability so that he didn't have to form close bonds, even with people whose minds he found congenial, like Chandra. Because of his ability, he knew individuals well enough, and therefore did not have to work to get to know them any better—and in the process allow them to get to know him. He did not have to give anything of himself.

If he did not give of himself, then no one could take from him. No one could hurt him again.

"I don't think I could afford to get the console removed," he muttered.

"Okay, Jeff." Chandra nodded, letting the matter drop. "Hey, don't forget about tonight. We'd really love to see you."

"Yeah, right." Vaughan cut the connection, ordered another beer, and reached for his chora.

NINE

The party was just beginning to liven up when Jimmy Chandra's handset chimed. Sumita, glass in hand, raised her eyes to the stars.

"Chandra here," he said.

Commander Sinton's face appeared on the screen. "Chandra, I want you on duty in ten minutes."

Chandra glanced at his watch. "At one in the morning, sir?"

"You heard what I said. There's been another shooting. It bears many similarities with the Bhindra case."

Sumita was looking at him, lips pursed in an attempt not to smile. He covered his handset. "I'm sorry, Sum."

"Am I saying anything?" she smiled.

"Where is it, sir?" Chandra asked.

"Lt. Vishwanath's already there. Ship Seven, on the Boulevard of Voidships. Report to me with the details before dawn, will you?"

Chandra cut the connection.

Sumita draped her arms around his neck and kissed him on the lips. "Take care."

The Boulevard of Voidships had been a money-spinning venture developed by the Commander in charge of the 'port before Weiss. Instead of having the old decommissioned ships towed off and scrapped, he came up with the idea of utilizing them as accommodations for wealthy citizens willing to pay exorbitant rates for something a little dif-

123

ferent. A long cantilevered shelf was added to the southern margin of the 'port, and two-dozen voidships were welded into position overlooking the ocean. The old, three-man voidships were transformed into single accommodation units, while the larger freighters were subdivided into individual apartments.

Ship Seven, a squat, three-man explorer dating back to the turn of the century, sat in a well-manicured lawn, its silver carapace gleaming in the light of the moon. It looked to Chandra, as he climbed from his flier on the boulevard, as if the explorer had just touched down in paradise.

The homicide scientists were filing down the ship's ramp, their work done at this particular crime scene. The clean-up boys were kicking their heels on the lawn, waiting to be given the all-clear to go in and remove the corpse. Vishi met Chandra at the foot of the ramp, a screader tucked under the Lieutenant's arm.

"I don't know if Sinton told you, sir, but it looks like the same killer shot both Bhindra and this victim, Marquez."

"He mentioned there were similarities."

Vishi ushered Chandra up the ramp, through the carpeted foyer of the ship, and into a spacious lounge that had once been the bridge. A long, curved viewscreen looked out over the ocean.

Vishi crossed to a red velvet chesterfield, knelt behind it. Chandra stood behind him, staring at the dead man for longer than was wise. He was suddenly aware of the meal he'd consumed earlier that evening.

Like Bhindra, Marquez had suffered the fate of having had his head blown away with the impact of the shot. The messy decapitation robbed the corpse of character and dignity; it might have been a shop mannequin lying face down on the thick pile carpet, up-flung arms parenthesizing the puddle that had been its skull.

"Who was Marquez, Vishi?"

"Miguel Jose Marquez—a spacer with ESA, the European Space Agency, from the age of twenty-five until his retirement at fifty. The last twenty years he's lived on the Station, first in New Mumbai and then here. It's the ship he flew on his first exploration mission."

Chandra glanced at him. "Which Agency did Bhindra work for?"

"The Asiatic Space Corporation."

"So what are those similarities?"

Vishi proffered the screader. "These are the findings of the scientists, cross-related to those in the Bhindra case."

Chandra accessed the screader. Vishi kept up a running commentary. "The projectiles in both cases were fired from the same weapon, a high-caliber Steiger repeater. According to forensic, the weapon used is a make favored by hired assassins."

Chandra nodded. "Very good, Vishi."

"There's more, sir. We have a witness to the arrival of a black Ferrari flier outside the ship two hours ago, minutes before Marquez was shot. The witness reported seeing an indistinct male, probably Indian, climb from the flier and enter the ship. The same witness saw the man leave a couple of minutes later and take off. The flier had a taillight malfunction, causing it to flicker. I've put the description out Station-wide."

"Excellent."

"As regards the Bhindra case, sir, witnesses also reported seeing a black Ferrari flier passing the apartment at the time Bhindra was shot. It looks like we're looking for the same man in both cases."

Lost in thought, he walked around the lounge. On walls,

125

shelves, and desks were the mementos of a lifetime: graphics of ships, crews, landscapes of wonderful and exotic planets, a haphazard collection of extraterrestrial rocks. Like Bhindra, Marquez collected model spaceships—a touchingly juvenile hobby for grown men to indulge in after a lifetime among the stars.

He paused before a writing desk, the centerpiece of which was a signed photograph of three uniformed spacers, arms about each other's shoulders. He stared at the man in the center of the pix, then read the names of Bhindra, Marquez, and a spacer called Essex.

His pulse racing, he turned to Vishi. "I thought you said Bhindra worked for the ASC?"

"That's right, sir, according to records."

"Take a look at this." Chandra indicated the signed photograph. "They're all wearing ESA uniforms, Vishi. Not only were Bhindra and Marquez both spacers, they worked together back then."

"Do you think—"

"Get to records. I want to know what missions they flew on together."

Vishi nodded, walked to the viewscreen, and spoke hurriedly into his handset.

Chandra gazed around at the stacked possessions, the miniature spaceships, and the rocks, then back at the body. He wondered if someone so engrossed in the acquisition of possessions had ever thought about the inevitability of death, the possibility that it might all end like this.

Vishi turned from the viewscreen, consulting the text on his handset. "Bhindra was seconded to the European Space Agency for a year in '98. He flew with Marquez on two exploration missions."

"Do you know which planets they explored?"

Vishi nodded. "The first mission was to a planet designated L56b, Capella. It was found unsuitable for human habitation and never investigated further."

"And the second?"

"A world designated M68a, Riga—found to be Earthnorm, eventually colonized and renamed Verkerk's World."

"Verkerk's World . . ." Chandra echoed.

Vishi shrugged. "That's what records say. Do you think it might mean anything?"

"It might, Vishi. Get back to records. I want to know the name of the third pilot on the Verkerk's World mission, where he is and what he's doing now."

While Vishi spoke into his handset, Chandra returned to the desk and stared at the photograph of the three handsome, laughing spacers, young and ambitious and with all their lives before them.

Verkerk's World . . . The place was cropping up too frequently of late for it to be a mere quirk of coincidence. First the shielded container and the Chosen One from Verkerk's, then the link with both the drug and the religion to the planet, and now this . . . But why would an assassin be targeting two of the three spacers who had explored the world over forty-five years ago?

"The third pilot was a Brit by the name of Patrick Essex," Vishi reported. "And . . . this is a bit of a coincidence—he now makes his home on Verkerk's World. Must have liked the place."

Chandra nodded. "He must indeed." He picked up the photograph, and stared at the tanned, laughing face of the British spacer, Essex.

"I think we've learnt all we can here, Vishi. Let's get the clean-up boys in."

He returned the police HQ and for the next hour he

compiled a report of the night's events, then shunted the file through to Sinton. He sat for a long time after that, quiet in his darkened office, and considered his next move.

He made his way to Sinton's office and paused outside the door, collecting his thoughts. His boss was a big Australian, blunt and often caustic, who worked on the principle of keeping himself distant and aloof from the men in his command. Consequently, he was feared and loathed by many.

Chandra never came out of a meeting with Sinton without feeling that his every word and gesture had been scrutinized and found wanting. He knocked on the door and entered.

Sinton was scrolling through Chandra's report. He looked up from behind his desk, stared at Chandra without the slightest hint of a smile.

"So what now, Investigator?" Sinton said, sitting back in his chair and lacing his fingers across his stomach. "How do you intend to proceed?"

"I've been giving it some thought, sir, and I'd like to request that we move the focus of inquiry to Verkerk's World. The political situation seems to have stabilized, so there'd be no danger in that respect."

Sinton nodded, non-committal.

"It seems the obvious place to continue the investigation," Chandra continued. "I'd like to look into the Church there, question Elly Jenson's father. Also the pilot Patrick Essex, the third man in Bhindra and Marquez's team that explored the planet at the turn of the century—he makes his home there now. I'd like to question him about the killings, see if he knows why his team-mates were targeted."

Sinton was watching him, silent. Chandra feared the worst—that the Agency could not fund such a trip, that the crimes committed thus far did not warrant such extensive investigations. He expected to be told to wrap up the case—consign it to the "unsolved" file—and move on to other things.

Sinton surprised Chandra by saying: "I think that might be a good idea, Investigator. Book passage aboard the next flight to Verkerk's. Are you taking Lieutenant Vishwanath?"

"Actually, I was wondering if I could take Vaughan—the telepath who first brought the irregularities concerning Weiss to light."

"Hasn't he been assisting you with your investigations?"

"In an unofficial capacity, yes, sir."

"He can be trusted?"

Chandra nodded. "Without a doubt."

"We'd have to employ him for the duration of the trip, put him on the payroll."

"I'll arrange that side of things."

"Very good." Sinton nodded again, impassive. "Report back to me on your return. That will be all, Chandra. Good luck."

"Thank you, sir."

Chandra returned to his office, thinking that for once he had done something worthy of his commanding officer's praise. He sat at his desk in the darkness and thought back to the young, ambitious boy he had been. Never, in his wildest imaginings, had he ever dared to dream higher than the upper-deck. He wondered what the ten-year-old Jimmy Chandra would have said to the idea of a voidship journey to the stars.

He called Jeff Vaughan.

His handset showed Vaughan bleary-eyed and obviously drunk. By the evidence of the background noise—the clash of cutlery and babble of voices—he was still in Nazruddin's.

"Jimmy . . ." Vaughan tried to focus. "I'm sorry I didn't make it. Meant to come . . . You know how it is."

"Forget it, Jeff. Look, something's come up." He told Vaughan about the murders of Bhindra and Marquez. "Yet another link to Verkerk's World." He paused. "How would you like a trip out to the colony?"

Vaughan peered up at him with red-rimmed eyes. "Say again?"

Chandra repeated the question. "Can you get time off from the 'port?"

Vaughan smiled. "I've just taken a couple of weeks' leave."

"Excellent," Chandra said. "You'd be working for the Agency, getting paid for the trip. Of course, you'd have to bring along your augmentation."

"Of course. Hell . . ." Vaughan rubbed a hand across his face, as if trying to sober up, gather his thoughts. "Christ, Jimmy. When do we leave?"

"There's a voidship leaving for Verkerk's in twenty-four hours. I'll contact you before then to make the arrangements." Vaughan was still shaking his head when Chandra signed off.

He sat in the silence of his office, staring into the darkness. He asked himself why he'd requested that Vaughan accompany him. Obviously, as a telepath, his ability would be valuable. But he could think of more personable travelling companions—Vishi, for instance.

As he sat at his desk and stared out at the coming dawn, he considered Vaughan. They would be together for the next few days, perhaps a week. As the telepath was unwilling to divulge anything about his background, then Chandra felt that it was up to him to find out the facts, if possible, for himself.

It was time to investigate Vaughan's shadowy past.

TEN

Sukara was late for her shift at the Siren Bar.

Fat Cheng sat at the bar, a bottle of beer in his huge fist. He was wearing his multi-colored Hawaiian shirt and Bermuda shorts tonight. Spilling out of his seat, he looked like a Sumo wrestler on vacation.

"Little Monkey, there you are. What happens? You late!"

"Sorry! Metro so busy!"

Fat Cheng waved this away. "Strange thing. I get call. Customer, he want see you tonight. Eleven o'clock."

"Which customer? Ee-tee?"

"Maybe Ee-tee. You go to Astoria hotel, Silom Road."

"Astoria hotel?" She whistled. "Rich place, Fat Cheng. Eleven o'clock?" She looked at the clock behind the bar. "After ten now. Silom Road long way. Won't make it."

"You will. Customer say you take flier. He pay."

Sukara stared. "Flier?"

"Go now. Hurry."

She ran from the bar, plucking her mask from its peg in the cloakroom and fitting it over her nose and mouth. She felt a flutter of excitement in her belly, and at the same time a little apprehension. She had often imagined what it might be like to ride in a flier, the speed and the power, the sight of the city from so high up. Never before had she gone out to a smart hotel to see a customer—that privilege was left to the beautiful girls, who were always going out to expensive hotels and clubs, balls and parties. Now, *she* was going to see a rich customer in the Astoria.

She arrived at the taxi rank. A dozen sleek, jet-black fliers waited on the ramp like hungry, carnivorous fish. She climbed the steps, feeling as though she were trespassing, that at any second a cop would grab her by her t-shirt and haul her away, and leaned in through the open window of the first flier. "Astoria hotel, Silom Road."

The pilot hardly glanced at her. She climbed into the back seat, sinking into the plush upholstery. She had to sit up to peer out through the window as the flier climbed. Inside, the noise of the jet engine was muffled. She watched the street, the flashing lights, and the crowds of people fall and tilt away beneath her as the cab banked. And then, so suddenly that Sukara was forced back into her seat, breathless, the flier accelerated. Buildings flickered by in a quick rush, then disappeared as the flier gained cruising altitude. Below, Bangkok was spread out for her inspection, a stretch of individual lights fusing into a continuous, hazy glow on the horizon. The Chao Phraya lay to her left, a dark swath winding its way through the illumination. She sat back in the seat, bouncing once or twice and caressing the soft leather, her worries forgotten for now.

She wondered who had summoned her like this tonight. She could think of two or three regular customers she thought it might be. Always, though, they had come to the bar. She wondered why tonight was different. Could it be that it was an Ee-tee, which had only a short time in Bangkok before taking off again for the stars?

The pilot adjusted the volume on the radio, and Sukara heard that yet another young girl had been murdered in the city, her body dumped in a klong. Victim number eight. She blinked down at the brilliant array of lights. From so far up, it looked so innocent. It was hard to imagine that down

132

there, somewhere, a murderer was going about his business, killing occasionally, then slipping back into hiding.

A towering, light-spangled building came into view, and the flier slowed down. They landed in the forecourt, and a footman in an ancient Thai costume ran up and opened the rear door. "Chintara Sukarapatam?"

She could only stare out at him, nod wordlessly.

"Room twenty-five, tenth floor." He assisted Sukara from the flier, then leaned inside to pay the driver.

Sukara crossed the forecourt and entered through sliding glass doors that ran with liquid like a waterfall made rigid. In the foyer, rich citizens stood about in groups of two or three, chatting casually. Conscious of her inappropriate dress, her sweat-soaked t-shirt and scuffed sandals, she hurried across to the elevator, eyes staring straight down at the crimson carpet. A young uniformed boy opened the door for her and operated the controls once they were inside. "Floor ten!" he repeated, glancing from her scarred face to her bare legs, seemingly fascinated by both.

The elevator rose quickly, stopped with a sedate bounce that made her stomach flip. The doors swished open. Sukara stepped out, surprised to find the long, thickly carpeted corridor eerily empty. The doors of the elevator closed and she was suddenly alone.

She walked down the corridor, reading off the room numbers, then realised she was moving in the wrong direction. She turned and hurried the other way, blushing even though there was no one around to see her mistake. She passed room 30, increased her pace, then slowed as she passed room 28. She stopped and stared at the door bearing the number 25, as if it might give some clue as to the identity of its occupant.

Her legs wobbly with apprehension, her mouth dry, she

reached up and knocked on the door. She realised what a feeble tap she'd given, then knocked with more force. The door opened before she had finished, leaving her with her fist in the air. Her arm fell to her side as she stared.

"Mister Osborne?"

He smiled. "Su, it's nice to see you again. Come inside . . . Drink?"

He was gallant enough to pretend not to notice her nervousness as he ushered Sukara into the spacious lounge. He was dressed in a slick black suit, high-collared, cut away at the front to reveal a brilliant white shirt. His smile, even more devastating than she recalled, was enough to melt her insides.

"Can I get you a drink, Su?"

"Ah . . . beer? You got beer?"

He opened a wooden cabinet, which turned out to be a cooler, pulled out a Singha, and unscrewed the lid. He poured the beer into a glass, passed it to Sukara.

She stood in the middle of the room, sipping quickly and nervously, while Osborne poured himself a brown drink in a glass as big as a goldfish bowl. She hugged herself, shivering despite the warmth of the room. She asked herself, over and over, what he might want with her.

He turned and raised his glass. "It really is nice to see you again, Su. I enjoyed our conversation the other night. I was—" He was interrupted by a bleeping sound coming from his sleeve. He pushed up his cuff, spoke angrily into a device that encircled his forearm.

He looked at Sukara. "Excuse me. This won't take long."

He moved into another room. Sukara heard him speaking, but could not make out the individual words.

She wiped her sweat-soaked palms down the front of her

t-shirt. She recalled that, on their first meeting, Osborne had said that he did not want to go with her. She wondered if he'd changed his mind.

She kicked off her sandals, sat on the arm of a big sofa, and scrunched her toes into the lush crimson velvet.

Osborne emerged from the connecting room, touching the back of his head as if arranging his hair.

"I'm sorry. Business. We won't be interrupted again."

"Nice see you, Mister Osborne," Sukara blurted. "Big surprise. Never thought I see you again. I put two hundred baht in savings account, for rainy day."

"That's a good girl. I'm glad you're careful with your money."

"Working girl, Mister Osborne. Must be careful."

He crossed the room, glass in hand, and sat on the sofa. He turned sideways, staring at her. His eyes seemed to lose themselves in her face.

She wondered if she should reach out, touch his dark, strong jaw, or leave him to make the first move. She wanted to touch him, but could not bring herself to move. She wondered why she trusted this man, this stranger.

"I confused," she found herself saying. "Why me? I not beautiful, not like—"

"You're beautiful to me, Su. No, you're not like the other girls."

"Other girls, they beautiful. They have light skin, long legs, perfect faces. Just what men want."

"In here," Osborne said, reaching out and cupping her skull in his big hand, his thumb caressing her temple. "In here, you're what I've been looking for, for a long, long time."

That smile again, that lopsided, easy grin which reassured her despite the obsessive quality of his words.

She avoided his eyes. "You like me, Mr. Osborne?"

He took her hand, drew her gently toward him. She arranged herself on his lap and pressed her head to his chest as he held her. She closed her eyes, wished this moment would go on forever, just like this, the pure physical pleasure without thought of motives or consequence. She realised that this was what she had been missing for many years, for as long as she could recall, an embrace that wanted nothing other than to communicate affection without demanding sexual gratification . . . She would not let herself look further than this moment, to the time when he would leave her, the moment over, and she would be alone again.

She said, in a whisper: "Okay like this? We not go to bed?"

"No," he whispered in return. "No, Sukara. It's fine like this."

She felt the moist heat of his lips on the top of her head. She closed her eyes, and the movement of her lids squeezed hot tears down her cheeks.

They remained like this for an hour—Sukara watched the time elapse on his wristwatch—though it seemed to her a matter of minutes. She wondered if this was what love felt like. She had never allowed herself to believe in love before, never expected anyone to show her love or to feel it herself.

She told herself not to be so ridiculous. She hardly knew the man called Osborne, and how could he really know her? But whatever it was, she told herself, she would enjoy it while it lasted.

At last he positioned her on his knee so that he could look into her face. He thumbed the tears from her cheeks, caressed the line of her jaw with his knuckles. Sukara responded by pushing against his hand like a cat, laughing tearfully at his affection. The golden pendant that he wore around his neck nestled against her cheek, warm against her skin.

He pulled her to him, running his hands through her hair, kissing the top of her head. "Oh, sweet Jesus Christ," she heard him whisper.

She reached out, linked her arms around his neck. She stopped when she felt something cold, metallic, at the base of his skull.

He looked into her eyes. "It's nothing," he said. "I had an operation a long time ago. It's nothing, Sukara."

He kissed her forehead, her cheeks, her nose, burying his face in her hair. She caught brief glimpses of his face, as he pulled away, a swimmer coming up for air, and she realised that he too was in tears.

He held her face in his hands, his fingers spanning her temples. "Tomorrow I leave Bangkok," he told her.

A wild, pounding panic seized her heart. She wanted to scream that it wasn't true, that the pleasure she had experienced with him so briefly could not be over so soon.

He said, "I can't let you stay at the Siren Bar, get beaten up by drunken Indians."

She stared at him. "How you know?"

He ignored her, went on: "I couldn't let you go on working there. I want you to come with me."

Her heart missed a beat. "You do? I go with you?"

"You will come, won't you?"

"I will," she stammered. "I come. Of course I come . . ." She shook her head, the movement restricted by the vice of his fingers. "How long? How long you want me stay?"

He smiled. She reached out, touched the silver tears on his cheeks with her fingertips.

"I want you to stay with me forever, Su."

They held each for a long time. It seemed so right, she told herself. It seemed that she had waited all her life for just this moment. She looked into the future—and told herself that the events of the past, the beatings and the taunts, she could finally put behind her.

He perched her on the summit of his knees. "Tomorrow, we leave Bangkok," he told her. "We'll live together. During the day I'll do the work I must do, and at night we will be together."

"What work you do, Osborne?"

He hesitated, then said, "I'm looking for someone. A man I worked with a long time ago."

She nodded. "We go tomorrow," she whispered, "but where we go?"

He looked into her eyes, into her head.

"Bengal Station," he said.

ELEVEN

Vaughan leaned back in the couch before the bulging viewscreen as the *Spirit of Riga* made its transition from the void to the airspace above Sapphire Falls, Verkerk's World. The inky, starless blackness was replaced by the quick, almost subliminal, flash of blue sky and a range of jagged mountains. Then the black of the void returned, before disappearing again. The viewscreen flickered for ten seconds with alternating scenes like images on a defective hologram. Vaughan had only ever witnessed transitions from the ground, watching voidships come and go above Bengal Station. To behold a world come into being, the birth of a reality he was soon about to join, was an altogether more startling experience.

The ship made its final jump and the magnificence of the view was revealed. The crystal screen curved beneath the couch, and Vaughan sat forward and stared down between his feet at the silent, drifting landscape far below. They were passing above the foothills of the mountain range, the hills buckling in a series of rucks and folds, flattening out gradually as they gave way to a vast, cultivated floodplain. Ahead, he could see the outskirts of the city of Sapphire Falls, big timber houses laid out on a grid pattern of streets. It was dawn, the sun rising above the mountains, and Vaughan was amazed to see that the streets of the city were almost deserted. His sensibilities, geared to conditions on Bengal Station, could not help but compare: he supposed that this was the first of many imminent culture shocks.

He was still trying to gauge his reaction to Chandra's invitation to join him on the investigation. Chandra had met Vaughan at the 'port, and introduced him to Commander Sinton. "Jeff Vaughan, sir, the telepath. He's the best man for the job."

They had chatted for a while, Sinton obviously trying to assess his worth. Sinton had been shielded, common for a man in his position. Chandra had told his commanding officer that he had worked with Vaughan before, and that he was sure that he would prove invaluable on the case.

But Vaughan suspected that Chandra had other reasons for the wanting him along. He recalled Chandra's expressions of concern over the past few days. He wondered if Chandra thought a sojourn to another world might bring about a transformation of Vaughan's personal situation. Christ knew, Chandra was naive enough to assume that different scenery might prove a palliative for depression. Vaughan found himself resenting Chandra for his patronizing presumption. He feared that Chandra would probe him about his past, as he had done once or twice recently, attempt to play the amateur psychologist.

However, during the forty-eight-hour journey to Verkerk's World, Chandra's manner had struck him as rather odd. He seemed wary of Vaughan, not the usual friendly, forthcoming Chandra of old. Also, he'd been fastidious with his mind-shield, ensuring that he had it on him at all times, as if he had secrets which he did not want Vaughan to share.

Not that Vaughan had worried. He'd spent time alone at the bar, avoiding the other twenty passengers, and muting their mind-noise with copious doses of chora.

The *Spirit of Riga* banked over the city. Vaughan spotted a few tiny roadsters, like trilobites, moving slowly along the streets. To the left, parallel with the mountain range fifty kilometres inland, was the geological feature that gave Sapphire Falls its name. Over millennia, the escarpment that was the termination of the floodplain had been eroded by the work of a thousand streams. From a series of fissures, waterfalls tipped in spectacular arcs to the rocks a kilometre below, sending up great billowing drifts of rainbow-spangled spray.

Vaughan had spent a couple of hours at the start of the journey scrolling through a screader advertising Verkerk's World. The planet was vast, with almost four times the continental surface area of Earth, and the new government was eager to promote travel and tourism. The screader flashed graphics of spectacular geography, boasted unexplored terrain in swaths the size of Asia.

Vaughan found it hard to believe that only a million people made their home on Verkerk's World. The screader had explained that for decades the Verkerk-Scherring Company had limited immigration, preferring to keep the planet as the exclusive, and expensive, preserve of the rich. Also, lack of major industry had curbed work opportunity. Even now, Verkerk's World was reliant on neighboring industrial planets for the supply of certain hi-tech materials.

The spaceport was a tiny affair three kilometres outside Sapphire Falls. The ship banked toward a docking berth, one of only four scattered across the weed-laced tarmac. One other voidship stood on the 'port, a bulky freighter from one of the nearby worlds. The place had the run-down air of a colonial backwater.

The other passengers were filing through the lounge behind Vaughan, making their way to the foyer for disembarkation. He heard the thunking percussion of a dozen connecting-leads snap into the skin of the ship, the gurgling of siphoned fuel, and an arpeggio of musical notes indicating function shut-downs. He had lost count of how many ships he had boarded at this stage, scanning new arrivals. Too busy with the job at hand, he had never paid much attention to the sounds of a resting ship at journey's end.

As he stood and headed for the ramp and the 'port officials waiting there, it struck him as strange to be on this side of security. He looked through the hatch, trying to catch a glimpse of the Verkerk's World law enforcement officer on hand to meet him and Chandra.

Chandra appeared from the lounge, carrying his case, and joined Vaughan. Out of uniform, he cut a dapper figure in a dark suit and white, high-necked shirt. His smile suggested an effort to improve relations. "This is an historic moment, Jeff. The first time either of us have stepped on extraterrestrial soil."

Vaughan tried to find a suitable response to Chandra's statement of the obvious, but not wanting to resort to sarcasm, he remained silent. He knew that his own reaction to Chandra's cool manner during the journey—his avoidance of the cop, his disinclination to start conversation—had been noted by the other man.

An official passed through the crowd, casually checking papers. He arrived at Chandra and Vaughan, gave their passcards a cursory glance, and pointed through the exit to the terminal building. "You'll find Lt. Laerhaven waiting for you, gentlemen. Pleasant stay on Verkerk's World."

They passed down the ramp. Despite the bright, early morning sunlight, the air was sharp and cold. A rime of frost scintillated across the tarmac, bringing to mind a host of long-forgotten memories of childhood in Ottawa. It was the first time in ten years that he'd seen his breath plume in the air: Chandra, mesmerized by the effect, was chugging like a steam train. Vaughan felt a sudden pang of longing for the familiarities of Bengal Station, the heat and humidity, the hurly-burly activity of the crowds.

One advantage of the sparse population was the pleasing lack of a concentrated mind-hum. Here, the noise of human thought beyond the port was dilute, tolerable.

Chandra *brrr'd* his lips and hurriedly led the way to the terminal building.

Lena Laerhaven was a tall, big-boned woman, her handsome face severe between smiles. She wore a green military-style uniform and carried a carbine slung casually over her shoulder. She strode across the blue and white checkered tiling and introduced herself. "Investigator Chandra, Mr. Vaughan, welcome to Verkerk's World. I'm Lieutenant Lena Laerhaven. I've been assigned to liaise with you for the duration of your stay. If I can help you in any way . . ."

They shook hands, Laerhaven smiling with what seemed to Vaughan like unforced openness. He caught a predominant mood of confidence from her mind: she seemed a woman self-possessed, sure of her place in the scheme of things.

"If you don't mind my asking, which one of you is the telepath?"

"I am," Vaughan said. "But don't worry, I'm not reading at the moment."

Laerhaven nodded uncertainly at Vaughan's tone. "Thanks for the reassurance—it's just that I've never met a telepath before. The use of augmentation-pins has been proscribed on Verkerk's World for the past twenty years."

Vaughan managed a smile. "Are you surprised to find I look relatively normal?"

Chandra shot him a quizzical look.

Laerhaven changed the subject. "Oh, before I forget—a

little present from the Agency." She reached into one of the many pockets in her military fatigues and handed Vaughan and Chandra each a small, velveteen-covered box, smiling as they accepted the gifts in puzzlement. Vaughan opened his case, discovering a handsome watch within. At first glance it appeared no different from any other old-fashioned timepiece with minute and hour hands. Then Vaughan noticed that it was numbered from one to eight.

Laerhaven explained. "We have a sixteen-hour day on Verkerk's World. Approximately nine hours of daylight and seven of darkness. I hope these will assist your acclimatization."

While Chandra thanked the Lieutenant, Vaughan strapped the quaint device onto his left wrist. It was years since he had last worn a watch; handsets had made them redundant long ago.

"If you're ready, gentlemen, I'll drive you to the house we've set aside for you. When you've got your bearings, you can move about at will and make your own plans. This way."

The passed from the building and walked across a deserted parking lot to a police roadster, the same dark green as Laerhaven's uniform. Vaughan sat in the back.

Laerhaven clipped her carbine into a holder on the inside of the door and revved the engine. She swept the car from the lot, accelerating along a straight road raised between fields ploughed like corduroy.

"First time on Verkerk's World, gentlemen?"

Chandra nodded. "Our first time off Earth."

"Which country do you come from?"

"I was born on Bengal Station," Chandra said.

Laerhaven glanced over her shoulder. "And you, Mr. Vaughan?"

He ignored the question and turned his gaze through the window. The frost was burning off with the ascent of the huge, fiery ball of Riga. A haze of steam hung over the land.

Laerhaven went on, ignoring his snub: "Your accommodation is on the edge of the Falls, with an incredible view across the lowlands. Because of the temperature differential—twenty below zero at night, in the nineties at noon—the plant life of the planet has adapted accordingly. During the night and early morning, the blooms hibernate, then come out in a rush when the day warms up. It's called the Blooming, and it'll happen over a few minutes in a couple of hours from now."

Vaughan wondered when was the last time he'd seen—really bothered to look at—a living flower. Some of the parks on the Station were planted with gardens, but he had to admit that he'd never paid them much attention.

They sped along the elevated road. Vast fields of some grain crop, perhaps corn, stretched away on all sides like a golden ocean. From time to time timber farmhouses, still and silent, appeared on the horizon, like galleons becalmed in an agricultural sargasso.

Chandra was quizzing Laerhaven about the political situation on the planet. "All I know is that there was a popular revolution a week or two ago," he said.

"I suppose you could have called the deposed government a benign dictatorship, though that makes them sound blacker than they really were. They were a council of a dozen old businessmen who had ruled the planet for the last thirty years. There were no democratic elections, as such. New leaders of the cantons were appointed by the council when incumbents died or became too feeble to make decisions. They were against change and all for the status quo that maintained the world as a backwater out of touch with the rest of the Expansion."

"And the new people in power?"

"The new order comprises businessmen and social philosophers who want the planet to progress, open up. Of course, curbs have to be kept to ensure industrialization and immigration don't get out of hand. But the new government has instituted local elections so that the people will have a say in the future of their planet."

"I read that the population is barely one million."

"That's right. We're the descendants of Dutch, Danish, and German settlers. The local language is an amalgam of Dutch and German. But English is widely spoken. I think you'll find it a friendly place."

"Unfortunately we won't have much time for sightseeing. We're due to return on the next ship to Earth, four days from now."

Laerhaven nodded. "What exactly are you investigating, Mr. Chandra, if you don't mind my asking?"

"We're looking into the activities on the Station of a cult that originated here."

Laerhaven smiled across at him. "That sounds like Verkerk's World, all right. It has something to do with the size of the place. Communities of settlers are so far-flung and isolated that strange belief systems and religions spring up every few years. For the most part, they're harmless schisms of the Judeo-Christian traditions."

Vaughan leaned forward. "For the most part? That sounds like something more sinister rears up now and again?"

Laerhaven shrugged. "Once or twice since I've been with the force—that's almost six years, now—we've had trouble with cults. Reported kidnapping and brainwashing of youngsters, that kind of thing. Nothing we couldn't soon get straightened out."

Chandra said, "That wouldn't by any chance have been the Church of the Adoration of the Chosen One?"

"I think I might have remembered a cult with a title like that," she said. "No, it's a new one on me."

"We'd like to question a suspected cult member, a man by the name of Lars Jenson. He has a daughter, Elly—she was taken to Earth against her will. We understand he's resident in the Falls."

Laerhaven nodded. "I'll look up his address when I get back to headquarters and pass it on to you."

"We'd appreciate that," Chandra said. "There is one more thing. Two ex-spacers were killed on Bengal Station during the past few days—Rabindranath Bhindra and Miguel Marquez."

Laerhaven repeated their names. "The same spacers who first explored the planet?"

"The same. There was a third pilot, a man by the name of Patrick Essex. We understand that he's a resident of Verkerk's World. Of course, we'd like to question him."

"I'll get back to you with that one, too," Laerhaven promised.

They drove into the city of Sapphire Falls—though the term "city" to describe so spacious and uncrowded an urban center seemed a misnomer to Vaughan. Wide streets were flanked by sprawling houses—A-frames, ranch-style villas, bungalows—and each was constructed of the same material, a dark brown timber that glowed in the sunlight with the warm lustre of old brandy.

The road passed through the city and climbed, and suddenly, to their right, the land fell away in a spectacular series of deep gorges and fissures, silver waterfalls like perfect arcs of mercury tipping themselves from level to level. Laerhaven pulled up in the drive of a long timber building perched on the very lip of the escarpment.

"Here we are, gentlemen," she said. She indicated a gray roadster parked in the drive. "For your convenience while you're on Verkerk's." She presented the ignition card to Chandra. "I'll show you inside."

The long, low house comprised a lounge with a big window looking out over the gorge, a kitchen and bathroom in one wing and the bedrooms in another. It seemed far older than it could possibly have been—the planet had been settled for only thirty-odd years; yet the rooms were constructed of a dark timber that appeared ancient.

"How old is this place?" Vaughan asked.

Laerhaven stood in the lounge by the window, having shown them through the rooms. "These houses were grown about ten years ago."

"Grown?" Chandra echoed.

"The wood is still living," she said. "Feel. It's called warmwood."

Vaughan crossed to the window, laid his hand on the wide grain of the frame. The wood glowed with heat beneath his palm.

"It is warm."

"But cooling. During the night it warms, heating the house. And during the day, as the temperature outside steadily climbs, the wood cools. By midday it will be cold to the touch."

"Is it naturally like this?" Chandra asked.

Laerhaven nodded. "The original trees were from the cold climes of the north—they warmed up and cooled down as an aid to survival. The Verkerk-Scherring Company, who bought the rights to develop the planet from the agency who discovered it, genetically altered the wood to grow into all sorts of useful shapes. This is one of them."

"Frost, fast-blooming flowers, and living houses," Chandra said. "What next?"

"I'll leave you to explore the area for yourselves, gentlemen. Enjoy your stay, and please contact me if you need anything at all."

Chandra saw her to the door, then picked up his case and carried it to the first bedroom. "I'm going to lie down for an hour or two. See if I can catch some sleep."

Alone in the lounge, Vaughan stared through the window. The sun cast its light into the gorge below, and the waterfalls, transformed from silver, glowed with the lustre of poured gold. In the delicately rising mist, rainbows appeared fleetingly, then winked out, to reappear as if by magic further along the gorge. Far below, the plain of the lowlands stretched away for kilometres.

He saw a precarious path fall steeply away from the house and down the side of the escarpment and decided to take a look around.

He emerged into the dazzling sunlight and followed the path around the house until it dropped down the face of the rock. As he descended, picking his way with care over loose rocks and down roughly chiseled steps, he moved from the intense heat into cool shadow and felt immediate relief.

The path zigzagged, approaching a vast sink constantly supplied with water from a fall pouring over a lip of rock high above. As the house disappeared from sight, he stopped and looked about him. For the first time in years he was in a natural landscape and unable to see the artifacts of man. Even the minds, dulled by the mass of the escarpment between him and the city, were barely audible. He continued his descent and arrived at the brimming lip of the sink; on the far side, over a depressed lip worn down throughout the aeons, the water discharged itself slickly beneath an unbroken quicksilver meniscus.

As the sun rose further, finding him, the terrain of the gorge suddenly transformed itself. What he had taken before to be no more than a unique patterning in the rock, a million fossilized stems and leaves, began to writhe. All around, from buds that seconds before had seemed as frozen as stone, flowers snapped open. Vaughan stared about him, his head moving constantly to catch the next bloom in the instantaneous process of expanding its magnificent petals to the light of the sun. Up and down the gorge, a complex tapestry sprang into life. Beside his head, nodding with the momentum of its sudden explosion of petals, a great trumpet bloom blared a blood-red cacophony of pigment. He was amazed that something so cold and seemingly dead as the iron-gray buds could have, with the right stimulus, transformed into something so vital.

Within seconds of the Blooming, the air was filled with a million silver insects. With a deafening hum of wings they descended *en masse* to gather pollen, then rose and moved on, a swarming pointillism of activity that often blotted out entire swathes of scenery. The swarm passed Vaughan by and moved further along the gorge, trailing a patch of darkness across the land like the shadow of a cloud.

He sat beside the sink for perhaps an hour, then started the slow climb back to the house. He was exhausted by the time he crossed the veranda of living wood, cool now to his touch. He checked his new watch. It was almost eight—midday on Verkerk's World—and Riga was at its zenith. The thermometer on the veranda read a hundred and five Fahrenheit. He entered the house, washed, then retired to his room and lay down.

He had no idea how long he slept. He was awoken suddenly, surprised that he had slept at all, and it was seconds before he realised what had brought him from sleep. He heard the chiming from the lounge, rose, and hurried from his room. The summons stopped suddenly: Chandra had reached the communications set before him. He knelt before the screen, pressing the control panel. A face expanded from a white horizontal band, as sudden as one of the flowers outside.

"Gentlemen," Lena Laerhaven said. "I have the address of Lars Jenson here . . ." Chandra thanked her and typed it into his handset.

When Laerhaven cut the connection, Chandra turned to Vaughan. "We might as well not waste any time, Jeff. Let's go see what Jenson has to say for himself."

Chandra inserted the ignition card and rolled the roadster down the incline, heading for the center of town. Vaughan stared through the windscreen at the lengthening shadows of the silver-leaved trees. It was three-thirty and the sun was setting rapidly, and it seemed that the day was drawing to a close before it had hardly begun. Five minutes after leaving the house, daylight was replaced by a gorgeous, orange-skied twilight.

They passed along wide, tree-lined streets. The citizens of Sapphire Falls were hurrying home, bundled inside thick, insulated jackets and trousers.

Chandra checked his handset. "Renstraas. This is it." He turned down a tree-lined avenue and drew to a halt outside an imposing—spuriously ancient-looking—two-story warmwood house.

As they stood on the porch, waiting for Jenson to answer the bell that chimed through the house, an icy wind sprang up from nowhere. Through the stained glass of the door, Vaughan saw the tall, broad shape of a man eclipse the hall

151

light—but there was no accompanying mind-noise. Even unaugmented, as he was now, he should have picked up something.

"He's shielded," he said.

"What?"

"I said the bastard's shielded."

Lars Jenson pulled open the door. He was a large, silver-haired man in his sixties who Vaughan instantly recognised from the images he had read in Elly Jenson's mind aboard the freighter.

Jenson peered at them, suspicious. "Yes, gentlemen?"

Chandra displayed his identity. "Investigators Chandra and Vaughan, Bengal Station Law Enforcement Agency, Earth."

Jenson hesitated, quickly calculating his options, before deciding on hospitality. "Gentlemen, please. It's getting cold. Come in."

He led them into a comfortable lounge, an open log fire radiating warmth. He indicated an overstuffed sofa, saw Vaughan looking at the flickering flames in the hearth. "A hologram, I'm afraid. But very realistic, yes?" He seated himself in an armchair, an authentic book laid print-down on the arm where he'd left it to answer their summons. "Gentlemen, how might I help you?"

Chandra cleared his throat. "We're investigating the abduction of your daughter, Elly, from Verkerk's World."

On the mantle-shelf above the fire, Vaughan saw half a dozen framed graphics of Elly and Lars Jenson. In all of them she was smiling, a pretty blonde-haired girl in the arms of her father. He looked at Jenson, an ungovernable emotion, somewhere between anger and incredulity, building within him. He would have given anything at that moment to have been able to read the man's mind.

"But I assure you," Jenson was saying, "that my daughter's departure from Verkerk's was totally legitimate."

"We believe she was selected by the Church of the Adoration of the Chosen One as the Chosen One."

Jenson inclined his head. "That is correct. Of course, I was both honored and amazed when it was found that she was the Chosen."

"You yourself belong to the Church?"

"I am a member, yes, Mr. Chandra. Unfortunately, my time being strictly limited with my business commitments, I cannot worship as often as I would like."

"Your daughter went willingly to Earth?"

"Of course. Do you think I would have sent her otherwise?"

Vaughan almost interrupted, but stopped himself. He recalled Elly Jenson's terror at being taken from Verkerk's World.

"Did she travel alone?" Chandra asked.

"Of course not—she was accompanied by two highly respected members of the Church."

"Can I have their names, please, Mr. Jenson, and their present whereabouts?"

"By all means. They were a Jen Freidrickson and his wife, Olga. They will be on Earth now, of course, with Elly."

Chandra tapped their names into his handset. "You don't have their current address on Earth?"

"Unfortunately, no. You see, they will be travelling from church to church over the next few months."

"Mr. Jenson," Vaughan spoke for the first time, staring at the man. "You mean to tell me that you let your daughter travel to Earth, stay there without you—you agreed willingly to this?"

"Mr. Vaughan, you don't seem to understand what a

great privilege it is to have one's daughter selected to be the Chosen One. It is the equivalent, in Buddhism, of having one's son pronounced the incarnation of the Dalai Lama."

Chandra said, "How is the process of selection made, Mr. Jenson?"

"The Council of High Priests retires for three days and undergoes a long, rhapsody-induced trance. In this trance they are contacted by the Godhead, and the Godhead informs them of His choice. This time, praise be, Elly was Chosen."

Chandra stared at his manicured fingernails, at a loss for the next question. Vaughan stood and took a pix of Elly from the mantelshelf. With her bright blue eyes and blonde curls, her resemblance to Holly was quite remarkable.

Vaughan turned to Jenson. "Do you make it a habit to wear a psi-shield around the house?"

"I beg your pardon?"

"If you have nothing to hide, Mr. Jenson, then get rid of your shield."

Jenson looked indignant. "As a matter of fact I have certain information—involving my business transactions here on Verkerk's—that in the hands of competitors from neighboring systems would be highly disadvantageous to my home planet's economic security."

Chandra shot Vaughan a look. "Well, I think that concludes our business here, Mr. Jenson, though we might have need to call back at a later date."

Vaughan strode down the hall and pulled open the front door. An icy blast of wind met him, chilling the exposed flesh of his hands and face. He could hear Chandra inside the house, taking his leave of Jenson.

He heard footsteps behind him. "You were a bit abrupt in there, Jeff."

Vaughan said, "How could he? How the hell could he let

his daughter go like that? If you'd seen her in the freighter
. . . He's lying, Jimmy."

"Okay, so he's lying. We'll get to the bottom of this and
nail him before we leave the planet. Come on, it's freezing
out here. Let's get back to the house, ah-cha?"

They climbed into the car. Vaughan said, "And how
come the guy was shielded?"

"Like he said—business interests—"

Vaughan snorted. "Bullshit. You heard what Laerhaven
said, pins are verboten here. Don't you think it a bit suspicious that Jenson was wearing a shield just as we turned up?"

Chandra thought about it. "Maybe . . ."

"Damned suspicious," Vaughan said, wondering how
Jenson could have known. Laerhaven? Had she told him?

On the way back, Chandra's handset chimed. It was
Laerhaven.

"Gentlemen, I've been talking with my colleagues in the
capital, Vanderlaan. I inquired about the ex-spacer, Essex."
She paused.

Chandra said, "And?"

"Well . . . he's currently under police protection in hospital in Vanderlaan. Apparently he approached the police
there three days ago, claiming that his life was in danger.
He was vague, almost incoherent. My colleagues dismissed
his claims, sent him away."

Chandra glanced across at Vaughan. "Don't tell me . . ."
he said into his handset.

"Two days ago an attempt was made on his life. He was
shot at close range by an unknown assailant in a park in the
city. Fortunately for Essex, a police patrol was passing
nearby and heard the shot—they intervened, but the
gunman got away."

"And Essex?"

"Badly wounded, but he'll live."

"Did he say why someone wanted him dead?"

"He's been in no fit state to say anything, Mr. Chandra. My colleagues are hoping to interview him when he recovers."

"We'd like to question him, if possible," Chandra said.

There was a pause, then Laerhaven said, "I'll give you the address of the hospital, and the code of the officer in charge of the case. I don't foresee any problems."

Chandra thanked her and was about to sign off when Vaughan said, "Lt. Laerhaven, Vaughan here. Did you by any chance mention to Lars Jenson that we wanted to question him, and that I was a telepath?"

The reply was immediate: "No. No, of course not."

Chandra said, "Thank you, Lieutenant. We thought not." He cut the connection.

Vaughan glanced across at Chandra. "Did *we?*" Vaughan asked pointedly.

"You think she might have mentioned it to Jenson?" Chandra asked. "You don't think she's in with him?"

Vaughan shrugged. "Not necessarily—but she might have mentioned it inadvertently."

They continued the drive in silence.

Later that evening, after a passable curry cooked up by Chandra with the meager ingredients available in the house, Vaughan stepped through the French windows and stood on the frost-crackling lawn.

Alerted by movement above him, he stared into the sky. He laughed, the sound harsh in the silence. Snow was falling and, through the sudden flurry he could see—like snowflakes that had elected, *en masse,* to defy gravity—the still points of light that were a million stars. Unbidden, the recollection returned of a night very much like this almost twenty years ago, when he had stood beneath the vast Canadian night sky and stared up into the heavens. Now he was overcome with the recapitulation of the feeling he had experienced back then—the overwhelming optimism of a young boy at the start of life, with all of the hopes and none of the fears, with all the cosmos at his fingertips.

He thought of Holly and Tiger. He wanted to be able to stand with them now and stare up at the teeming stars. He wanted to experience, however vicariously, their delight at being young and alive.

It came to him that the tragedy of their deaths was not so much the termination of what they had been, but the ultimate and irrevocable termination of all that they would have become. That was the terrible tragedy.

The wind blew, bitter cold, and at last Vaughan turned and walked into the sanctuary of the warmwood house.

He lay on his bed and listened to the muted thrum of mind-noise from the city. It was nothing like as concerted as what he experienced on Bengal Station, but he told himself that he could do without it, nevertheless.

He reached for his chora, poured a dose into his beer, and drank.

TWELVE

Jimmy Chandra had expected Vanderlaan, the administrative capital of the northern continent and the largest city on Verkerk's World, to look something like the cities of Earth: sprawling suburbs, a busy, built up center. He should have guessed that, with a population of little over fifty thousand, it would be just another, slightly larger version of Sapphire Falls. As he drove into town along the coast road, two hours after setting off at dawn, he wondered if he'd been somehow turned around during the journey and was arriving back in Sapphire. There were a few differences to assure him that he was in Vanderlaan, however: the sea, to the left, filled the bay with a million scales of reflected sunlight, and there were fewer warmwood houses here—for the most part, the buildings were constructed of polycarbon in gold and silver, reflecting the sun like some inland, mirror-image of the bay.

Vaughan sprawled out across the back seat, asleep. As Chandra drove through the city, following directions to the hospital he'd received from the officer in charge of the Essex case, he considered what he had discovered about the telepath on police files back on Earth.

Jeff Vaughan was not Jeff Vaughan at all, but someone who had taken on the identity, the personal files and records, of a deceased Bengal Station citizen named Jeff Vaughan. Chandra had always thought he'd known Vaughan well enough to second-guess his reactions, his opinions—his sardonic take on reality. But the telepath had

158

rarely spoken about his past, only once letting slip that he was Canadian, and that his parents had died when he was young.

And Vaughan's obsessive interest in the Elly Jenson case? How did that square with his usual apathy, Chandra wondered.

After their meal last night, Chandra had heard the French windows open. He'd moved into the lounge and looked through the window. Vaughan had been standing in the middle of the lawn, in the snow, staring up at the stars and weeping.

That morning, Chandra had inadvertently stumbled upon what might have been a little piece of the puzzle to Vaughan's past. At dawn, ready to set off, Chandra had knocked on Vaughan's bedroom door. Five minutes later he'd knocked again and shouted and, getting no response, had opened the door and looked in. Vaughan was sprawled on the bed, fully clothed and snoring. Beside him, spread across the rumpled sheets, were about two dozen pix of Elly Jenson—miniatures of the graphic that Vaughan had taken from Genevieve Weiss's studio. Then Chandra noticed something else: all the pix were not of the Jenson kid. Some were of a girl who bore a striking resemblance to Elly, and in one or two of the pix—Chandra could not get close enough to be sure—the girl was with a man who might have been a younger Jeff Vaughan.

Riga hung high above the sea to the east, four hours from setting. Already, a cool breeze had sprung up to temper the fierce heat. Chandra found the short day, the accelerated time-scale, hard to accommodate. They had been on Verkerk's World for almost twenty hours, yet had experienced a night and almost two days. He longed for the familiarities of Bengal Station, where you could get a full day's work done without the premature arrival of night.

"Jeff," Chandra called. "We're here."

Vaughan hung his head through the gap between the front seats, looking dog-tired. "I'll never get used to the short night, Jimmy."

Chandra smiled. "Tell me about it."

The city hospital was in the oldest quarter of Vanderlaan, the area constructed over thirty-five years ago by the first wave of colonists. Despite the relative modernity of the old town, the area had the look, with its warmwood buildings bedecked with creepers and blooms, of having been settled for centuries.

They parked outside a low, modern building and made their way to reception. An officer, Sergeant Hengst, greeted Chandra and Vaughan and ushered them along a corridor. "Lt. Laerhaven instructed me to help you however I can in your investigations, gentlemen," he said in stilted English.

"We can interview Essex?" Chandra asked.

The Sergeant nodded. "He is showing signs of recovery," he said. "His doctor says that you can have thirty minutes." He paused. "As a matter of security, and in order to aid our own investigations, I must tell you that your interview will be recorded."

Chandra looked at Vaughan, who shrugged. "No problem," Chandra said.

Hengst smiled. "Excellent."

Vaughan asked, "Have you any idea who might have wanted Essex dead, Sergeant?"

Hengst shook his head. "Our investigations so far have come to nothing. Please, this way . . ."

He led them into a small room overlooking a garden. The shrunken figure of an old man, not at all the image of the ex-spacer Chandra had expected, lay in a recovery pod. Essex was thin-faced, bald. His thin chest was encased in a glossy layer of synthi-flesh, and from the pale flesh of his arms snaked the leads of a dozen monitors and intravenous tubes.

He stared at Chandra, wide-eyed, as the three men approached the pod. He tried to sit up, but failed and slumped back into the cushioned interior. He said feebly, "If you've come to kill me, then kill me!"

Hengst said, "Mr. Essex, officers Chandra and Vaughan are here to interview you. If you could assist them by answering their questions, we would be grateful. If at any time you wish to terminate the interview, just say so. Do you understand?"

Vaughan took a sat beside the pod. He reached out and touched the old man's arm and said in a surprisingly soft and reassuring voice, "We're friends, Mr. Essex. We're police, from Earth."

Essex's nervous glance shuttled between Vaughan and Chandra, disbelief evident on his open-mouthed face. "You're not going to kill me?"

"We're on your side. We're from Earth, here to investigate what's been going on. We mean you no harm."

Hengst whispered, "I'll be outside if you need me." He slipped from the room.

Chandra drew up a chair and sat beside Vaughan.

Essex licked his lips. "I . . . I've been expecting them at any time. That was the most frightening thing, you see. Not knowing when—when they'd turn up and kill me."

"It's okay, you're safe now." Chandra reached out, took the old man's hand. "Why are they trying to kill you?" he asked.

Essex licked his trembling lips. "It's because of what I found out about them, you see. They don't want it getting out."

Chandra looked at Vaughan. "What did you find out?" he asked, soothing.

Essex nodded, his glance darting between the two men, still distrustful and unable to believe in the luck of his reprieve. "It's . . . it's all so vague . . ."

"Easy. Take it easy and tell us in your own time," Chandra said.

Essex nodded. "I was a well-respected naturalist when I was younger. Specialized in the study of migration patterns of species on newly colonized planets. I worked for some of the biggest space agencies. They didn't want colonists wreaking havoc on the migration patterns of the native fauna. I charted major routes, so the colonists could avoid the animals . . ." He trailed off, shook his head in confusion.

"You and your team explored Verkerk's World," Chandra reminded him.

"Verkerk's World . . ." Essex repeated the name as if speaking it for the very first time. "Nearly fifty years ago now. New world, you see, new and interesting wildlife. I returned from time to time after the place was colonized, made studies in the northern continent." He shook his head. "Strange thing. Periodic drop in localized indigenous population of certain species in the northern ranges. Couldn't explain it. Larger animals, high in the food chain, animals with no natural predators . . . almost wiped out periodically. It baffled me. I wrote up a paper, published it on Earth, forgot about the whole thing. Lots of work to do out in the Expansion. That was what . . . twenty years ago? I didn't come back to Verkerk's for years and years." Again, his vision lost focus. He seemed confused as to where he was and why he was speaking of the past. "I was on Earth a few months ago. I looked up Marquez and Bhindra, my exploration colleagues, and we got talking about Verkerk's and what we found there. That got me thinking. I decided to come back, try to work out what was happening . . ."

"What did you find?" Chandra prompted.

The old man shook his head. "It was a year after the last periodic two-year 'cull.' Whatever had occurred, I'd missed it. I talked to a few locals, but they were unwilling to tell me anything . . . I ran tests on the water from the mountains, discovered minute traces of the drug known today as rhapsody. I found it gains in potency every two years. It flows from the north, through the floodplain of Sapphire Falls. Its molecules bind themselves to the cells of certain plants. These plants are harvested by locals—it's what forms the basis for the cult they have here, the Church of the Adoration. Anyway, that's by the by. It has no real effect down here, we're too far away—it's up there, up in the mountains, where it has its *desired* effect . . ."

Vaughan reached out, touched the old man's hand. "What effect, Essex?"

He screwed his eyes tight shut, opened them, and stared at a point between the two men. He began shaking his head in a slow, side-to-side motion that Chandra thought might never end. "I'd been visiting the remote mountain communities in the north. It was there I met a sociologist from Vanderlaan, man by the name of Kuivert. He told me he was doing some work on population figures. From time to time we'd meet, go through our findings. One day, he showed up here. He was agitated—no, more like petrified. Had every right to be. He'd been doing some poking around in the mountain communities in the north, checking claims that citizens had moved south . . . You see, there's no census here on Verkerk's. Massive planet. Relatively few settlers, thousands of self-sufficient communes—how many, nobody really knows. So it's not easy to keep a record of all the comings and goings . . . But my friend, he produced these figures and claimed that citizens of the northern mountains have been disappearing with the same frequency as the animals up there."

With shaking fingers he prodded tears from his eyes, took a breath, and continued. "So, six weeks ago, when the periodic disappearances were due to begin, we obtained a sample of some rhapsody and set off up north. You see, there had to be two of us, one to take the stuff, the other to stop him from following the call."

He fell silent again. His eyes were wide, his lips trembling.

"What happened?" Chandra asked gently.

Essex swallowed, nodded as if to acknowledge that he was strong enough to continue his account. "We drove north as far as we could, then left the car and trekked into the mountains. We were heading for the center of the disappearance phenomenon, place above the Geiger Caves." He scrabbled around on the table beside the pod, found a map, and pulled it toward him. He stabbed a long-nailed forefinger in the approximate area of the northern range. "We took along insulated tents and spent the night in the mountains. In the morning we prepared ourselves.

"We drove a stake into the ground, deep so it couldn't be pulled out. Kuivert handcuffed me to it. There was no way I could move, get away. Then I took the rhapsody." His eyes misted over, and a slight smile played around his mouth. "First, I felt dizzy, nauseous. I had to lie down. Then I felt . . . euphoric. I was united with . . . I can only call it God. I was part of a wholeness, united with all that ever was and will be . . ."

After long pause, he went on: "The trance lasted about thirty minutes. Then, suddenly, I had to move. I had to join the source of that euphoria. I could feel something calling to me, telling me that if I joined it then I'd be granted the sensation of unity with the oneness. All I can recall is trying to get free, and failing, and feeling that I would have given anything to follow the call. According to Kuivert, I begged him to let me go, threatened him that if he didn't release me I'd kill him. He didn't give in . . . Thank God.

"After an hour or two, the feeling diminished. I slept. When I came to my senses, I recounted the experience to Kuivert. We decided to trek further into the mountain, see if we could locate the source of the calling. I had a notion, a memory from the trance, of where it came from—the Geiger Caves.

"It was almost sunset by the time we got there." Essex closed his eyes and wept. Chandra laid an ineffectual hand on the old man's shoulder.

"Take your time," he said. "There's no hurry."

Essex sat up with difficulty. He gestured to a jug of water beside the pod and Chandra poured him a glass. Essex drank quickly. "You see, what was so terrible . . . We thought—all along we thought that it was a natural phenomenon. We thought that the locals were drinking the water and submitting to the call. But . . . we reached the entrance to the Geiger Caves, concealed ourselves behind boulders . . . And down there, in the mouth of the cave, down there was a service, a religious service of some kind. People stepped up from the congregation and approached some priest in robes at the head of the gathering, and the priest would offer a chalice, and the people would drink, and then pass into the cave. Even then we didn't understand what was happening.

"When everyone had passed into the cave, Kuivert said that he was going to follow them. I tried to stop him, tried to argue him out of it. But he was having none of it—he

165

wanted to find out what was happening in there. There was nothing for it—I had to go with him. I couldn't let him go alone. So we crept into the cave. We had flashlights, in case we were caught out on the mountainside in the darkness. We followed a worn path deep into the mountains.

"We . . . we followed the sound of the congregation as they descended. We were careful, very, very careful. I think we both knew that if we were caught . . ."

Essex paused there, shook his head. "We came to a gallery overlooking a massive chamber. It was dimly lit, but even so we could make out . . ."

He stopped, his eyes staring straight ahead at whatever he had seen in that subterranean chamber.

Chandra exchanged a glance with Vaughan. He felt sweat trickle down his chest, over his belly. Vaughan was staring at Essex, his bloodshot eyes wide.

The naturalist went on: "I saw a line of people, men and women and even children . . . they walked toward it and . . . and were absorbed. There are no words to describe what happened to them. They were just . . . *absorbed*."

Chandra cleared his throat, spoke gently: "Absorbed by what, Essex? What was *it*?"

Essex was shaking his head. "I know what I saw . . . but Kuivert disagreed. I saw a . . . a silver thing—a creature resembling a Palaeozoic *orthoceras,* a kind of giant squid. They just walked up to it and were absorbed. But Kuivert saw something different—some kind of huge amorphous quadruped like a pachyderm. What we both agreed on was that it was *taking* those people. Later, we decided that the creature appeared, in some way, different to every observer. As I was specializing in crustacea at the time, it appeared as a prehistoric squid. To Essex, who'd worked with elephant-analogues on Addenbrooke in his youth, it appeared as some kind of mammoth . . . Don't ask me how it did it. "We made our way from the cave. We didn't stop until we got back to our campsite, then packed up and returned to the car and drove back to Vanderlaan." Essex smiled bleakly at Chandra. "I can't begin to make you understand the horror we experienced that day."

"What did you do?" Vaughan asked. "What then?"

"Kuivert returned to the Geiger Caves, filmed the proceedings. He wouldn't let me see the film, and he wouldn't tell me whether he'd identified the culprits. He said that the less I knew, the safer I was. And, like the coward I was, I didn't argue. He did tell me, though, that he'd discovered about half a dozen sites where the ritual was enacted—he guessed that there were that many . . . *beings* dwelling in the mountain. He suspected that the priests of the sect were controlled by the creatures—or rather *motivated,* and rewarded with the euphoria of oneness for their actions.

"He discovered that the drug, the rhapsody, was only really effective—only provided the illusion of the union—within a ten-kilometre radius of the lair of the creatures, which was why the drug had little effect down here. He suspected that the beasts excreted the drug into the watertable, and from there it found its way into the streams that ran from the mountains."

Essex paused. "I thought Kuivert would turn the evidence over to the police, the government—" He shook his head. "But he wouldn't. He suspected that people high up in the police or the government were part of the sect."

Essex fell silent, stared into space.

Chandra said, "We need to talk to Kuivert. Do you have his address?"

Essex shook his head. In a small, frail voice he said, "Last week he packed up and drove into the northern

ranges. I begged him not to, I pleaded with him to stay
here, but he said he wanted more evidence." Essex shook
his head and wept. "Please believe me, I begged him to stay
here, I pleaded with him . . ." Essex stared at Chandra, his
eyes wide. "It was no good. I heard from him just one last
time."

"He contacted you?"

Essex nodded, gathered himself. "It was late at night . . .
Kuivert called me from high in the mountains. He said that
he'd seen people lead the beasts from the caves, load them
into containers, and ferry them away aboard cargo-fliers.
They were taking them somewhere. He sounded . . . my
God he sounded terrified." He finished in a whisper: "He
never came back. They must have found him and, and . . ."

Chandra stood and walked to the window, taking great
breaths of cooling air. He stared out at the lawned garden.

Essex said, "I fell to wondering where they might be
taking these . . . these monsters. I thought they might be
transporting them to Earth, to widen the net of the calling,
to spread the word. So I contacted Bhindra and Marquez,
told them what I suspected, and asked for their help. I
haven't heard from them since . . ."

Chandra looked at Vaughan and shook his head. It
would serve no purpose to tell Essex what, thanks to him,
had happened to his ex-colleagues.

He returned to the old man in the pod. "Do you know
what happened to the tapes Kuivert made, the records he
kept?"

Essex gestured. "When he didn't return after two days, I
went across to the apartment he was renting. I had a spare
key, so I let myself in. There was nothing . . . either he took
everything with him, or someone had got there before me
and destroyed the evidence. I left my flat, moved to a hotel

in town. I was planning to leave Verkerk's for good when they found me."

Vaughan leaned forward. "You said that these . . . these 'culls' are periodic, every two years or so. But do you know how long they last?"

Essex stared at the telepath. "Kuivert estimated that they went on for about two months—long enough to allow the monsters to have their fill."

Vaughan nodded, then said, "And how long has the calling been going on this time?"

Essex calculated. "I'd say about six weeks."

Vaughan stood and drew Chandra to one side. "The calling has roughly two weeks to run," he whispered. "The sooner we can stop the Church of the Adoration, the more innocent lives we can save . . ."

Chandra felt a cold weight settle in his gut. "But how do we stop them?"

Vaughan hesitated, then said, "We should go into the mountains, Jimmy."

Chandra said, "Do you really think we ought to?"

"We need a recorder, tapes. Once we have evidence, then we can get back to the authorities on Earth. That's the only way to eradicate the Church."

Chandra nodded. "Of course, you're right. It's just that . . ."

"Frightened, Jimmy?"

Chandra smiled. "To death," he admitted.

THIRTEEN

They set off for the mountains just after sunset and Vaughan drove throughout the seven hours of darkness, Chandra sleeping beside him in the passenger seat.

It was a novel experience to be heading into such a vast and depopulated wilderness. Rapidly the low mind-hum from Vanderlaan, the only concentrated noise for kilometres, receded into the distance. Vaughan had purposefully held off the chora so as to be fully alert during what lay ahead, and he had expected the noise to follow him for a long time. After two hundred kilometres, however, he experienced the blessed balm of total mind-silence. He leaned back in the seat and drove with his arms outstretched, gripping the apex of the wheel, staring straight ahead at the unwinding road, silver with frost, in the glare of the headlights.

He turned off the coast road and headed inland, through farmland at first, and then through undulating, uncultivated plains. The silence persisted. The nearest centers of population, villages located in the foothills of the central range, were three hundred kilometres distant. At one point the silence became so strange an experience that he slipped the case from his jacket and inserted the pin into his skull console, wanting to relish the silence all the more by contrasting it to any noise he might pick up.

In scan-mode, he read occasional signals in the vast and empty distance—the low hum of single, sleeping minds, the occupants of sequestered farmhouses. They were so distant that he perceived no mental images, just faint music. He drove through the cold, dark night, warmed by the heating in the roadster, half-listening to these slumbering minds as a driver half-listens to the radio, played low. He wondered if he found the evidence of these minds reassuring, in contrast to the emptiness of the northern mountains and what they might contain.

He looked ahead, considered the events that would inevitably occur in the hours to come.

He told himself that it was wrong to classify as evil the deeds done by the creatures in the Geiger Caves—they, after all, were merely fulfilling the demands of the biological imperative to survive. Even the humans in proximity to the troglodyte creatures, slaves to the promise of eternal euphoria, no doubt had little control over their actions. It was the Church hierarchy, expediting the transfer of the aliens to Earth, whose actions were reprehensible. And even then he warned himself against finding easy solutions to something he did not yet fully understand. Perhaps even people like Weiss, Dolores Yandoah, and Jenson believed that they were delivering the victims of the creatures to some ultimate oneness with the Godhead . . .

He thought back to the euphoria he had experienced at the Holosseum, and compared it to the experience he had had with the rhapsody he had taken in his apartment after the service. Then, he had achieved a dulled, torpid state, without any of the euphoria . . . He considered what Essex had said about the drug being effective only in a ten-kilometre radius of the mountains—in proximity, in other words, to the creatures that issued the summons. Did that mean that, in the Holosseum, he had been close to one of the aliens transported to Earth?

But why, then, had he not experienced the calling, the second stage of the effect described by Essex, that followed on from the euphoria?

He wondered if it was something to do with the strength of the drug administered at the service. Perhaps the drug given out then had been a sampler, designed to hook the congregation into coming back for more, and passing on the word of the thrill of communion. Later, when the ranks of the faithful had swelled, the dose would be increased and the congregation would experience the calling, and the alien would feed upon the faithful.

The creatures had fed on Verkerk's World, and now they were about to feed on Earth. Vaughan wondered how many of the things had been smuggled off-planet.

Essex said that the calling had about two weeks to run. The next ship left in two days, with another two days of flight time before they reached Earth. That would leave approximately ten days in which to locate the aliens on the Station, and wherever else they might be, and eradicate the danger they posed.

He had discussed tactics with Chandra for the first hour of the journey. They would approach the Geiger Caves and attempt to film, at a distance, any activity that might be taking place. They had decided to err on the side of caution. Better to come away with nothing than suffer Kuivert's probable fate. They had come prepared. They had a vid-camera in the back of the car, and weapons, thermal clothing, and tents should they be caught out in the open come nightfall.

Vaughan drove on, his mind active with speculation, and before he knew it the short, dark night was at an end.

Dawn arrived with the rapidity of an activated holo-set. The period of half-light seemed to last only seconds, and then the rising sun beamed up from behind the mountain range like the rays of a searchlight. The land was revealed as an idyllic panorama etched in every shade of silver, from the dull pewter of the metalled road to blinding white magnesium of the snow-capped mountains.

He pulled off the road. Chandra, still sleeping, shifted and muttered at the discontinued lullaby drum of tires on tarmac. Vaughan eased himself from the driver's seat and closed the door quietly behind him. The cold clamped itself around him, bracing and bone-gripping. He took a deep, invigorating breath, feeling the tiredness that had built up over the hours flee, leaving him clear-headed and alert. He walked away from the car along the side of the narrow road, stretching his legs. There was not the slightest sign of human presence. He was surprised to discover, when he raised a hand to his console, that his augmentation-pin was still jacked in. He stood in the middle of the road and turned in a full circle, taking in the undulating hills, sparkling in the frost; the distant, flat line of the coastal plain; and, in the opposite direction, the rearing ramparts of the northern mountains. He turned and scanned, concentrating on picking up the slightest human signal out there, however weak. He had never in his life had to scan with such diligence; usually, in scan-mode, he could do nothing to keep the minds from encroaching. Now there was nothing out there, no mind-hum or individual signatures, nothing but absolute silence.

He stood in the middle of the road with his arms raised to heaven as if in supplication. The silence of the night, his first experience of this kind of mind-silence, had hardly prepared him: never before had he experienced such a peace, such a profound and ringing silence. It was amazing to be alone with one's own thoughts, to have the fragmented identities, the angst-ridden detritus from the minds of a million souls, the scraps of psychoses, paranoia, and neurosis, banished from his sensorium. Once tasted, the silence would haunt him forever with its promise of peace. Now that he knew that such cerebral relief was possible, he told himself that he could go on, could endure the agony of being a telepath, just so long as he could return from time to time to the silence.

The cold drove him back to the car. He slipped into the driver's seat and pulled the map from inside his jacket, opening it out across the steering wheel. He judged that they were less than a hundred kilometres from where the road passed closest to the Geiger Caves. From that point, it was a hike of another twenty kilometres through the foothills to reach the source of the call.

He returned the map to his pocket. Beside him, Chandra stirred again. It was strange to have experienced such profound mind-silence and yet be in the presence of another human being. He thanked himself for insisting that Chandra should take Weiss's mind-shield back at police headquarters.

He was about to start the roadster and set off when a thought occurred to him. Chandra was fast asleep, snoring gently. If he reached into Chandra's jacket pocket, removed the shield, and carried it the requisite distance from the car . . . Chandra's mind would be revealed to him in blazing clarity, his every memory, his every hidden secret.

Chandra's manner since arriving on Verkerk's World, his reserve and attitude of suspicion, quite apart from the fact that he was careful never to be without his shield, suggested to Vaughan that he was hiding something. Vaughan wondered if it were possible that Chandra had found out something about his past. He could scan Chandra, find out exactly what he knew and so assess the danger.

As he contemplated the sleeping Chandra, he wondered

how much of his reluctance to scan him was because he did not want to know what Chandra really thought of him. There had been times, over the past few days, when Vaughan had made cynical jibes at Chandra's expense, and Chandra had regarded him with an expression little short of loathing, and quite justifiably so. Vaughan could do without a mindful of Chandra's dislike.

He started the roadster. As he drove off, he wondered whether he should just simply ask how much Chandra knew of his past. But that would mean he would have to come clean, explain to Chandra why it had been necessary to change his identity. Years ago, he might have trusted the Indian, but he could not let himself trust anyone that much now.

The sun climbed, turning the frost to dazzling quick-silver on the surrounding meadowland. The road wound into the foothills, and the rearing mountains filled the width of the windscreen with a range of blue-gray flanks and snow-covered summits.

Chandra woke an hour later, stretched and yawned. "Oh, the mountains . . . How far have we come?"

"Five, six hundred kilometres."

"You should have woken me, Jeff. Stop and I'll drive."

"Relax. We're almost there. You could pass me a coffee, though."

"Coffee coming up." He passed Vaughan a steaming bulb of black coffee and sandwiches of the tasteless, plastic cheese popular on Verkerk's World.

Thirty minutes later he pulled off the road and parked the car beneath a concealing stand of fir trees. He opened out the map and indicated the route to Chandra. "It's by foot from here. I reckon around eighteen, twenty kay."

"You sure you don't want a rest?"

He was feeling wide-awake, the combination of caffeine and the mind-silence invigorating him. "We'll stop and rest when the heat gets too much. Let's get going."

Vaughan opened the boot of the car and broke out the supplies: two backpacks, one containing a tent and insulated clothing, the other food and water. He took the pistols from their case—two automatics—and passed one to Chandra. He strapped his own pistol beneath his jacket, ensuring he could reach it without hindrance.

They drank a bottle of water, consulted the map, and then set off up a long, wide valley.

It was mid-morning and the heat increased by the minute, though the ground underfoot was still hard with frost. All around, Vaughan saw the unopened buds of a thousand flowers. He imagined the green meadow in an hour or two, when the sun climbed and the blooms decided to open.

The gradient increased; the last few hundred metres before they reached the head of the valley were littered with the rocky deposits of the glacier that had torn through the land millennia ago. They walked between boulders, and then the rocks became so closely packed that they were forced to climb them, jumping from boulder to boulder. Soon they reached the opening to a side valley, this one narrower and steeper than the last.

Vaughan stopped and unfolded the map. "This is the one. And when we get to the top—" he indicated the second valley, "—there should be a trail through the rocks for a couple of thousand metres."

He turned and surveyed the terrain they had crossed so far. The valley fell away steeply, a broad green sweep between two fingers of rock. In the distance, beside the twisting course of the road, was the stand of tiny fir trees behind which their roadster was hidden. Beyond the road and the vast, spreading expanse of the plain, the coastline was obscured by a morning mist that stretched the entire length of the horizon.

Chandra was shaking his head. "I've never been anywhere like it, Jeff. To someone brought up on the Station . . . you can't imagine. The silence, the openness—it feels almost threatening." He took a deep breath of the clean, cold air, turning three hundred and sixty degrees in a kind of disbelieving wonder. "Not a soul in sight for kilometres. Wait till I tell Sumita about this."

Vaughan smiled to himself, oddly pleased by Chandra's childish exhibition of wonder. He closed his eyes and scanned. Silence filled his mind, a void in which the only thoughts in his head were his own.

Down in the valley, the flowers were opening. The comprehensive transformation, from the uniform green of the meadow to the multi-colored tapestry of the writhing blooms, was so sudden that it reminded Vaughan of something programmed—like a color sweep on a computer screen. A swarm of insects buzzed over the land, a million individual pixels of iridescence scintillating the light of the sun.

From behind them, long-beaked birds darted down the valley, heading for the bounty of pollen on offer. Vaughan was reminded of the scene reproduced at the Holosseum.

They set off again, jumping down from the vantage point of the tumble of rocks and heading up the narrow valley. The sun was almost directly overhead now and the increased temperature, combined with the steeper gradient, made for an arduous two-hour climb. They persisted doggedly, no longer exchanging talk, Vaughan aware that a decade of relative inactivity was taking its toll. They stopped frequently to rest and drink water. The head of the valley, a steep cutting in silhouette against the snow-covered mountains beyond, seemed to remain just as distant no matter how far they walked. He spurred himself on with the incentive of a long, well-earned rest when they reached the head.

Chandra forged ahead, reached the cutting, and sat against a rock. Vaughan dropped his pack unceremoniously and collapsed against it, hanging his head back and gulping in the mountain air. He pulled out a water bottle and chugged the cold liquid.

"Ten minutes, Jimmy. For chrissake don't set off before then, okay? I need time to recover."

"When you get back to the Station, Jeff, I'll book you into a gym."

"Don't bother. I don't intend to be doing this too often in the future."

He pulled out the map and passed it to Chandra. He traced their L-shaped route up the valleys, then indicated the winding track to the mouth of the Geiger Caves. "It's less than three kilometres from here, Jimmy. We should be there in an hour."

Chandra looked up from the map. He stared down the valley. "Beautiful," he said to himself. "It must remind you of Canada?"

Vaughan shrugged. "Toronto was much flatter."

Chandra hesitated, then said, "You never told me much about what you did before you came to the Station . . ."

Vaughan pursed his lips around a mouthful of water, feigning concentration on the label of the plastic bottle. He swallowed, nodded. "That's because it's a time I don't talk about, Jimmy. Simple as that."

"It must have been a bad time, if you can't talk—"

"Quit it, Jimmy."

Chandra opened his mouth to speak.

This is it, Vaughan thought. *This is where he comes out with what he's discovered.*

He was aware of conflicting emotions within himself—the burning desire to know what Chandra knew, and at the same time the disinclination to open up and admit his past.

Chandra closed his mouth, shook his head.

Quickly, Vaughan stowed away his water bottle, lifted his pack, and swung it onto his shoulders. He looked up, scanning the way ahead. "Let's get to it, Jimmy," he said, as if nothing had come between them. "The sooner we set off, the sooner we get there."

He strode off up the rocky, winding track. Silently, Chandra followed.

As he climbed the path between great, tumbled boulders and craggy overhangs, it came to him with a startling jolt why the track was so well defined. Over the years, the sacrificial victims, the faithful who had obeyed the calling, had come this way by the hundreds. They had sought union with the One, and instead had joined with oblivion.

Thirty minutes later, the path opened out onto a sloping, meadowed incline. Over the rise, according to the map, was the opening to the Caves. Vaughan scanned ahead.

"It's okay. We're alone. Let's go."

They hurried up the greensward toward the crest where a series of flattened rocks jutted from the earth. From the cover of these sloping rocks they had a clear view down into the dell where the mouth of the Caves, gaping as if in surprise, showed dark against the blue rock of the mountainside.

Before the cave mouth, the hollow of grass had been churned in the not too distant past by the passage of the faithful.

Chandra hunched, shivering. "What now? Can you read anything?"

"Not a thing." He pulled the map from his jacket, studying the system of caves marked by Essex. "See these, here? They're a couple of kilometres away. Maybe we should try there." He looked at his watch. "We've about another hour of daylight left. What do you think?"

Chandra smiled. "Sure. Why not?"

They set off again, climbing the steep incline between the gray rocks. Vaughan remained vigilant, constantly scanning ahead for the first signature of human presence. The warmth of the sun dissipated and the wind from the mountaintops was razor-sharp.

"We'll make it to the caves, change into our thermals, and camp the night," he said. He made sure his pistol was handy, checked his flashlight.

They climbed quickly, moving faster in the cool of dusk. Vaughan led the way, consulting the map from time to time but for the most part following the well-worn track up the side of a rock-strewn valley.

Forty minutes after setting out, Vaughan stopped. Something, some quick, sharp signal, had pulsed in his head like the mark on a radar beacon. He closed his eyes, concentrated. There were more of them, a whole cluster. Too far away to be read as individual thoughts, they registered as a lively buzz of intelligence—human intelligence.

"Jeff?" Chandra said, watching him.

"There's someone up there," he whispered needlessly. From the strength of the signal, he judged the people he was scanning to be about a kilometre away.

"More than one. Perhaps . . ." He grimaced, concentrating. "Perhaps ten, fifteen. Come on, we can make it before dark."

They continued along the trail. The buzz of human presence was located at the head of the next valley, the area around the entrance of the caves toward which Vaughan and Chandra were heading. As they climbed, taking exaggerated care not to dislodge rocks, the signal gained in strength. There were thirteen individuals, nine men and four women. The contents of their minds became discernible. He flitted from mind to mind, searching for any information that might prove valuable. Their thoughts were fuzzy, hazed with something he was unable to make out at first—then he realised that he was scanning the minds of addicts.

Suddenly, Vaughan was granted a glimpse of the truth.

These people were . . . Disciples, as they thought of themselves, and their God was the One God, the gestalt unity of the Vaith. The Vaith, he discovered, the extraterrestrial beings that had arrived on Verkerk's World millennia ago—taking their fill of the local fauna until humans happened along—were no longer present on the planet. The long-planned transfer had been successfully completed. Vaughan dived deeper into the mind of the closest woman, tried to work out from her drug-addled recollections if the Vaith had instigated the transfer, or if it had been the idea of the Disciples. He read a frightening loyalty to the Vaith, a loyalty that would have involved sacrificing herself for the welfare of her God, and he read too that the Vaith had willed their transfer so that they might more fully experience human civilization and so facilitate the communion with the One for the legion of human faithful. Vaughan picked up brief glimpses in the woman's memory of how the creatures had appeared to her, and brief glimpses were all he wanted: great crab-like shapes of midnight chitin, flashing claws, moist pink mouths equipped with ancillary claws with which to draw in their victims. To the woman, the sighs of the sacrificial faithful were the sounds of salvation itself: she lived for the day when she too could give herself to the One.

He pushed the images aside and scanned the woman and others, trying to find the destinations of the alien demigods. He found that three were on Earth; the three others had been transferred in the last week to the colony planets of Harmony, Zalspar, and Greenwood.

They climbed the valley, keeping in the cover of the rocks. When they gained the crest of the valley, Vaughan ordered Chandra into a crouch and edged forward, peering over the tumble of rocks into the sloping sward before the mouth of the cave below.

The Disciples were busy dismantling a series of extruded polycarbon dwellings, flattening them out and loading them into the hold of a cargo-flier, their mission accomplished. They were dressed in silver insulation suits, the uniform design giving them the appearance of an army. Beside him, Chandra had remembered their original plan and was filming the proceedings. Vaughan felt his heart beat deafeningly in his ears, aware of the danger if they were discovered now. It came to him that the threat would have been grave enough if the Disciples had been acting on their own initiatives: driven as they were by drug-induced loyalty to the Vaith, the danger was maximized.

Vaughan scanned the Disciples below, searching among the minds for the exact location of the Vaith on the colony planets, on Earth, and specifically on Bengal Station. But in every mind he drew a blank. The Disciples were aware of the individual planets to which the Vaith had traveled, but not the precise locations. Next, he scanned for knowledge of the ringleaders on Earth and the colonies, but again he scanned in vain. The Disciples were organized in a system of highly disciplined cells, with only the cell leader having contact with commanders in higher cell structures. None of the Disciples down below knew of others beyond their own cell of eighteen.

He told himself, later, that he should have known at that moment. Eighteen, and he had counted thirteen down below . . .

Then he read something in the mind of a Disciple: >>>*Where the hell is Jenson?—we're almost ready for off* . . .

Jenson . . . Elly Jenson's father?

He knew, of course, that Jenson possessed a mind-shield—and with the sudden realization came the sudden awareness of danger.

There was no time to get away. He seemed to be moving in slow motion: it took an age to gesture to Chandra to stop filming and flee, an age to turn and begin the descent of the valley.

Even the arrival, seemingly out of nowhere, of the silver-suited Disciples—their sudden appearance from the shadows all the more shocking for the fact they all wore mind-shields—even their attack seemed to happen over a period of protracted seconds, their movements slowed in his perceptions with shock and the futile awareness that this should never have happened.

And then the Disciples were upon Vaughan and Chandra in an instant. Someone knocked him to the ground, a fist in his face. He felt blood trickle, thick and hot, down his cheek and into his mouth. A Disciple kicked him in the stomach. He groaned and curled up tight against the ice-cold ground, pain exploding through him.

Seconds passed, and then he felt callous hands turning him over and searching for weapons. He struggled, but was held in position by more than one person. A Disciple pulled the pack from his back and grabbed his jacket, tearing pockets and sleeves. They found his pistol, took it.

Two men dragged him to his knees; the same number held Chandra. Jenson stood over them. His expression was impassive, his mind unreadable.

"Sir?" a Disciple said.

"Get rid of them," were Jenson's only words before he vanished into the shadows.

Then Vaughan was upright and borne through the air. He put up a token struggle, but the hands restraining him were unshakable. He was carried up the valley toward an outcropping of rocks. Vaughan closed his eyes, ready for the bullet in the back of his head.

Instead, the hands released him and he was falling through the air, and it came to him that they had saved a bullet and had thrown him from the mountainside. He experienced the stomach-churning sensation of falling, and hoped that the impact would kill him outright. It came after brief seconds, ramming his thighs into his chest and winding him. He rolled, falling on his shoulder and yelling in pain. Chandra arrived next, thudding down beside him.

Vaughan rolled onto his back, gasping for breath. He could hear Chandra nearby, sobbing quietly. He looked up, made out a ragged circle of twilight sky between the rocks.

Seconds ticked away, became an interminable duration Vaughan spent waiting for the *coup de grâce*, the bullets from above. As the minutes and the silence stretched, a slow realization came to him.

Beside him, Chandra said, "What are they waiting for? Why don't they get it over with?"

Vaughan pushed himself into a sitting position, his right shoulder protesting. "Why should they? Think about it. How long do you think we'll last before freezing to death?"

In the darkness of their prison, Chandra said, "Why didn't we change into our thermals earlier, Jeff? We might have stood a chance . . . ."

Vaughan leaned his head against the rock, massaging his injured shoulder.

Chandra was on his feet, a dark shadow in the pit beside him. He was moving around the confines of the pit, feeling the rock.

"You're wasting your time," Vaughan said.

Chandra turned on him. "How the hell do you know!"

He closed his eyes. "Think about it. They put us down here to freeze, Jimmy. There's no escape."

"There might be a way out. If we help each other, one climb on the other's shoulders . . ."

Vaughan laughed. "Have you seen how deep this place is? See that overhang? Even if we did get up that far, we couldn't scale it."

"I'm not giving up!" Chandra moved around the circular pit, trying footholds, handgrips.

Vaughan had seen such desperation before, witnessed the tragic human optimism more terrible than despair. He felt a profound sadness on Chandra's behalf. *What must it be like to so desperately want to live,* he asked himself, *and to know that in all likelihood you will die?*

"Chandra . . . Sit down. You're wasting your time."

"I'm not giving in, Jeff. I'm not just going to sit here and wait to die."

Vaughan felt a quick pang of guilt, then, for ridiculing Chandra's futile efforts to escape. For the cop, who had everything to live for—his wife, his career—life was all; death an unthinkable end to what had been a worthwhile existence. Who was he, Vaughan, to gainsay the worth Chandra placed on his own survival?

"Jimmy, listen to me. Take it easy. You're exhausting yourself. Sit down and get your thoughts together, okay?"

Chandra had made a circuit of the sheer rock face, arrived back where he had started. "I can't find the smallest toe-hold . . . But there's got to be some way out of here." There was an edge of desperation in his voice. He sank to the ground next to Vaughan, hugging himself.

He told Chandra about what he'd read in the minds of the Disciples, more in a bid to occupy his own mind than to appraise Chandra of information that might be useful in future. There was no future, or rather only a limited future.

He thought of the oblivion which awaited him in death, the oblivion to which hundreds, even thousands, of Disciples had given themselves willingly. If only they could have experienced what he had lived through all those years ago in Canada . . . He felt a sudden rage toward his captors, a desire to revenge his death even before he had died.

He scanned. The minds of the Disciples were distant now, and growing ever more faint as they headed down the valley toward a waiting vehicle.

A voice in the darkness said, "An hour's passed, Jeff. I'm freezing. Let's . . . let's do something. We've got to try . . ."

Vaughan opened his eyes, aware that he'd been on the verge of sleep. He scanned: silence.

He stood, his shoulder throbbing painfully. It was almost pitch black in the pit, the light of the strange constellations overhead providing little illumination. Chandra joined him and Vaughan knelt.

"Climb on my shoulders, Jimmy. Careful—!" He cursed under his breath as Chandra straddled his shoulders, his weight increasing the pain.

He took a breath and stood, his knees wobbling with the

strain. Chandra's weight eased from time to time as he tried the occasional hand-hold. Vaughan moved slowly clockwise around the pit, Chandra giving a running commentary.

"There's nothing around here at all . . . Move right, further. Stop. There's something here. I can't get a decent grip. Damn!"

As they completed the circuit, Chandra became quiet. Vaughan stopped, lowered himself into a crouch. Chandra climbed down and Vaughan felt suddenly buoyant with the release of the burden. He sat down with his back against the rock, kneading his shoulder.

He closed his eyes, felt himself drifting off. He awoke with a start, what felt like minutes later. He was shivering with the cold, the bone-gnawing chill that had forced him awake. His hands were numb, lifeless. He clamped his fists into his armpits, drew his legs up to his chest, and tried to bury his face in the material of his trousers.

He became aware of a low sound. He listened. It was Chandra, singing. No . . . he was chanting a mantra, a prayer. A dull, monotonous drone in Hindi. The sound, irrationally, infuriated Vaughan.

"Jimmy, for chrissake will you quit it . . . ?"

The drone continued.

"Jimmy . . . what the hell?"

"I'm preparing myself, Jeff. I'm preparing myself for the next life . . ."

"Oh, sweet Jesus Christ," Vaughan said. He could not stop himself: "Why do you sound so goddamned frightened, Jimmy? If you're going onto another life, why the fuck do you sound so shit-scared?"

He heard the sob in Chandra's voice. "Because . . . I am scared, Jeff. I'm scared for Sumita. I'm scared for all those innocent victims of the Vaith . . . I'm even scared for myself."

Vaughan shook his head. "Cheer up—you'll get another turn, right? What about me? What have I got to look forward to? I'll tell you—endless oblivion. Nothing. Zero."

Chandra's mantra ceased. The silence stretched. At last, in a small voice, Chandra asked: "What turned you into such a bastard, Jeff? Or were you always a bastard?"

"Is my bastardy genetic or conditioned? There's an interesting one. Maybe a bit of both, Jimmy. But mainly conditioned."

Chandra remained silent. Vaughan was aware of him in the darkness, looking his way. At last Chandra said, quietly: "Who the hell are you?"

The question hit Vaughan like a blow. He had not been expecting that, a counterpunch from someone he had thought he had beaten into submission.

He rode the silence, hoping Chandra would not press his advantage. Seconds later, a tentative jab: "Well?"

"Well, what?"

Another silence, taunting him. Chandra took a breath. "I . . . I accessed your files on a system we have at HQ," Chandra said, stuttering with the cold. "Before we came here. I wanted to know more . . . more than you'd told me. I wanted to know who I was working with."

A freak wind corkscrewed itself deep into the bottleneck of the pit, giving a razor edge to the cold. Vaughan felt something icy prick his cheek. He looked up. High overhead, against the starfield, he made out a flurry of snow.

Chandra went on: "According to the files, Jeff Vaughan died six years ago in a flier accident."

Vaughan stared into the darkness, trying to make out the shape of Chandra. He told himself that in the brightening light of the stars he could see the whites of the Indian's eyes, staring at him.

He could never have told anyone about his past, until now. To open up, admit to his other, hidden identity, would have been to endanger himself needlessly. Yet now, with only hours to go before the end . . . what was stopping him now?

"My real name doesn't matter," he told Chandra at last. "I no longer think of myself as anyone other than Jeff Vaughan."

Overhead a keening wind howled across the opening of the pit.

"Why did you need the new identity? What did you do?"

What the hell . . . "I worked for the government of the Federated Northern States of America," he said. "Not voluntarily. I had no choice in the matter. When I was twenty, I tested psi-positive. I was given the chance to volunteer . . ." He laughed at that. "Volunteer? There was never any doubt about it. They told me they could make me into a mind-reader, that they'd pay me fabulous wages . . . I was twenty, for chrissake. I signed on the dotted line. I had the operation, the cut. They only told me later . . . they said that during the op they'd discovered I had a special talent, which with augmentation could prove beneficial to the government . . . I don't know. They probably knew all along." He fell silent, cursing the psychiatrist who'd smooth-talked the impressionable twenty-year-old into thinking he could become a superman.

Chandra said, "Knew what, Jeff?"

"Knew what they could make me into." He stopped; he wanted to weep for the boy he had been, the wreck he had become.

"A telepath?" Chandra asked.

"A . . . a special kind of telepath, Jimmy. Ever heard of a necropath?"

189

Chandra repeated the word. In the shadows, Vaughan could see him shaking is head. "A necropath? No, I've never . . . Necro—something to do with the dead?"

Vaughan nodded. "Right. You're right, Jimmy. They made me into a telepath who could read the minds of the dead. I worked for the Toronto Homicide Department."

Chandra's silence, this time, was shocked. After seconds he said, "I . . . I don't understand."

So Vaughan told him about the many oblivions he had vicariously experienced.

He would never forget his first case.

The victim was a young woman, attacked and stabbed to death during a robbery at her apartment. He was rushed to the scene of the crime, hurried through the crowd of investigators and forensic specialists who looked upon him with gazes of awe and pity that Vaughan had failed to understand at the time.

He had inserted his pin, knelt before the corpse, and scanned.

He accessed the women's fading awareness, the core of her sensorium still erratically firing one hour after death, and he relived her last memories, saw the face of her killer, and more importantly found that he was known to her, in fact lived nearby . . .

But more than that, more terrible than being privy to the women's terror at the attack, he had ridden her failing mind toward oblivion, the total negation of everything she had ever known in life.

And he had cried and pushed himself from her, clawed the pin from his head, and rolled into a fetal ball in the corner of the room, trying to banish the hell of oblivion from his mind.

He was counseled after that, told that the first time was always the worst, and sent back out . . .

He read more dead and dying minds, and he developed a technique to try and minimize the pain. He would dive, and find what he wanted, and then hurry to get out before the pain became too much. But always he experienced the terror, to varying degrees. Every day he knew what it was to die. He knew what awaited him when his own brief existence came to an end.

For a while he harbored a desire to kill his instructor, and the surgeon who had made him like this, and the psychiatrist who had first discovered that he possessed psi-ability.

The desire passed, and the pain continued, and he waited for the chance to get away and start a new life without fear of being discovered. Five years after his very first case with the Toronto police, during a job that went very wrong, he knew that he had to get away, or kill himself.

Two days later he boarded an orbital shuttle to Beijing . . . and he had been running, with occasional stops, ever since.

Chandra was silent for a time, then said, "It must have been hell, Jeff."

"Hell? *Hell* . . . You've hit it in one, Jimmy. You asked what made me into the bastard I am, remember? Well, that did, Jimmy. Reading dead minds did . . ."

The cop murmured: "I'm sorry, Jeff."

"And you know what else? There's no white light. There's no Nirvana or heaven or Valhalla—no afterlife of any kind. You know what there is? I'll tell you. There's one fucking big black ocean of oblivion. I've ridden hundreds of minds on that final journey, I've read their terror. Christ, I've shared that terror, felt it myself, the soul-destroying

191

terror of knowing that the only thing awaiting is a cold, empty nothingness for all eternity, of knowing that life is over, for good, no more warmth or love or anything we take for granted, just oblivion."

He stopped there, aware that he was shaking uncontrollably.

Chandra did not respond for what seemed like long minutes, and then he said nothing to counter Vaughan's interpretation of the dying experience, as Vaughan had thought he might. Instead he said, "So you quit? Changed your identity?"

"I had to change my identity. A necropath can't just quit, leave the government. You're a valuable commodity—they've spent millions on you, you've solved crimes that otherwise would have gone unsolved. The only way to get away is either to kill yourself—and I considered that often enough—or to drop out, find yourself a new identity."

"And if they found you now?"

"They'd kill me." He said it before he realised the irony of what he'd said, then laughed aloud. "They'd kill me, Jimmy. I know too much. I'm too much of a security risk. If I fell into the hands of my government's enemies . . .

"They have someone, a telepath called Osborne. A bastard. A bounty hunter, a trained killer. Whenever a telehead has had enough and gets the hell out, they send him out to track down and kill those strays . . .

"First five years I spent moving from city to city around the world, frightened, paranoid. I saw Osborne everywhere. Then I cooled down. Knew I was seeing shadows. I thought, where am I least likely to be discovered? I'd heard about the Station. I thought I'd give it a go. During the five years, I'd not worked as a telepath—I specialized in security software systems, knew it'd come in handy. When I got to the Station, I hacked into files, found a suitable identity. Took the name of Vaughan. Then I applied to the 'port for a job as a 'head." He paused, considering. "I don't know. Maybe I'd had enough. Maybe a part of me wanted to be found. It'd be quick and painless."

He could see Chandra, watching him, his eyes highlighted in the illumination of the stars.

"You were married?" Chandra asked.

Vaughan released a breath. "No, but there was someone. Didn't work out."

Chandra asked: "Kids?"

Vaughan tipped his head back and stared at the silent stars. He shook his head. "No," he said, "no kids."

He closed his eyes and hoped that Chandra would ask no more questions. He buried his head between his knees, willing an end to the cold. He knew that if he slept, he would die. He tried to sleep, but the cold worried at his face, gnawing at him like a hungry rat.

Perhaps an hour passed; Vaughan could not see his watch to check. Chandra began his chanting again, unconvinced by Vaughan's testimony of the void that followed life. Faith, Vaughan thought to himself. He wished he had faith, wished the bastards at Ottawa Psionics had not discovered him. He had often wondered how things might have turned out, if he had not undergone the operation.

He must have drifted off to sleep. He awoke, startled, some time later. Chandra was shaking him. There was a note of desperation in his voice. "Jeff. Jeff, for pity's sake."

Vaughan looked up. His whole body felt frozen. He had never felt so cold, never realised that cold could be this painful. "What?"

"Jeff, we can't give in. We can't die down here."

He stared at Chandra in the meager light of the stars. "Why not?"

Chandra gestured in exasperation. "We're the only ones

who know," he said. "If we die, who'll be left to stop what they're doing?"

Vaughan's initial response was to find some wisecracking rejoinder to Chandra's concern. Then he considered the man, and what he'd said. In extremis, facing death, Chandra had thought beyond himself, considered the fate of the victims of the Vaith.

He nearly said, "Does it matter?" but stopped himself. It mattered, obviously, to Chandra.

"Jeff . . ." Chandra's voice sounded small, far away. "Look, why don't we hold each other, share our warmth? Then in the morning . . . maybe then we can find a way out."

Vaughan heard the words, felt a sudden despair at the futility of Chandra's suggestion. But he stopped himself from commenting. Instead he said, "Okay, Jimmy. Okay, we'll do that."

He held out his arms, and Jimmy came to him. They hugged each other. For a minute, Chandra's body heat warmed Vaughan, lessened the pain of the cold. Then, as he became accustomed to the added warmth, the all-encompassing iciness invaded again, creeping up his arms and legs like an army of biting insects intent upon devouring his very heart. He felt Chandra, in his arms, weeping and shivering uncontrollably. He caught the scent of the Indian's hair oil, the garlic on his breath, and almost laughed aloud at the stupidity of their situation. If only he'd been more aware while scanning, if only he had thought to suggest they change into their thermal gear earlier . . .

He felt Chandra relax, his breathing become even.

"No!" Vaughan yelled, shaking Chandra. "Don't sleep! If you . . . if you sleep, you'll die."

"I'm so . . . so cold, Jeff. I'm so tired."

"Hang on in there, Jimmy. A few hours. That's all. Hang on for another few hours, okay?"

He tightened his embrace around the little Indian, crushing Chandra to him. He felt himself slipping, growing ever more tired with every passing second as the cold registered no more as cold but as a scalding heat, a perverse warmth that permeated his every cell, calling to him to relax, submit, close his eyes, and sleep.

He lost all concept of duration. He nodded off, shook himself awake, stared up at the stars, as if by concentrating on the scintillating points of brightness he might stave off the siren of sleep.

Then a greater wave of tiredness overcame him, and he told himself that it would be okay if he slept for just a few minutes—he would be woken by the cold, anyway, just as all the other times. But even as he thought this, he told himself that he could not submit . . . He admitted that he did not want to die, even though to fight against it was an exercise in futility: he did not want to experience the terrible oblivion he had so often shared vicariously in the past.

Despite himself, against his will, he felt himself slipping into unconsciousness.

Much later, something made him open his eyes.

He blinked, stared in disbelief.

The night had come to an end; a new day had arrived on the mountain. It was light in the pit. He held Jimmy Chandra to him, almost laughing tears of delight at their survival.

For the first time he could look about him and see his prison. He scanned the rock walls that contained them. He made out possible foot- and hand-holds in the sheer face. The sun struck a beam down into the pit, as warm and welcome as a flame.

Perhaps, after all, they would be able to escape.

A few minutes later Vaughan heard the faraway sound of a helicopter's rotor blades, and hope turned to despair. The rhythmic *blatt-blatt* of rotors grew louder, nearer, and Vaughan almost laughed at the irony of surviving the night only to fall victim to the Disciples' bullets this morning.

He held the sleeping Chandra to him, steeling himself for the end.

The sound of the chopper became deafening, then cut out on landing. The only sound then was the pounding of his heart, as he waited. Brief seconds later he heard footfalls on the rock above, muffled shouts. He held onto Chandra, willing the Indian to remain sleeping rather than wake and be aware of his end.

He scanned, and at first he did not believe what he was reading . . .

He heard something being thrown into the pit. A length of black fiber hung from the opening. Instantly it changed shape, became a ladder: memory carbon.

Someone was climbing into the pit. Dark shapes appeared in the patch of sky above, peering down.

"In here! We've found them!"

A young man in the uniform of the Vanderlaan police jumped from the ladder and hurried across to him. The officer stared, then turned and yelled for medical assistance.

Vaughan began laughing, a mad sound that echoed eerily in the confines of the pit. He shook Chandra, trying to wake him. "Jimmy! Jimmy, we're safe!"

Someone was climbing into the pit, someone familiar. She turned and hurried across to where Vaughan huddled with Chandra in his arms.

He stared up at Lt. Laerhaven. "How . . . ?"

Her mind exploded with delight at finding them alive.

"The watches I gave you are tracking devices, Vaughan. I wasn't altogether sure we needed to keep tabs on you, but as things worked out . . ."

The pit was full of people now, kneeling beside him, examining him. Their mind-noise was becoming painful. Quickly he withdrew his pin.

"Vaughan," Laerhaven squatted before him, her expression solicitous. "Vaughan, you can let go of Chandra, now. There's nothing you can do, I'm sorry . . ."

He stared at the cold bundle in his arms. With his eyes closed, his face set in a peaceful expression, Jimmy Chandra might have been sleeping.

"Jimmy . . ."

"Vaughan, there's nothing you can do."

"No!" he yelled. He had the absurd idea that if he were to hold Chandra all the tighter, never let him go, then he might imbue the Indian with some of his own vitality.

The officers were all around him, pulling at Chandra, trying to part Vaughan from the frozen corpse. For the first time, Vaughan realised that he was shivering, though whether with cold or shock he was unable to tell.

"Let him be!" he screamed at the officers. "Please . . ."

Then he felt the blast of a hypo-ject in his neck, and no more.

He came to his senses in a hospital room. He felt weak, feverish. Lt. Laerhaven sat on a chair beside the bed. She spoke to him—at least, he saw her lips move, but heard no words. He lapsed into unconsciousness.

When he next awoke he was in a different room, this one flooded with bright morning sunlight, and he no longer felt ill. He pushed himself into a sitting position, called out.

Laerhaven hurried into the room.

"Jeff . . . You've been through a hell of an ordeal. Lie down. You need to rest."

He recalled what he had scanned in the minds of the Disciples. The Vaith were on the Station, elsewhere in the Expansion . . . He needed to get out of here, back to Earth to warn the authorities.

"When's the next ship to Earth?"

"Tonight. But you're in no fit state to be on it. You had a close escape. We're not going to endanger you further by releasing you ahead of time."

"Jimmy . . . ?"

"We've arranged his transportation to Earth on tonight's ship—"

"I need . . . Do you have a screader? I need to make a report for the Enforcement Agency on the Station. It must go on tonight's flight, okay?"

Laerhaven looked at him dubiously. "If you're sure you're up to the mental strain of reliving what—"

"Just get me a damned screader!" he yelled, and fell back on the bed.

Later, alone in the room, Vaughan stared at the blank screen of the screader and wondered where to begin.

FOURTEEN

Sukara decided to take each day as it came.

She sat in the back of the taxi-flier as it cruised high above the ocean, Osborne dozing beside her. She had never seen the sea before, never really understood how vast it was; in every direction all she could see was the blue and white expanse, its size made apparent when a tiny ship came into sight below, marking the perfection of the surface with its feathery wake. She had expected Bengal Station to be just off the coast of Myanmar, observable from the land. When they had flown out over the long line of the coast, she had leaned forward between the front seats and stared ahead in search of the artificial construct where her sister now made her home.

"I no see it," she had complained.

Osborne had opened one eye. "See what?"

"Bengal Station."

He smiled. "You won't. It's still five hundred kilometres northwest of here."

"Five hundred kilometres!" She shook her head. "And we go all way in taxi-flier?"

Osborne had just smiled again and settled himself further into the seat, trying to sleep.

She had been amazed that morning when Osborne had told her they were going to the Station by flier—and at that time she had thought it was only a matter of fifty or so kilometres from Bangkok. She tried to imagine how much the fare might be for a journey of more than five hundred kilometres.

It made her wonder again who Osborne was. He had

199

told her very little about himself—that he worked for the government of Federated America, and that he was trying to locate an old work-colleague on Bengal Station. She had worked out for herself that he was rich, most likely unmarried, and lonely. What concerned her most of all, though, was why he found her so attractive.

Last night at the hotel they had slept together in the king-sized bed, but they had not made love. Sukara had been willing, but when she had reached out for him in bed he had shook his head and stroked her hair. They had spent the night separated by an expanse of cool linen, holding hands. Sukara could not understand him: he professed affection for her, and yet seemed afraid or unwilling to be drawn into sexual intimacy. She had always understood that the first step on the way to keeping a man was to sleep with him. Osborne's refusal worried her on more than one count: she feared that without sex he might tire of her, and worried that the reason he didn't want to sleep with her was because he found her ugly. Last night he had said that he never wanted her to leave him, had held her and caressed her like a lover. She told herself that she should be thankful that he wasn't like her customers who had wanted from her only one thing.

In the early hours of the morning, staring at his profile in the light of the moon that slanted in through the window, she had sensed that he was awake.

"Osborne?"

"Mmm?"

She found his hand, held it tight. "Why me? Why I special?"

He was a long time before replying. "When I walked into that bar and . . . and saw you. Do you believe in love at first sight, Su?"

She frowned. "Don't know."

"There was something about you . . . who can say why they are attracted to people? Some chemical thing. Does it matter?"

"Suppose not."

"Good. What matters is that we have each other, okay?"

"Mmm." And she had fallen asleep to pleasant dreams, and on waking that morning had wondered, for a quick second, if the events of the night before had been nothing more than part of the dream. And then she had seen Osborne sleeping quietly beside her, and everything had come back to her: that her worries were over now, that she was going to Bengal Station, and that the man called Osborne loved her.

She told herself that she would try not to love him, as a safeguard against emotional catastrophe, and take each day as it came . . .

In the morning he had taken her by flier to pick up her belongings, and then they had left Bangkok aboard a taxi-flier without even saying farewell to Fat Cheng.

As the flier carried her away, she told herself that whatever happened she would not come back, she would never again be a working girl. She would find Pakara on Bengal Station and start a new and happier life.

She was dozing, the muffled roar of the jet engines lulling her on the edge of sleep, when she felt Osborne's touch. "We're almost there, Su."

She woke with a start of excitement and peered through the side-window. Ahead and to the left, Sukara made out a massive shape on the face of the ocean. It was a monumental square structure, a jet-black block that rose sheer from the foaming waves around its base. It seemed out of place, an obviously artificial object contrasting with the natural element of the ocean. As they approached, it increased amazingly in size, as if magnified, and Sukara made out a hundred details that turned the Station from a lifeless architectural block to what it was: a great, hive-like city teeming with life. The upper three levels on the eastern flank were open, a deep shelf of towerpiles and hanging gardens, with the tiny shapes of pedestrians occupying plazas and escalators. Lower down, the flank was sealed, one long black wall interrupted by the silver rectangles of windows and viewscreens.

Hundreds of boats and ships converged on the Station, from dhows to ocean liners, and overhead a constant stream of airborne traffic came and went like so many bees around a hive. To the south, Sukara made out the ponderous bulk of a voidship moving slowly toward the spaceport. Even as she watched, another materialized over the horizon, blinking on and off before finally solidifying into reality.

Their flier banked, coming in over the upper-deck, and Sukara gasped at the sight of the crowds below. She had thought Bangkok crowded, but down there each street seemed packed with people, a solid flow of humanity like so many millions of iron filings following the tug of some invisible magnet. How did individuals fight their way through such a crush? It was a thrilling and frightening prospect to realise that soon she would be down there. She wondered how she might find Pakara among so many people.

She pointed. "Look! Millions of people!"

Osborne smiled. "We'll be staying in the north, Su. It'll be a bit less crowded there."

The flier dropped, came in low between ranked towerpiles, the occasional green area of a park. Five minutes later they banked, slowing, and landed gently in the forecourt of a golden, pyramidal building bearing the title: Hotel Ashoka.

They booked into their room, showered and dressed, then took the elevator to the restaurant. After a light lunch—Chinese noodles and fried fish, better than anything she had ever tasted—Osborne took her shopping in the hotel mall.

He bought her two pairs of shoes, three dresses, skirts and blouses and t-shirts, a watch and jewelry—a necklace, a ring, and a ruby brooch—and gave her dollars to buy underwear and anything else she might want. He helped her back to the room with her purchases, smiled at her like a father on Christmas Day as she tried on first one dress, and then another.

He kissed the crown of her head. "I'm going out for a few hours. I'll be back around six. Then we'll go for something to eat, okay?"

She lowered the dress she was holding up against the one she had just tried on. "I go out, too. Things I need to do, people to see."

Osborne looked at her with that intense, penetrating gaze. He nodded. "But take care. Buy a map and travel by flier." He gave her a stack of dollars, kissed her head again, and left the room.

She sat on the bed surrounded by her new clothes and thought ahead to the meeting with her sister. For so long it had been an impossibility, a dream she had never really imagined would come true, and now the inevitability of their reunion, in just a few hours, was a fact she could allow herself the luxury of savoring. She decided to take her time, rehearse what she would say to Pakara, go over and over what it might be like, together again after five years. It was still only midday. She had plenty of time. She lay on the bed, staring at the ceiling and trying to imagine her little sister's reaction to seeing her after so long.

What should she wear? She jumped up and held her dresses to her body. There was a mirror on the wardrobe door, but she avoided that. Somehow, her new clothes did not seem quite right for the occasion. From her backpack she pulled the clothes she had brought along: a few pairs of shorts and t-shirts, two short skirts. She picked the shorts and a red t-shirt. It was what she would have worn back in Bangkok, when Pakara had known her.

In the pocket of her shorts—tucked away and forgotten until now—Sukara found a pix of Pakara and herself, taken in a pix-booth six years ago. It showed two cheeky-faced girls, ten and fifteen, faces squashed together and poking their tongues at the camera. She smoothed the pix out over her knee, stared closely at the face of her little sister. She would no longer be so little. She would be sixteen now, a young woman, and beautiful. Sukara wondered if Pakara would recognize her with the scar disfiguring her face, how she might react. Then she wondered what her sister was doing now. A year ago, in the stitched message on the silk scarf, she had said that she was working—but working at what? Perhaps she had got a good job, was not working in a bar or club. She pulled out the scarf, read Pakara's message for perhaps the thousandth time.

Dear Sister, I am on Bengal Station, keeping well and working. I think of you every day. When you have money, come to the Station. I will be outside Nazruddin's Restaurant, Chandi Road, Himachal sector. I am well and hope you are. Love, Pakara.
P.S. My friends now call me Tiger.

Sukara walked to the window and looked out. Somewhere out there, among the many millions of people, was her sister. She wondered if it was time now to go and find her. The longer she delayed, the more excited she became, and the excitement she felt burning in her chest was like a powerful drug to which she could become addicted.

She decided to leave the room now, but to take her time. She would go down to the mall, where she had seen a shop selling plastic maps of the Station. She locked the door behind her and carried the key-card down in the elevator. The act of passing it to the sari'd woman at reception filled her with pride and importance: she was doing things now which she had only seen actors performing in films. She walked along to the mall, among strolling crowds of Indians and Thais, found the shop, and asked the assistant for two maps printed in Thai: one of the whole upper-deck, and another of just the Himachal sector.

She wondered whether to take the maps and study them in a cafe over a coffee, or to go outside and sit on the grass. She decided to go outside, and then saw an open-air cafe in the grounds of the hotel, with people sitting around tables beneath colorful parasols. She found an empty table and ordered a *cafe au lait*.

When it came, and while she waited for it to cool, she unfolded the maps and pored over the intricate design of highways, streets, and alleyways; train-routes and flier lanes marked in broad sweeps of different pastel colors. She came to terms with a dozen strange symbols, indicating flier-ranks, train stations, 'chute stations, police stations, parks, and more.

She studied the Himachal map, and eventually found Chandi Road. In the key to symbols, a small letter R in a triangle indicated a restaurant. She found an R on Chandi

Road, and stared at it for a long time, sipping her coffee and enjoying the odd feeling of knowing that her sister would have no idea that she, Sukara, was on her way.

Osborne had told her to use a flier, but she noticed that there was a train station just outside the hotel, and that it travelled south all the way to the spaceport. The last-but-one station before the 'port was at one end of Chandi Road. She would be able to get off there and walk down the street, looking out for Pakara on the way.

To hire a flier, to arrive in minutes, would be to rush into the reunion and in some way devalue it. A part of her wanted to meet Pakara *this minute*, but another part was enjoying the slow build-up. She folded the maps, paid for the coffee, and strolled from the grounds of the hotel.

She was unprepared for the ambush—in affluent Bangkok, beggars were rarely seen. After the sumptuousness of the hotel, the reality on the street was shocking. Sukara was immediately surrounded by half a dozen boys and girls, naked but for soiled shorts, jabbering at her in Hindi, palms outstretched. They tugged at her t-shirt, their whines plaintive, staring at her with massive, beseeching eyes. As she approached the station, she handed them dollar notes, watched their faces light up as they ran away waving their wages.

She bought a ticket and waited on the southbound platform. Ten minutes later a bulky, rattling train—altogether different from the sleek bullet trains she was used to in Bangkok—eased itself into the station. The only similarity with Bangkok was that the carriage was packed. She hung on a strap for thirty minutes before a seat became free, then slipped into it gratefully and stared through the window.

Parks and polycarbon towerpiles flashed by, interspersed with streets at right angles to the track, all packed with regimented rivers of people. The train carried her though alternate districts, predominantly Thai and Indian, signaled by shop signs bearing the different script. Some areas, with street-stalls and shops selling Thai goods, crowded with her small, lithe fellow-countrymen, could have been districts of Bangkok. She felt she could easily make her home on the Station.

She opened her map of the upper-deck and checked off the passing stations, at every stop obsessively counting how many stations remained before Chandi Road. "I'm coming, Pakara," she said under her breath. "You don't know it, but not long to go now."

The sense of anticipation, of excitement, built as the train neared Chandi Road. With only two stations to go, Sukara felt like shouting her delight to the whole carriage. They pulled from the last station before Chandi Road and she climbed to her feet and made her way toward the sliding doors, her legs almost giving way with excitement. When the train slowed and drew into the station marked Chandi, she thought her heart would burst with joy. She felt pressure behind her, and as the doors opened she spilled out at the front of a crowd. She found herself carried along with them, through the station and down the steps. She remembered to turn left, struggling through the press on the street, and made her way south, toward Nazruddin's. By her estimation, she had half a kilometre to walk before she reached the restaurant. The crowd thinned, became almost negotiable. She realised that hers was the only Thai face among so many hundreds of Indians, and that the majority of them were men. From time to time the press parted to make way for the passing of a ramshackle, khaki-colored cow. She experienced a surge of amazement that this was where she would find Pakara.

Then ahead, to the right, she saw an unlit neon light spell out the word "Nazruddin's" against the old, cracked polycarbon façade of the restaurant.

She slowed down, buffeted by those behind her. She moved to the far side of the road, where the rate of flow was slower, like the shallows of some great river. She stopped by a stall selling sugar cane juice, bought a cup of the sickly sweet syrup, and stared across the street.

Half a dozen stalls occupied the sidewalk before the building, selling cooked foods and ice cream, plaster models of the Hindu gods and stacked boxes of incense. Sukara examined each stallholder in turn, and his or her helpers, but could see no one even slightly resembling her sister. She looked further along the line of stalls, to those on either side of Nazruddin's, but in vain. Next she walked from stall to stall on this side of the road. It had not occurred to her before, but in the year since she had received Pakara's message it was possible that she had moved.

She crossed the street, fighting her way through the current of humanity, and arrived before an incense stall directly outside the restaurant.

The stallholder saw her, beamed a mercantile grin. He waved a box of joss-sticks. "Wonderful scent, lady. Light an incense stick for Hanuman. Very cheap."

"I look for girl," she said in English. "My sister. You know her? She called Pakara—also called Tiger. She Thai, like me. Sixteen-year-old. You see her?"

The Indian pulled a frown and shook his head. He bellowed in Hindi to his neighbor. They exchanged a dialogue involving exaggerated gestures and much head shaking and nodding.

"My friend says over there you might find her, outside Nazruddin's." He pointed over his shoulder, to an area beneath the restaurant's striped awning.

Sukara pushed through a knot of arguing men and stopped outside the restaurant. A dozen street kids, resting in the shade of the awning, stared at her with pleading eyes.

She looked around at the kids, boys and girls, Indians and Thais, and the feeling of elation she had enjoyed all day suddenly and sickeningly evaporated.

"*Baksheesh!*" a young boy cried. A little Thai girl approached Sukara and forlornly tugged at her shorts. "You give me baht, lady?" she said in their language.

Sukara, her legs weakening, sat down on the steps to the restaurant and looked from one beggar-child to the next. They were all, without exception, missing limbs. Most were without legs, their limbs removed above the knee, the wounds repaired with a messy cross-hatching of stitches. A couple of girls had arms missing. They presented a pathetic sight as they gazed at her, silent now, wondering what she was doing here.

"I'm looking for Chintara Pakarapat," she said to the little Thai girl. "Do you know her?"

The girl slowly shook her head, watching her.

Sukara looked around the other children. "Perhaps you know her as Tiger?"

A little boy stared at her with wide eyes. "Tigerji?" He glanced around at his friends, talking to them in Hindi.

"Do you know her?" Sukara asked, her heart skipping.

The boy nodded. He spoke rapidly in Hindi. The Thai girl translated. "He says, he knows Tigerji. She's not here any more."

"Does he know where she is?"

When the Thai girl translated, the boy shrugged, avoiding Sukara's eyes. Another boy spoke up: "I get Prakesh, bring him here?"

"Prakesh?"

"He Tigerji's friend. He tell you what happened."

She stared at the crew-cut Indian boy. "What happened? What do you mean?"

The boy shrugged, ran off into the crowd.

Sukara said, "Did Tiger . . ." She pointed to the Thai girl's stump. "Was Tiger like you? She have no . . . ?"

A boy offered: "She have leg chopped off. Thunk! Here." He gave his thigh above the knee a swift karate chop, grinning at her.

Sukara felt her stomach turn, her thoughts in turmoil. She wondered what might have been worse: life for Pakara as a working girl in Bangkok, or life here as a crippled beggar. She wanted to see Pakara, hold her, tell her that from now on everything would be okay.

She gestured for a stallholder to bring her a soft drink, and when he did so she noticed the eyes of the street kids on her. She ordered a dozen more and handed them out, then took a sip of the syrupy cola. The stuff nearly made her sick.

The crew-cut boy emerged from the crowded street, dragging someone behind him. Sukara glanced up, heart thumping, but the someone in tow was not her sister. A thin, gangling one-armed boy of about twelve gave her a quick glance, looked at the floor.

"You know Tiger?" she said in English.

Mute, Prakesh nodded.

"You know where she is now?" When he failed to reply, she went on: "You tell me, I give you dollars, okay? Where Tigerji?"

He would not lift his gaze from the ground.

Sukara pulled a crumpled dollar note from the pocket of her shorts, passed it to Prakesh. "Tigerji," he said in a whisper, "she not here."

"You know where I find her?"

Another shrug. Sukara wanted to take the boy by his shoulders and give him a good rattling. "You know anyone who know where she is?" she said.

Prakesh looked up, gazing into her eyes. She thought that he looked frightened. He nodded.

"Good. Take me see this person, okay? You do that?"

Prakesh spoke in Hindi to another boy, who flung a gesture along the street with a handless arm.

Prakesh told her: "I take you see Dr. Rao. He at Nawob Coffee House. He tell you." He paused, said, "You give me more dollars, okay?"

"Take me Dr. Rao, then I give dollars."

He nodded. Sukara left her unfinished cola on the step and followed Prakesh as he slipped quickly through the crowd, stopping occasionally to look back and ensure that she was following. They moved with the flow of humanity along the street toward the train station. Sukara looked up alarmed as, overhead, the colossal shape of a low-flying voidship eclipsed the sun and plunged the street into premature dusk. She dodged the gold-tipped horns of a cow as it tossed its head, almost losing her footing. Prakesh disappeared up ahead; Sukara ran on desperately. He was waiting for her on the corner of the street. Across the road she saw a painted sign: Nawob Coffee House. Prakesh took her hand, led her through the street and up the steps into the building. The cool interior, after the heat of the day, hit her immediately and made her shiver. Indian gentlemen in suits sat at tables with tablecloths and drank coffee from tiny white cups. Prakesh led her to a table at the back of the room, situated in a raised alcove. He spoke in rapid Hindi to a small, balding man, turning to indicate Sukara.

The old man spoke quickly to Prakesh, then turned and

resumed his conversation with three other Indians.

Prakesh jumped down the steps. "Dr. Rao see you in two minutes, okay?"

She pulled a handful of dollars from her pocket and handed them to the boy. He took the notes, stared at them as if in wonder. He glanced at Sukara, an indecipherable look in his big brown eyes, almost as if he did not want to take the money, but could not bring himself to give it back to her. Avoiding her eyes, he clutched the notes in his fist and ran from the restaurant.

Dr. Rao called out: "Girl! Take a seat. I will be with you presently."

Nodding meekly, Sukara found an empty table and sat down. Dr. Rao gestured to a waiter, who brought her a cup of coffee. Sukara gazed around the room, aware that she was the only girl among so many men. From time to time she felt their scrutinizing eyes on her. She stared at the frothy disc of her coffee, wishing that Dr. Rao would quickly finish his business and join her.

She thought of the anticipation with which she had set out from the hotel. Things had not gone the way she had expected. But how could she have foreseen that her sister would have ended up as a beggar girl with one leg? The more she thought about it, the more she wanted to cry.

She wondered if legs could be replaced with modern surgery. Many miracles could be performed now, if you had the money . . . She thought of Osborne. Surely he would help her? Surely he would agree to repairing Pakara's missing leg? The thought made her smile with delight.

A shadow crossed the table. Sukara looked up at the tiny Indian in an ochre suit jacket and tight white leggings. He sat down opposite her, his hands resting before his chin on the handle of a walking stick.

He stared at her from behind old-fashioned spectacles, taking in her scar. "And you are?"

"My name Chintara Sukarapatam, sir. I look for Pakara—Tiger, my sister."

He removed his spectacles, massaged his eyes. He replaced them and stared at her, blinking.

"The world is a very cruel place, Chintara Sukarapatam," he said. "Do you work?"

She blinked at the question, surprised. "Yes, sir. I working girl—was working girl."

"A gentlemen's lady." He nodded. "Then you do not need to be told of the many and various iniquities that fate places in one's path."

Sukara smiled timidly. "Sorry . . ." She gestured with a small shrug of her shoulders that she did not understand.

"When Tiger came to me, she had recently arrived from Thailand. By all accounts the journey was precarious and life-threatening. She was lucky to survive the crossing. As fortune had it, she found her way to my sanctuary. She did not wish to return to her former profession as a working girl, which I found quite understandable. Instead I found her other work." He pushed his glasses further up the bridge of his nose in a gesture of self-importance.

"Tiger—how she lose leg?" Sukara asked.

"It was . . . infected. There was no option but to amputate."

She repeated the word. "What it mean?"

"Remove, girl. Chop off. From then on, she worked on the streets."

"She beggar girl, like others?"

"A honorable and noble profession. Tiger had a good life in my sanctuary. She wanted for nothing."

Sukara frowned, stared at her empty coffee cup. She could not understand much of what the little man said, but something made her wonder why he was not telling her where Pakara was.

"Dr. Rao—you know where my sister is?"

It was not his words that alerted her to the truth of what had happened, but a certain gesture. He reached his hand across the table and placed it protectively on top of hers, and in that instant, she knew.

"I am very sorry, girl, but your sister has passed on."

She heard the words but all after that was silence. Dr. Rao might have uttered more empty consolations, but she was deaf to all sound. All she could hear was a great, distant roaring in her ears, and she felt removed from the proceedings. The phrase "passed on" didn't seem right to describe what had happened to Pakara, at once informing her of what had happened, and yet telling her nothing.

"Pakara . . ." she whispered, "Pakara dead? My sister dead?"

Rao patted her hand. "I'm very sorry."

She felt unable to respond physically, cry or shout or jump up and hit out, though she wanted to do all these things. It was as if a giant hand was holding her in paralysis. She thought of Pakara's message, which had said she was well; she thought of the hope with which she had left the hotel. It was impossible that her hopes had been dashed so rapidly, impossible that her little sister was dead.

"Pakara tried a drug," Dr. Rao was saying, "a very lethal drug. She overdosed and slipped away peacefully six days ago."

Sukara echoed: "Six days, just six days . . . ?"

"She was in no pain, of that I can assure you."

Sukara was shaking her head. Six days ago, her sister was alive, and now she was dead. If only she had reached her sooner . . .

The world was cruel—to offer her so much, and then to take it all away.

"Where are you staying?" Dr. Rao asked her.

"What?" The question did not make sense, had no relevance to what she was experiencing.

"I said, where are you staying? I'll take you to a flier rank."

She had to force herself to concentrate on the name of the hotel. At last she said, "Ashoka, the Hotel Ashoka."

Dr. Rao nodded. He paid the bill, took her hand, and led her from the restaurant. As they made their way down the crowded street, Sukara gripped the old man's hand even tighter, and it was as if she were a girl again, holding the hand of her father as he took her to the morning market in the village.

They arrived at a flier rank and Dr. Rao assisted her into the back seat, then spoke to the driver and handed over rupees.

Before the flier took off, he looked in through the open window and said, "Pakara had a special friend, a man named Vaughan. He was with her when she passed away. He arranged her funeral. If you wish to speak to him, he spends the evenings at Nazruddin's Restaurant. I'm sure he will talk to you if you wish."

Then, before she could thank Dr. Rao, the flier took off. She sank into the seat as the flier accelerated, and closed her eyes.

A flood of memories returned, of Pakara, so small in Bangkok, a tiny waif. She pulled the pix from the pocket of her shorts and stared at it: Pakara, aged ten, poking her tongue in mischievous glee. Sukara felt a surge of grief painful in her chest.

Back at the hotel, she hurried to the lift, endured its agonizingly slow ascent, then sprinted along the corridor. She realised, too late, that she had forgotten the door-card at reception, but barged against the door anyway. It was open—which meant that Osborne was back. Her heart swelled in pain and gratitude. She ran into the lounge and stopped. Osborne was at the window, and turned when she entered. He stared at her, and his expression crumpled into the mirror image of the anguish she knew contorted her own features. He reached out. "Su, Su—I'm so sorry." And without asking how he knew, only grateful that he somehow shared her grief, she ran across the room and into his arms.

He carried her to a chair, sat down and held her in his lap while she clung to him like the survivor of some shipwreck, and sobbed.

"I know," he said, smoothing her back through the material of her t-shirt.

"I know . . . there's nothing you can do, you're right. Yes, that's why it hurts all the more . . ."

Sukara felt his arms around her, strong and comforting.

"She wasn't in pain, Su. Isn't that what Dr. Rao said? He told you that she passed away peacefully."

She nodded, trying to control her sobbing.

"She was better off begging than selling her body. Dr. Rao said that he looked after her, that she had a good life."

Sukara wiped tears from her eyes with her wrist.

"There was nothing you could have done . . . But you *didn't* arrive any sooner, so it's no good trying to edit the past. You must try to look back at the good times . . ."

She felt the muscles of his chest through his silk shirt, and was hit by the thought that Pakara had probably never felt this, never felt real love for a man.

"I'm sure she did," Osborne tried to comfort her. "I'm sure she had friends and lovers."

At the thought that her sister would never again have the

opportunity to experience *anything,* Sukara choked on her sobs.

"You *will* get over it," Osborne said. "It just takes time. Believe me. I know words mean nothing now. There's nothing I can say to make it any better, but time does heal the wound. I've lost someone close to me—I thought I wouldn't survive, I didn't want to survive. Life seemed pointless . . . But, Su, we go on. We do survive. And you have me. Never forget that, Su. You have me."

I love you, she thought.

He held her to him. "I know you do," he said.

Time passed, and under the ministration of his soothing words, words which answered her every anguished thought almost before those thoughts were fully formed, Sukara calmed herself. She knew that somehow her mind was open to him, and instead of feeling vulnerable and exposed—as she would have done if anyone else could have read her mind—she felt a joyous relief that he could see into the very core of her being and still want her.

She held Osborne, never wanting to let him go.

He stroked her hair. "I am a telepath," he said, in answer to her thoughts. "I work for the government of Federated America."

She took his golden pendant in her palm. It almost pulsed with a strange, lustrous warmth. She realised, then, that she had never seen him without it.

He smiled. "It's a shield," he said. "A mind-shield. It prevents other telepaths reading my mind."

She thought, *You looking for friend on Station?*

"Not a friend. A colleague, once. A traitor to my country. I know he's here, somewhere. I discovered that he worked at the 'port. Eventually I will track him down, and punish him."

Will you kill him?

He kissed her head. "That need not concern you, my little one. All that matters is that you have me, okay?"

And she thought, *Mmm*.

As the sun set and the room slipped into darkness, and Osborne held her in arms like reassurance made physical, Sukara closed her eyes and eventually slept.

FIFTEEN

Vaughan stood before the viewscreen as the voidship materialized over the Bay of Bengal. The mind-noise of the Station increased as they approached the 'port. He should have realised that, after the relative mind-silence of Verkerk's World, the Station would be intolerable; he should have saved enough chora to get him through his first few hours on Earth. He thought back to the absolute silence he had experienced north of Vanderlaan, and longed to enjoy it again.

The ship landed, and thirty minutes later Vaughan joined the procession of passengers as they crossed the deck to the terminal building. As a citizen of the Station he was processed rapidly. He passed through the cursory customs check with business-people and tourists returning from vacation. The main foyer, a plush marble chamber, was thronged with visitors recently arrived. Vaughan saw travellers in the distinctive dress of a dozen different colony worlds, and even some aliens among the crowd: the tall, blue beings of Barnard's Star, a party of adipose ancients from Ophiuchi.

He'd taken the first available flight from Verkerk's World as soon as he was released from hospital, and he calculated that he had about four, maybe five, days in which to locate and destroy the Vaith on the Station before its feeding cycle ended for another two years.

Of course, if Sinton had acted on his report and instituted a search worldwide, then the danger might have passed.

"Mr. Vaughan!"

He turned, alarmed at the summons.

A young Thai police officer approached him. "Mr. Vaughan? Commander Sinton wants to see you at Investigator Chandra's funeral, about what happened on Verkerk's."

"What a damned welcome to Earth," he said. "Yes, of course. What's the local time?"

"Five in the evening, sir. The funeral is just about to begin."

He left his luggage in a locker at the 'port and followed the pilot across the forecourt to the flier. As the vehicle rose, engines whining with the rapidity of the ascent, Vaughan leaned back and closed his eyes.

Minutes later the flier banked over the edge of the Station and came down on the ghats beside the ocean. The pilot indicated a funeral underway, and Vaughan climbed out and crossed the deck toward the assembled mourners and their attendant mind-noise. He remembered Tiger's funeral, over a week ago now, and it came to him that the only similarity between the two services was the funeral pyre itself. Whereas Tiger's service had been attended by Vaughan and three or four of her friends, there must have been three or four hundred mourners here. Which, he supposed, was to be expected: Jimmy had died valiantly in the line of duty, and was accorded a full police service in consequence.

He eased himself through the crowd until he stood near the front. The pyre had already been lighted by Chandra's widow, Sumita, in the Hindu tradition, and the flames licked through the stack of wood-sub built about Jimmy's body. As Vaughan stared into the pyre, sweating in the heat from the blaze and the summer sun, he thought back quite involuntarily to Jimmy's death in the pit on the mountainside, and not for the first time since the incident he realised how pointless was the complex charade of existence.

He looked around the mourners for Commander Sinton, and spotted him in the front row of the gathering.

He watched Sumita step back from the pyre as a holy man began a dolorous chant. She appeared calm, composed: a slim, oval-faced Indian woman in her mid-twenties. Jimmy had never spoken of her, had kept the personal side of his life strictly private, and that had been fine by Vaughan.

He looked around at the mourners, mainly Indian civilians and a few Thais: their expressions were not ones of grief, rather a stolid, expressionless acceptance of the consequences of karma accrued from life to life.

How wonderful it would be to share such a belief, he thought. He wondered how he had gone on for so long with the knowledge of the oblivion that awaited him . . . though that, indeed, was probably why he had not taken his own life in the darkest days of his existence just after escaping from Canada: life was hell, but the alternative was not much better.

Thoughts of Canada turned his mind to the telepath called Osborne, their last mission together, and what had occurred then to dictate the course of their futures. Osborne was a boosted-telepath; due to unique neurological make-up, his powers of mind-reading were considerably greater than Vaughan's, both in range and clarity. Vaughan had been seconded to Osborne's tactical unit from time to time, when his own specialization was not in demand. Osborne was an assassin, trained to take out whomever his government considered a threat to national security. On the very last mission, just before Vaughan realised that he could take no more, they had formed a two-man team sent out to trap and eradicate the cell of terrorists suspected of being responsible for the bombing of the assembly buildings a few months earlier.

He moved his gaze around the mourners. A fellow police officer was standing at a microphone before the pyre, his eulogy interrupted from time to time by the static of the crackling fire. He spoke in Hindi and Vaughan understood not a word, for which he was thankful: no doubt he would have to endure platitudes in his own language soon enough.

He eased himself back through the crowd, earning looks of censure from mourners more pious than himself. The heat of the day, and the migraine-sharp memories he had managed not to dwell on for a long time, were making him nauseous. There were rows of seats at the back of the ghat, for the elderly and infirm. He sat down gratefully and gave a passable imitation, to whomever should be looking, of someone concentrating on the eulogies.

A dozen officers in khaki uniform lifted their rifles and let off a salvo of laser fire, the crimson vectors cross-hatching the air above the ocean with a lingering tartan pattern.

The gathering broke up, some mourners drifting away, others moving to where Sumita was receiving words of consolation.

Vaughan almost stood and crossed to her, but something stopped him. Maybe later, in a few days, when the affair of the Vaith was over. He would contact Chandra's widow then and give her a euphemistic version of her husband's death.

He left his seat and walked around the smoldering mound of ashes, to where Commander Sinton was standing on the edge of the deck, looking out to sea. The stench of the cremation stung his nostrils, brought tears to his eyes. He reached Sinton and stood beside him, watching the lazy rise and fall of the waves a couple of metres below.

BENGAL STATION

The Commander nodded. "I read your report, Vaughan."

He was a big man, tall and broad, with graying hair and a humorless ruddy face. As on their first meeting, at the 'port before he and Chandra had left for Verkerk's World, Sinton wore a mind-shield. He turned and watched the priest brush the embers from the deck. Ashes rose up in a gray cloud and drifted out to sea.

"I don't like to lose men," Sinton said, "and I especially don't like to lose good men." His gaze, which he turned on Vaughan for long seconds, held more than a hint of accusation.

Vaughan detected something false in the Commander's statement. "Don't give me that," he said evenly. "Chandra was just another foot soldier. There's thousands like him on the Station, willing to give everything for a good wage and a police apartment."

"Are all telepaths as cynical as you, Mr. Vaughan?"

"Occupational hazard. We get to read a lot of crap."

Sinton glanced at him. "As I'm shielded, I'd kindly ask you not to guess at my thoughts and sentiments on the matter."

"Then put your shield aside and let me read the truth," Vaughan snapped.

"And have you privy to sensitive and classified information, Mr. Vaughan? I wouldn't trust you as far as I could spit."

"Is that a prejudice against all telepaths, or just against me, Sinton?"

"All telepaths," Sinton said. "But the prejudice I have against you is more specific."

Vaughan looked up, surprised by the turn of events. He rarely wished to be able to look into a mind, but he would have scanned Sinton with pleasure now.

Sinton fixed his gaze on the far horizon, his eyes narrowing. "It was going on information supplied by you that Chandra made his decision to request the Verkerk's World operation."

"And I'm as cut up about what happened to Jimmy as the next man."

"I don't doubt it," Sinton smiled. "Or should I be more cynical and doubt the sincerity of your sentiment, just as you doubt mine? But I won't indulge in character assassination, Mr. Vaughan. The problem I have is with the accuracy of your information."

Vaughan felt his pulse quicken. "What do you mean?" He disliked the trick Sinton had of never looking him in the eye, of staring out to sea and addressing his barbed comments as if to no one in particular.

"I mean, Mr. Vaughan, that your reasons for going to Verkerk's World were invalid."

"You mean the girl, Elly Jenson? And whatever was in the container? You think I was lying?"

"Lying is perhaps too strong a phrase to use—but I certainly think you were . . . shall I say, misguided?"

"And what about what we found on Verkerk's? You don't think for a minute that I was 'misguided' in everything I put in the report?"

Sinton shook his head. "I don't know. I probably think that you genuinely believed what you saw and heard. But no one is infallible—"

"Just a minute, there's evidence for every statement I made in the report. I gave names and sources for you to contact."

"But that's just my problem, Mr. Vaughan. You see, I have absolutely no evidence at all to suggest that what you state in your report has any basis in fact."

Vaughan felt himself trembling. He knew the reality of what he had experienced on Verkerk's World, and he wanted to hit out at this smug bastard for having the gall to doubt him.

"We had only your evidence that there was a girl, an Elly Jenson, abducted from Verkerk's World and brought here—likewise the content of the crate. There were two murders of ex-spacers, both of whom happened to have explored Verkerk's World, but that was nothing more than a coincidence—"

"And the illegal use of rhapsody?"

"Okay, so a little class-two drug was being smuggled in from a colony—we have more lethal stuff coming in from Thailand every day."

Vaughan paced away from Sinton, along the edge of the ghat, stopped, and took half a dozen deep, mind-clearing breaths. He turned. "Let me ask you a question. I made a suggestion in the report, about how to deal with the Vaith you have on the Station. I trust you followed that suggestion?"

Sinton glanced at him. "Oh, yes—we followed it. I had a dozen officers, closely supervised, take a safe dosage of rhapsody and scour the Station, but of course we found nothing."

Vaughan thought about that. "Okay, it's possible that its period of feeding is over for another two years. If it's dormant now, and not sending out the call, then even with the rhapsody you'll pick up nothing. But that doesn't mean we should stop looking. This thing'll wake from dormancy in two years, and the slaughter will start all over again."

Sinton snorted in disgust. "What slaughter, Mr. Vaughan?" He almost laughed. "We have absolutely no evidence for any of the outrageous claims you make in your report. Lt. Laerhaven sent me a full report of her investigations. Her people found none of this 'evidence' you claim Patrick Essex came up with—no vid-recordings, tapes, or written evidence—"

"Then Essex himself, he'll provide first-hand—" Vaughan stopped when he saw Sinton shaking his head.

"He won't," Sinton said. "Essex died of complications from his injuries in police custody the day after you interviewed him. And in any case, in Laerhaven's opinion Essex was a paranoid schizophrenic whose evidence could not be trusted. Laerhaven sent a team of experienced cavers into the mountain where you said these creatures had their lair, and they found nothing."

"The Vaith have been moved," Vaughan said. "Of course they won't be found in the caves—they're on Earth and three other planets."

Sinton was shaking his head. He jabbed a stubby forefinger at Vaughan. "I want *proof*, Vaughan. I can't act on uncorroborated evidence and hearsay."

Vaughan stared out to sea, watching the progress of a hydrofoil bounce across the choppy waters. He tried to look at the situation from Sinton's point of view, work out if the Commander had a case. Going on the information he had, Sinton was following a logical and rational course of deduction. Of course, as Vaughan knew what he had experienced, and knew therefore that Sinton was wrong, there could be only one answer: that someone on Verkerk's World was covering up the evidence, manipulating Laerhaven to their own ends. But what chance did he have of persuading Sinton that this was so?

"I know what we experienced," he said quietly. "Jimmy Chandra died because they didn't want their plans known. Why else do you think they threw us into the pit?"

Sinton sighed. "Vaughan," he said, something like pity

226

in his tone, "my guess is that they were a drug syndicate, refining and distributing this rhapsody stuff. It's big business, big money. Of course they didn't want their plans known." He poked at something with the toe of his shoe. Vaughan watched him kick what appeared to be a piece of vertebra from the ghat. It turned over and over as it fell and splashed into the sea.

"What are your plans now?" Sinton asked at last.

"I don't know . . ." Vaughan shook his head. He hadn't thought of anything beyond returning to Earth, joining in the operation to eradicate the Vaith.

"The Agency could always use a telepath," Sinton said. "Good salary, police apartment . . ."

Vaughan looked at him. "I thought you didn't trust my judgement? Now you want to employ me."

"You'd come in useful at interrogations."

"Thanks, but no thanks."

Sinton nodded. "Well, if you should change your mind . . ." He set off, toward a waiting flier, paused, and turned to Vaughan. "Can I offer you a lift anywhere?"

"I'll make my own way, thanks."

He watched Commander Sinton walk toward the flier and climb carefully inside. The vehicle rose, turned on its axis, and climbed on a long diagonal toward the upper-deck.

Back in his apartment, seated in his chair before the window, Vaughan watched the sun set beyond distant India. He raised his handset and tapped in Carmine Villefranche's code.

Her small face peered out at him. "Oh, it's you . . ."

"Carmine, this is important. I need to know the time and location of the next communion."

Her face became pinched, suspicious. "I'm sorry. I can't tell you that—"

"Why not?" He felt suddenly sick. "I want to share the communion, Carmine."

She sneered. "Don't bullshit me, Vaughan. I know all about you—we've been warned—"

"What do you mean?"

"We know you're working against us. You're an unbeliever; there's no hope for you."

"Carmine, lives are at stake, for chrissake!"

She laughed at him. "We are giving ourselves willingly to the ultimate truth. Tomorrow at midnight I will be among the last Disciples to take the Communion for this cycle. You have no idea what a beautiful union awaits me, Vaughan."

"Carmine!"

She smiled out at him and cut the connection.

He tried to contact her straight away, but she didn't reply.

He sat in the rapidly darkening room, calming his breathing and thinking through what had happened on Verkerk's World. He considered Elly Jenson's father, and how he had been waiting, his mind shielded, when he and Chandra had turned up to question him. Jenson had *known* that a telepath was on his way, and later he and the Disciples had done their best to eradicate him and Chandra.

Who had known about their mission to Verkerk's World?

He raised his handset again and this time got through to Commander Sinton.

Seconds later the Commander's big, florid face filled the screen. "Ah, Mr. Vaughan. Have you changed your mind already and require work?"

"No fear, Commander. But I have come up with something I think you might find interesting."

"And that is?"

"Not over the air," Vaughan said. "When can we meet?"

"I'm rather busy at the moment. How about tomorrow? Let me see . . . Around noon?"

"Noon—by the gates of Himachal Park, okay?"

"I'll be there, Mr. Vaughan." Sinton cut the connection.

Vaughan sat in the gathering darkness of his room for a minute, considering. Then he made a second call.

"Dr. Rao. I'd like to do business again."

"I'd be delighted, Mr. Vaughan. What can I do for you?"

Vaughan told him. He haggled over a price and arranged to meet Rao at Nazruddin's at two tomorrow afternoon.

"One more thing!" Dr. Rao said before Vaughan cut the connection. "I was paid a visit earlier today by Tiger's older sister . . ."

"Her sister . . . I didn't know she had a sister."

"As you might imagine, the girl was distraught at the news of Tiger's passing. She is staying at the Ashoka Hotel, if you're interested in being charitable and consoling her."

Vaughan grunted something non-committal. He was tempted to tell Rao that he had more important things to do than console Tiger's sister.

Rao went on: "I mentioned your name and told her that you were close to Tiger. I think she might appreciate a few words."

"Yeah . . ." Vaughan nodded. "I'll look in on her sometime. And I'll see you tomorrow, Rao." He cut the connection and forgot about Tiger's sister and missions of consolation, and concentrated his thoughts on finding the Vaith.

SIXTEEN

It was almost midday by the time Sukara emerged from sleep. She awoke suddenly, blinking at the dazzle of sunlight that fell into the bedroom. She heard Osborne moving around in the adjacent lounge, the vid-screen on and the volume turned low.

Then, the recollections of the day before rushed to fill the vacuum in her mind. Pakara was dead; she would never again see her little sister, never again share the silly games, the sisterly intimacy, with the person on the Earth she had known for the longest time.

Last night Osborne had held her until well past midnight, and then he had carried her to bed. His words had helped her, his sympathy easing the ache of her loss. Every confused and grief-stricken thought that entered her head, he had countered with gentle words of counsel—it seemed that he had gone to the very core of her being and soothed her pain with exactly the right response. She recalled the night they had met at the hotel in Bangkok, and how Osborne had held her, wanting only to look deep into her mind.

Sukara wondered about his strange infatuation with her mind . . . She might have understood him had his obsession been with her body, if he craved sex with her like another customer. But why his obsession with her mind? She was a simple, uneducated working girl from the country, who knew nothing of the world around her, and even had difficulty making sense of the day-to-day incidents in her own sphere of experience.

She climbed out of bed and padded into the bathroom. She saw herself in the full-length mirror beside the shower, and instead of averting her glance as she normally would, she confronted herself head on. She was ugly. Her facial injury, which she had not seen like this for a long, long time, was not just unsightly in itself—a raised ridge of purple scar-tissue running down the center of her forehead, down the right side of her nose, and thorough both lips to the point of her chin—it also turned her nose to one side, and gave her lips a mismatched twist, as if they had been cut in half and then imperfectly re-joined.

As if this was not sufficient a burden to bear, she was short and squat, her skin a shade darker than what was considered the ideal. Fat Cheng had called her little Monkey—but little Ape would have been more appropriate.

Last night, lying in bed in his arms, it had occurred to her in a second of frightening awareness that Osborne knew her wholly and comprehensively, knew every last detail as to who and what she was, knew her every secret—and yet she knew nothing, absolutely nothing, about him.

She showered, washing the tears from her face beneath the jet of hot water. Then she stood beneath the drier, turning her body and avoiding the sight of it in the mirror. She returned to the bedroom and selected a dress, slipped it over her new silk underwear. When she examined herself in the mirror, tilting it so that the reflection showed only her body, she realised that the fancy dress made her look ridiculous, like a chimpanzee dressed up to mimic a girl. She pulled it off and dug a pair of shorts and a t-shirt from her backpack.

She moved to the window, sat on the cushioned seat, and stared out across the garden of the hotel. She considered what Dr. Rao had told her yesterday, about Pakara's special friend, Vaughan. Perhaps later today she would take the train down to the Himachal sector and go to Nazruddin's, where Rao had said Vaughan might be found. She wanted to know more about how her sister had died, reassure herself that Rao was telling the truth when he told her that she had died in peace and without pain. Also, she was curious about the man called Vaughan. Pakara's special friend, Rao had called him. She wondered if her curiosity did not contain just a tinge of jealousy that Pakara had had someone long before Sukara had found Osborne.

"You're up, Su." Osborne entered the bedroom, startling her. He came up behind her, held her shoulders, and kissed the crown of her head. Then he slipped his case from his pocket and inserted the pin into the back of his head. Sukara blushed with shame at her earlier thoughts.

He shook his head. "Su . . . trust me. I can't tell you about myself. I . . . there are secrets, information that my government—"

"I don't want know government secrets!" she cried. "Just about you. Personal things. You tell me nothing!"

"The past . . . my past, I don't like to talk about, Su. The memories are painful—can't you understand that there are things that people can't dwell on, much less tell other people, even those they love?"

"Why you love me! I ugly, no brain! Nothing!" She moved away from him and sat on the bed, staring through a blur of tears. "Why!"

He winced with the severity of her thoughts. "I love you because you're you, Su. As simple as that. You can't explain love, it's something you can't analyze. It just happens between people. You just feel it, and there's no explanation."

"I no understand." She shook her head. "I understand nothing."

He sat down beside her on the bed, stroked her cheek with his strong fingers. "Su . . . please listen to me. Last week, in Bangkok, I read your cerebral signature a hundred metres away. I read your mind, Su. Your purity, your goodness. You cannot begin to imagine what effect it had on me. You stood out from all the evil and brutality all around you. And I had to have that. I had to find you . . . I followed the signal of your mind all the way to the Siren Bar. And there you were . . ."

She looked up at him, saw the tears in his eyes. She recalled the night he had entered the bar, remembered the way he had looked at her, straight at her, as if he had been searching for her all along . . .

"Please, Su, don't doubt the love I feel for you. Trust me, please. Just trust me."

He kissed her gently, then withdrew his pin and returned it to its case. He moved to the next room, leaving Sukara feeling drained and empty. She stared at the pattern of the carpet, tried to work out if his words explained anything, if they made any sense.

What had been so terrible about his past that he could not speak about? She wished, then, that she could be made telepathic. She felt that that would make everything understandable. If she could just look into his mind for ten seconds, and read the truth.

He returned to the bedroom, paused by the connecting door. "I'm going out for a few hours, Su. I'll see you at five, okay? We'll go out for a meal, I'll show you the sights."

"You look for your government enemy, Osborne?" she asked.

He smiled. "That's what I do, Su."

Wordless, she nodded.

Osborne smiled and moved to the lounge, and seconds

later she heard the door open and close as he left the suite.

She moved to the window and stared out. She would leave the hotel, catch the train south to Himachal, and seek out Pakara's friend, Vaughan. It would be reassuring to talk to someone who had been close to her sister. She checked that she had dollars in the pockets of her shorts, and was about to leave the room when she saw Osborne. He was sitting at a table in the outdoors cafe on the lawn of the hotel, drinking something. She wondered why he hadn't invited her to join him, and felt obscurely betrayed. It occurred to her that he didn't want to be seen with her—then she told herself not to be so silly.

She would go down and buy a comic for the train ride south, then join him over breakfast. She left the room and took the elevator to the ground floor, bought a romance comic from a kiosk, and folded the plastic sheets into a square that fitted neatly into the back pocket of her shorts.

By the time she reached the cafe, Osborne was no longer there. She halted, forlorn, on the edge of the grass—then she saw him walking toward the hotel gates, and decided to follow him. Only when she reached the gates, and saw him merge with the crowd outside the train station, did she wonder if what she was doing was wise. How might he react to her turning up at his side, uninvited? She decided that she did not want to provoke his displeasure, or anger—and yet at the same time she was overcome with a sense of curiosity. He was trying to locate someone, a traitor to his country, but had been unwilling to tell her any more. She realised that she had no proof that this was his reason for being on the Station . . .

This area of the Station was not as heavily populated as the street outside Nazruddin's, where she had felt claustrophobic in the press of humanity. The crowds here were no worse than in Bangkok. She moved along a wide boulevard, ignoring the cries and tugs of the street kids and keeping Osborne in her sights.

He was walking at medium pace in the shade of the trees that lined the street, the only Westerner in sight. Beggars approached him from time to time, then fell away as he snapped something at them. Sukara found it difficult to reconcile this severe *farang,* the very image of a high-powered businessman, with the kindly lover who had soothed her in her hour of need.

She watched him turn right, into a public garden, and seconds later reached the gates herself. The gravel paths that cut through the lawns and raised flowerbeds were relatively quiet, and she waited until Osborne was a couple of hundred metres distant before she too entered the gardens. She didn't want to get too close, in case he had inserted his pin and read her presence. She adopted a casual stroll, admiring the flowers and trees, from time to time looking ahead to ensure that he was still in sight.

She began to feel guilty at following him like this—there was no way she would be able to keep it secret, when he returned tonight and read her mind. She decided that she would join him, tell him that she wanted to be with him, which anyway was the truth. She was about to call his name and run after him, when she saw that he had stopped and was talking to a group of street kids.

She moved into the cover of a tree, watching him. His attitude seemed easy, even affable. After a minute, most of the kids moved away, leaving Osborne alone with a white girl, small and fair, maybe ten years old. In an amazingly short time, they seemed to have struck up an amicable relationship. The girl was laughing and nodding her head, watching Osborne a little shyly from time to time. At one point, as he reached out and stroked the girl's cheek, the tableau seemed to freeze—or it might only have been Sukara's shocked perceptions refusing to acknowledge that this was the same gesture of care and concern that he had used with her. Her heart banged in her chest and she wanted to scream at Osborne that she would never, ever trust him again.

The little girl nodded, reached up, and took Osborne's offered hand. They walked around the park to a side exit. Sukara, a heavy sensation in her chest, followed at a distance. Osborne and the girl left the park and moved along the road, turning into a side street. Sukara hurried across the road, paused, and peered around the corner. The alley was packed with cheap hotels. Osborne and the girl were chatting away; they might have appeared, to a casual observer, to be father and daughter.

As Sukara watched, they paused outside the entrance of a run-down hotel, and then disappeared inside.

She leaned against the wall of the building, her legs weak. He had said trust me, trust me, and she had trusted him. And he had betrayed her, not had the simple honesty to admit that he found her unattractive, that he preferred little blonde girls, perfect and white.

Slowly, her mind confused with anger and self-pity, she retraced her steps back toward the hotel. Crying quietly to herself, she pulled out the bulky wad of her folded comic, stared at the familiar characters on the front page. Now the comic assumed an immense importance—a treasured possession that was hers and only hers—her only ally against a harsh, cruel world.

As she passed the train station, she realised why she had bought the comic—to occupy her on the journey south. She halted, staring up at the entrance to the station. She would take the next train to the Himachal sector.

Ten minutes later, as she tried to shut Osborne and his betrayal from her mind, the Himachal Express carried Sukara toward Jeff Vaughan.

SEVENTEEN

Vaughan stood in the cool shade of a cedar tree, staring out across the ocean. Behind him, Himachal Park was almost deserted in the extreme noon-day heat. A kilometre below, alone on the blue marble surface of the ocean, a dhow with a shark's-fin sail tacked toward the Station.

It was hard to believe that Tiger had died just a week ago, and Jimmy Chandra had called with information about Director Weiss. He looked back and realised that that had been the beginning.

He had the strange feeling, now, that today was yet another beginning—the beginning of the end, when the events of the past week would be resolved for good, one way or the other. He felt the weight of responsibility settle heavily upon him. If he acted with care and vigilance, he could eradicate the threat that hung over the Station. If he did not, and failed, then it would surely mean the deaths of hundreds, perhaps even thousands, of people around the Expansion.

For the first time in years, Vaughan felt that his existence had purpose and meaning.

He glanced at his watch. It was almost noon. He stepped from the shade of the tree, into the glare and heat of the sunlight. He had bought a fresh supply of chora last night, to drive away the demon mind-hum that had assailed him ever since arriving back at the Station, but he had resisted the urge to take a dose this morning: he wanted his ability unimpaired during the next few hours. In consequence, the collected noise of the massed citizens beyond the park pressed upon his head like a migraine.

He hurried through the gardens and paused outside the main gates. Chandi Road was not as busy as usual, the crowds thinned by the heat. He checked his watch again. It was twelve exactly—and, right on time, a police flier appeared overhead, descending slowly. It put down in a blast of hot jet engines and dust. Vaughan backed away, coughing, and watched Commander Sinton climb from the passenger seat.

Sinton strode toward the gates, nodded tersely. "Vaughan."

Vaughan gestured to the path that led through the park toward the rail by the cedar tree. Sinton fell into step alongside him, his mind-shield blocking his every thought.

"I hope I'm not wasting my time here," Sinton said, direct as ever.

"I'm sure you're not."

Sinton nodded. "Chandra regarded you very highly, Vaughan. I don't know why you don't agree to come and work for the Agency."

"I don't actually like being a telepath. It wasn't my choice in the first place, and I've resented the ability ever since."

"I should have thought the talent to look into the minds of one's fellow humans would be eminently rewarding."

Vaughan kept his smile to himself. "There's an old adage among telepaths—we never read what we want to read, but what we don't want to."

"Meaning?"

"Meaning, we read the truth, and the truth is often vile."

Sinton glanced sidewise at him, scowling. "You don't like your fellow man, do you?"

"As a rule, no, I don't."

Sinton's next question surprised him. "Are you religious, Vaughan?"

"No—are you?"

He watched for Sinton's reaction: the Commander never even blinked. "I have certain . . . beliefs, Vaughan, which I suppose could be described as religious. Haven't you read the religious impulse in your fellows, and been momentarily swayed?"

Vaughan shook his head. "The impulse is strong, but it proves nothing other than man's need to believe in something to counter the fear of death."

Sinton slowed his pace, staring across the park, eyes narrowed. "You might have something there. But that doesn't disprove the existence of something transcendent toward which we are all moving. Humanity might be vile, as you claim, but I believe in redemption." He looked at Vaughan. "Don't you?"

"I'm not sure I believe in anything, Commander."

They arrived at the western-most edge of the park. Vaughan moved into the shade of the cedar, Sinton beside him, and leaned against the rail. From here, the entrance to the park was obscured by shrubbery.

"Enough philosophy," Sinton said. "You said you had information I might find of interest?"

"I've been going over my time on Verkerk's World," Vaughan said. "Piecing together the incidents, trying to get certain things clear in my mind. I felt I owed it to Jimmy Chandra, to the other people who lost their lives to the Vaith."

Sinton appeared impatient. "You aren't still harping on that old theme?"

"Why not? It's a tune I find particularly fascinating. Even if I'm the only person who can hear it."

"You're not wrong there," Sinton snapped.

"You see, I know what I experienced. I know that I'm not wrong. I suppose we all have our beliefs, but I happen to know that mine are factual."

"We've been through all this yesterday. If you haven't got information more substantial than what you presented to me then, I don't see . . ."

"I told you—I have more information. I went over the events on Verkerk's. It struck me as odd that Lars Jenson was equipped with a mind-shield when I arrived to talk to him. You see, telepaths were proscribed from entering Verkerk's World under the old regime, and that statute still hasn't been amended. There would have been absolutely no reason for Jenson to fear the probes of a telepath, and so use a shield."

Sinton nodded. "Interesting. Go on."

"So, I reasoned that he must have known I was on my way to Verkerk's, and taken precautions. Later, Jenson and the Disciples followed us and threw us into the pit."

"I suppose it is possible."

"It's the only scenario that makes any sense, Commander. The next question was, who was his informant on Earth? I thought back to Gerhard Weiss, a native of Verkerk's World."

"But—"

"Please, hear me out. Five or six years ago he came to Earth, assumed a new identity, facilitated either by himself or by members of the Church already set up on Earth. He infiltrated the command structure at the 'port, rose through the ranks, and when he was high enough to influence things, the plan went ahead."

"But Weiss died well before you even knew you were going to Verkerk's World."

Vaughan said, "I know. It wasn't Weiss. But I thought that if a Disciple could infiltrate one organization, someone else could just as well infiltrate another—get themselves into a high up position—"

"We're back in the realm of wild speculation again."

Vaughan nodded. "Indulge that speculation just a little longer, Commander. So here we had a very efficient organization, capable of great duplicity and ingenuity to achieve their ends. They had infiltrated one important organization on the Station, so it occurred to me that it would be quite within their means to infiltrate another."

Sinton pursed his lips in a speculative frown. "That organization being?"

"The Law Enforcement Agency, of course."

"You aren't trying to tell me that one of my men . . . ?" He stared at Vaughan. "You don't mean that Chandra . . . ?"

"Of course not, Commander. Chandra was a relatively lowly Investigator. The infiltration went much higher than that."

"I must say that I find this most preposterous—" Sinton began.

Vaughan stared at him. "Do you really, Commander?"

In an instant, he drew his knife and looped his arm around Sinton's neck, pulling tight and choking the Commander. With his free hand he drew Sinton's pistol from his holster and worked the barrel into his back. Sinton gasped in pain.

"On your knees—"

"You're insane!" Sinton fell, breathing hard.

Vaughan moved around in front of the kneeling Commander, the pistol trained on the dead center of the man's forehead. He had the almost overwhelming urge to shoot Sinton through the head and in so doing go some way to avenging the death of Jimmy Chandra. He kept in control, however. To kill Sinton now would be counter-productive.

The Commander was working his fingers around the collar of his uniform, red-faced and spluttering with a combination of pain and indignation.

"This has gone far enough, Vaughan. I'll have you jailed—"

"Unfasten your handset and pass it to me. If you try anything, I'll shoot you."

Sinton glared at him, divined something of Vaughan's rage, and slowly unstrapped the handset. He dropped it at Vaughan's feet. "You're making a big mistake, Vaughan. Think about it. This is a serious offence. Let me up now, let me go, and I won't mention what happened."

"No way, Sinton. Or whatever your name is. You told Jenson that we were on our way. Only you knew I was going to Verkerk's World with Jimmy. You're responsible for his death, Sinton!"

"Preposterous!"

"I want to know where the Vaith are, on the Station and elsewhere."

"I don't know what you're talking about."

"One more time. Tell me, or you bleed."

"You wouldn't dare."

Vaughan lashed out with his knife. The front of Sinton's khaki shirt split diagonally, revealing a slash of fatty chest and belly, and within that slash another, this one leaking beads of crimson.

Sinton stared down at his wound, incredulous and for the first time showing real fear.

He looked up at Vaughan, the fire of the righteous in his eyes. "You might kill me, Vaughan. But I'm quite prepared to die for the cause. I know I will be received into the One."

With that pronouncement, Sinton seemed to change—he

shed the guise of the Police Commander and became something more, a man driven by an abiding mission and belief, which Vaughan found at once terrifying and impressive.

"Your One, Sinton, is nothing more than a drug-induced illusion. You, the Disciples, the poor fools you use on Earth, you're all the dupes of a force of nature, the biological means by which the Vaith gather their prey."

"And in so doing grant Unity to the sacrificial victims," Sinton called out with rage. "You do not know, Vaughan. You have never experienced the One."

"I know that the Vaith are carnivorous beasts. I know that what you are doing is wrong."

Sinton shook his head, his smile patronizing. "What we are doing is perpetuating the only true way. We give believers to the One, we nourish the Godhead of the Vaith so that future generations might know the truth. In two years, I give myself to the Vaith, my mission completed. Others, initiated into the way, will take my place and organize the rituals and services."

"Your god is evil, Sinton. The Vaith are using you. Your victims are no more than drug addicts needing their fix."

"The Vaith are truly demi-gods, Vaughan. They are an ancient race, the last of a species almost as old as the galaxy. They travelled between the stars in the early years of their evolution, seeking knowledge, seeking the truth. When they came upon it, when they discovered the universal truth of the One, they moved from star to star, bringing that truth to lesser races. They are wise beyond our belief, Vaughan— they are in contact with the ultimate reality that underpins this realm of illusion. Through them, and only through them, can we come to join in that truth."

"Your thinking is just as spurious as that of every other religious maniac on Earth."

"Spoken like a true ignoramus. You need to be initiated, Vaughan. Why not join us? We can initiate you with rhapsody that will allow you to share in the truth."

"We make our own truths, Sinton. I want none of yours. Now, tell me where the Vaith are."

Sinton smiled. "I would sooner die," he said.

"And by dying now miss out on the chance of unity?"

"I have been initiated. I am a true believer. I will be granted salvation without sacrifice to the Vaith."

"You're more the deluded fool than I took you for." Vaughan shook his head. "I pity you, Sinton. I really do. Now, give me your shield."

Sinton appeared unperturbed. "Take it from me, Vaughan."

"I'm warning you—"

"If you want the shield, take it."

Vaughan struck Sinton across the face with the pistol, knocking him to the ground. "Now roll over, face down!"

Sinton obeyed, grunting. Vaughan knelt beside him and, the pistol held to his head, frisked the Commander with his free hand. "Now roll over—slowly! Onto your back!"

Sinton turned, glaring. Vaughan aimed the gun at his temple, felt in the pockets of his shirt and trousers. He could find no shield. He searched again, Sinton watching him.

"You won't find it, Vaughan."

"Shut it!"

"I must warn you that my pilot was told to follow me after thirty minutes if I did not return. I should think that that thirty minutes is just about up by now."

"Turn over!"

Sinton glared at him, defiant. Vaughan prodded him with his knife, helping him roll onto his stomach. He tried again, searching everywhere for the small oval shield.

If Sinton wasn't carrying a portable shield, then he must have had one implanted. Vaughan placed a knee between the Commander's shoulderblades, pressing him further into the ground. He reached out and felt Sinton's scalp through his wiry gray hair.

Sinton cried: "No!"

"Quiet!"

He struggled, yelling. "Help! Please, some—"

Vaughan put all his strength into the blow, hitting Sinton across the back of the head with the butt of the pistol, stunning him. It had the desired effect of silencing his cries.

Vaughan pressed his scalp, searching in desperation for the subcutaneous shield. He found it, at last, located at the base of the skull.

Sinton was moaning.

Vaughan took his augmentation-pin and inserted it into his skull console. Then he drew his pocket knife, felt the raised area of the embedded shield, and sliced around it. Blood gushed over his fingers and Sinton cried out in pain. He made a three-sided cut, then applied pressure on the fourth side; slowly, a blood-smeared silver oval appeared from the back of the Commander's head.

Vaughan tossed the shield over the rail, into the sea, and as he did, Sinton's thoughts came crashing into his mind.

He read the Commander's intentions—but he was too slow to act. Sinton forced a hand free, then dug his fist beneath his jaw, just above the collar of his uniform. A chunky ring administered just enough rhapsody to end his existence, and Sinton sighed with relief as the drug coursed through him.

Vaughan shouted out and made a grab for Sinton's

spasming body, aware of the Commander's fading thoughts as they faded away in an inexorable diminuendo of death.

He knelt above the body, knowing that if he probed now, dived into Sinton's rapidly dwindling consciousness, then he would find what he wanted, where the Vaith were now located, and by doing so lives would be saved . . .

Bracing himself, crying in rage, Vaughan entered Sinton's consciousness.

Already much of the Commander's mind was dysfunctioning; great swathes of memory and intellection were dead and blackened—terrifying areas of moribund neurons and misfiring synapses where before had been energy, vitality.

What remained of his dwindling consciousness was like a shattered mirror. As Vaughan dived he caught fleeting glimpses of fragmented images, shards of memory, falling towards the blackness of oblivion. In pain he chased the images, the stray and failing thoughts.

Childhood on Verkerk's World: visions of mountains, the falls . . . the people he had known, his parents . . . These guttered, vanished like extinguished candles, and Vaughan experienced the Commander's terror at what was happening to him.

He dived deeper, frantic now, beset on all sides by the vicarious terror of death.

He was overcome by a great wave that was Sinton's faith: his devotion to the Vaith. He was bombarded by images of the Geiger Caves, of fellow Disciples worshipping the alien beings—together with the feeling of universal unity Sinton had gained from Communion.

He immersed himself in what remained of Sinton's consciousness and searched for his knowledge of the Vaith on Bengal Station. Images like darting silver fish turned and escaped from him: he chased.

The Holosseum at Tavoy . . .

The face of the Chosen One . . .

The case in which the Vaith had been transported to Earth . . .

The Vaith itself, which Sinton saw, improbably, as a tall and shining humanoid form . . .

But where was it concealed on the Station?

The longer he remained riding the dead man's mind, the greater the sense of impending personal annihilation became: he wanted to get out, to ascend to full consciousness and life once again. More than once he almost gave up, relinquished his hold on the fading awareness.

He experienced the disintegration of Sinton's belief—his dying terror at the knowledge that his faith in the Vaith, his assumption of some wondrous afterlife, had been no more than a cruel illusion. Despite himself, Vaughan felt an involuntary compassion for the man.

Then he had it.

Images of the Vaith's bronze casing . . .

A place of worship deep within the Station . . .

Between levels . . .

Restricted access . . .

Shards came at him like dream-images:

"No snooping guard will find it here . . ."

The final Communion . . .

"The blessed sacrifice that will unite us all . . ."

Level 12b . . .

Vaughan felt triumph surge through him. He liked the circularity of it; level 12b was, after all, where it had all began a week ago . . .

Sinton was almost totally brain-dead now, and Vaughan shared in the man's terror. He cried out, experiencing again that which he had vowed he would never undergo, the intellectual comprehension that beyond this life, this realm of vitality, was an all-engulfing territory of absolute nothingness.

He kicked off, away from the oblivion, and ascended through the fathoms of Sinton's failing consciousness in terror and in triumph.

He came to his senses to find himself kneeling above the body, taking in great breaths of air. He pulled out his augmentation-pin, felt an immediate and blessed relief. He regained his breath, tried to purge his mind of the events of the previous minutes.

He remained kneeling beside Sinton's body for what seemed like an age, paralyzed by fear and exhaustion. At last he dragged the body into the cover of nearby undergrowth, and tossed his knife and Sinton's pistol over the rail into the ocean.

He stood and emerged self-consciously from the cover of the shrubbery. He hurried around the perimeter of the park, stopping at a fountain to wash the blood from his hands. He checked his handset. It was almost two o'clock, the time he had arranged to meet Rao at Nazruddin's. He composed himself, left the park through a side entrance, and joined the crowd flowing along Chandi Road. He came to Nazruddin's like a desert traveller to an oasis, slipped into his booth, and ordered a beer.

By the second glass, he had managed to calm his nerves and stay his shaking hands.

Dr. Rao arrived ten minutes later.

He bustled into the restaurant, saw Vaughan, and signaled a greeting with his cane. He carried a small, black case and placed it carefully on the table between them. "Apologies for my tardiness, Mr. Vaughan. You cannot begin to appreciate the difficulty I had in obtaining the merchandise you requested."

Vaughan nodded, believing not a word of it.

Rao seated himself opposite Vaughan and ordered a lassi. "If you would care to inspect the goods . . ." he suggested.

Vaughan pulled the case from the table and placed it on his lap. He flipped open the two gold clasps and lifted the lid. Six silver grenades nestled like diamonds in the black velvet padding. Vaughan picked one out, weighing it in his palm; it had a satisfying heft, the weight of something that could wreak much destruction.

"The green button on the base is the primer. Depress that, and then depress the red button on the top. Six seconds later the grenade will detonate. I suggest that you put as much distance between yourself and your target, preferably with solid cover in between. It would be unfortunate indeed if I were to lose such a close business associate."

"Don't worry, Rao. I don't intend to blow myself up."

Rao cleared his throat, resting his hands on his cane and blinking at Vaughan through his spectacles. "If you don't mind my inquiry—just why do you need these devices?"

"You wouldn't believe me if I told you, Rao. But don't worry. I'm doing nothing to undermine the security of the Station. The only illegal act I'll be guilty of is the possession of these things in the first place."

Rao nodded. "I take it that you managed to raise the requisite funds?"

"I cleaned out my bank account this morning," Vaughan told him. "You see how good I am to you?"

Dr. Rao lifted the glass of lassi to his lips and sipped. "Your generosity is boundless. As to the fee we agreed on last night . . ."

"It's five thousand baht, Rao. Take it or get the hell out."

"You fail to understand the lengths to which I went to procure these highly dangerous and illegal items."

"And I thought you were a man of honor, Rao." Vaughan pulled the notes from his pocket and slid the bundle across the table.

"My supplier, at the very last minute, deemed that an exorbitant surcharge was necessary." Rao wore an expression of pained integrity.

Vaughan produced a plastic bank statement. "Take a look at this, Rao. Note the date—today's. Note the balance—zero. You've cleaned me out. I have thirty baht in my pocket to buy a few beers and a meal."

"Most unfortunate. Nevertheless, my supplier demanded payment of an extra two hundred and fifty baht."

"My heart bleeds. You can take the five thousand, or return the grenades." Calling Rao's bluff, Vaughan lifted the case onto the table and stared at the little Doctor.

Rao relented. He shook his head. "As ever, you show no charity to the hard-working, Mr. Vaughan. I hope you receive your just rewards in the next life."

"I'll look forward to returning as an insect, Dr. Rao. It's been a pleasure doing business."

Rao gathered his money and nodded his farewell. "Mr. Vaughan." He left a few coins to pay for his lassi and slipped from the booth.

Vaughan finished his beer and ordered another bottle. He sat back in his seat, watching the diners at the tables down below and considering the task awaiting him. His nervousness was made worse by the fact that he had forsaken his usual dose of chora today. The mind-hum of the diners, and the low-pitched background noise of the citizens of the Station beyond, made him jumpy and ill-at-ease.

Now that he had the grenades, there was nothing to stop

him from carrying out his plan. He had to act, destroy the Vaith before midnight, but something—fear and cowardice, perhaps—kept him at Nazruddin's drinking beer.

He saw the girl before he became aware of the music of her mind. She entered the restaurant nervously and glanced around at the diners, as if she had come seeking someone. She was a Thai—in her early twenties, dressed in shorts and a tight red t-shirt—out of place in the largely male preserve of the Indian restaurant. As Vaughan watched her, he received the distinct impression that something about her was familiar.

She approached the counter and spoke to Nazruddin. The burly restaurateur grimaced, cupping his ear and leaning closer. The girl repeated her question, and a look of sudden enlightenment spread across Nazruddin's features. To Vaughan's surprise, he turned and pointed across the room directly at him.

The girl looked at Vaughan, and in that instant he realised that this must be Tiger's sister, who Rao had mentioned last night. He felt a sudden wave of irritation that he should be bothered with her at this moment, and then she edged between the tables toward his booth and Vaughan became aware of the music of her mind.

There was a purity there, an innocence and vulnerability that reminded him of Holly, and at the same time a streetwise intelligence and determination that was all her sister, Tiger. To experience that music was at once agony and exquisite pleasure.

She approached him with painful hesitation, knuckles to her mouth in a gesture at once timid and at the same time designed to hide the lower half of the horrendous scar that divided her face. She was nowhere near as pretty as her sister, with none of Tiger's gamin precocity, but Vaughan was aware only of the signature of her mind, the music that gave a more truthful indication of her personality than did her physical appearance.

It seemed to him that he had been taken back years, to the first time he had encountered Tiger outside the restaurant, when he had been struck by the power and purity of *her* mind.

He found himself smiling at the girl in a genuine bid to put her at ease. She paused before the table, and he could see that her eyes were red from crying.

"You must be Tiger's sister," he said.

She nodded. "My name Sukara," she said in a small voice.

"Why don't you sit down and we can talk."

With painful timidity, she slipped into the seat that Rao had vacated, placed her hands on the table, and stared at her entwined fingers.

He ordered a lassi for the girl. When it came, she lifted the glass in both hands, leaving a moustache of white froth on her upper lip. She licked it off self-consciously, darting a glance at him.

In a barely audible whisper, she said, "Yesterday Dr. Rao, he tell me Tiger die. He tell me, you Tiger's special friend."

Vaughan found himself reaching across the table, covering her fingers with his hand. He wanted to do with the girl what he had never done with Tiger—use his augmentation-pin and dive into her vital mind, scan her identity, access her memories, and *know* the girl wholly. He had stopped himself from scanning Tiger for fear of becoming too close to her—and now, for the same reason, he could not bring himself to read Sukara's mental purity.

Intimacy, he told himself, *could only lead to pain.*

"I knew Tiger for around three years, Sukara, and I was with her when she died."

"She happy? She had good life?"

Vaughan smiled at Sukara in reassurance. "I think she had a better life begging here than she did working in Bangkok."

"She talk about me—Tiger tell you about big sister?"

How could he tell Sukara that Tiger had never spoken about her life in Thailand, reluctant to relive her memories of abuse at the hands of her customers?

"She said that she hoped you were well," he said.

Sukara was silent for a while, staring at Vaughan's hand on hers. At last she said, "When Tiger die, she feel no pain? She die peaceful?"

To spare the girl, Vaughan said that Tiger had died without pain and told her about the funeral attended by all her friends. Then, perhaps in a bid to assure Sukara, and himself, that she had had a good and full life, he told her how he had first encountered Tiger, how they had met regularly for years after that, sitting and chatting at this very booth. He told Sukara about her sister's infatuation with the Bengal Tigers, a skyball team, from which she had earned her nickname.

Sukara occasionally asked questions in her halting, broken English, and Vaughan did his best to answer truthfully, only lying where the truth would be too painful for the girl to bear.

She looked up at him. "Dr. Rao, he say, Tiger had bad leg, disease." She shook her head. "But I know: he cut off leg so she begs for him, so he get money, yes?"

Vaughan nodded. "Yes. Yes, that's what happened, and I know it sounds terrible. But Tiger wanted it that way, rather than having to go back to what she was doing in Bangkok."

She was quiet for a while. At last, her lips moved, but no sound came, or none that Vaughan could hear. Sukara looked up, something unreadable in her eyes as she stared at him. She tried again. "Did you . . . you sleep with Pakara?"

He could not tell whether she wanted him to answer in the affirmative, whether she would have been pleased that her sister had found a lover/protector/father figure, or if Sukara would have then despised him.

He shook his head. "I've used a drug called chora for five years," he told her. "I couldn't have slept with Tiger even if I'd wanted to. We were just friends, Sukara, good friends."

She smiled and nodded.

Vaughan changed the subject. "How did you get to the Station?"

She seemed reluctant to tell him. She stared up at him, her eyes as brown and large as Tiger's, as if assessing whether she might trust him. "Customer, he bring me. Buy me clothes . . ." She stopped, glanced down at his hand, still enclosing hers. "I think, he love me . . . He says, trust me, trust me . . . Then I see him go with other girl, young girl. He lie . . . He tell me, trust me, so I trust him, but he lie."

Vaughan watched her, aware of the beautiful tone of her mind, aware that he should offer words of sympathy, but afraid that if he did so she might think that he was offering more.

"Will you stay on the Station?"

She shook her head. "I don't know. Maybe." She glanced up at him, quickly, through her fringe. "I find work, somewhere live. I stay here. Make new life."

Vaughan nodded. "I hope you succeed." He hesitated. "Do you have enough money?"

255

She shrugged. "Some. Money I saved in Bangkok, money *he* gave me."

Vaughan reached into his pocket, unfolding the notes he had withdrawn from his second bank account that morning, to see him through the next month. He pushed a hundred-baht note across the table, and Sukara stared at it for long seconds before slipping it into the pocket of her shorts.

"Thank you," she whispered. "I go now."

Vaughan nodded.

Sukara said, "I go, say to customer, 'You lie, you go with girl, so goodbye.' I not stay with him, even if he begs."

Vaughan smiled, unable to bring himself to speak.

She glanced up at him again, that utterly vulnerable, pleading quick look through her fringe. "Mr. Vaughan . . . maybe I see you again? We meet here, like you and Tiger?"

He shrugged. "Maybe, Sukara," he said, and withdrew his hands from hers.

Her gaze downcast now, whispering an inaudible farewell, she slipped from the booth and hurried from the restaurant. Vaughan watched her go, something heavy and painful, easily identifiable as the incipient recognition of betrayal, expanding within his chest.

He ordered another beer and looked at his handset. It was four o'clock. He would give it another hour, until the sun was going down, and then leave and descend to the lair of the Vaith on level 12b. He considered it ironic that a week ago he had gone down there to be with the dying Tiger, and now he was going down to do the killing.

He sat alone and drank his beer and considered Sukara, wishing that he could have reached out and offered her hope, but knowing, because of who and what he was, that that would have been impossible.

EIGHTEEN

Sukara caught the New Mumbai Express north from Chandi Road. She sat beside the window and stared out at the passing streets and buildings, her fist clutched around the wadded hundred-baht note that Vaughan had given to her. She thought back over the meeting. Vaughan had done everything he could to make her feel at ease, and within minutes of meeting him she had received the impression that he was a good person. It was no wonder that Pakara had taken to him, and at the thought of her sister and her special friend, Sukara felt a strange, swift stab of jealousy. Right now, she would have given anything to have Vaughan as a friend—nothing more than that: she wasn't asking for love, or commitment, but just someone who would listen to her with sympathy. What she needed right now, she thought, was a friend.

When she had summoned the courage to ask him if he would see her again, she had been unable to interpret the look that had come into his eyes. It was as if she had struck him a blow. He had seemed pained, and at the same time almost pathetically grateful that she, Sukara, had wanted to see *him*. And yet his reply, an unsure, reluctant maybe, gave the impression that he would rather not get involved.

He was not the type of person she had first imagined when Dr. Rao had told her that Pakara had had a special friend. Sukara had expected someone older, and richer; someone more outgoing and at ease with the world. Vaughan had seemed . . . *haunted* was the first word that came to mind, haunted and beaten and on the verge of giving up. She wondered if he had suffered mental problems—there had been that strange look of frightened anguish in his eyes, contained there by mental effort and not allowed to infect his behavior. And yet his manner had been far from manic or obsessive: he was gentle and soft-spoken, almost, at times, seemingly on the verge of tears himself. She wondered if it had been Pakara's death that had affected him so badly.

She wished she had asked Vaughan more about himself, where he was from and why he was on the Station; what he worked as and where he lived. But perhaps, looking back on it, it was just as well that she hadn't been that inquisitive. He struck her as a lonely person, unused to talking about himself: she guessed that he would not have liked her questioning him. Maybe next time, maybe she would be able to ask him about himself when they met again.

As the train carried her away from Himachal sector and Vaughan, it was reassuring to know that someone who had known Pakara and grieved at her death was here to contact in the future.

Sukara looked ahead to her return to the hotel. She would pack her belongings and then tell Osborne that she was leaving. It would be hard to face him and tell him that she had seen him with the girl earlier, but it was something she had to do. She could pack and walk out without a word of explanation, avoid the emotional confrontation. But he had wronged her, he had taken her trust and betrayed her; he had taken from her mind what he had wanted and given nothing personal of himself in return. He had lied to her, and that had hurt. She could not let him get away without telling him what she thought of his betrayal.

At New Mumbai Station, Sukara left the train in a press

of commuters and crossed the street to the gates of the
Hotel Ashoka. The uncrowded, peaceful grounds seemed
like paradise after the chaotic hurly-burly of the streets. She
walked down the gravel drive, her heart thumping like a
drum. At reception she collected the door-card—which
meant that Osborne was still out—and rode the elevator to
the tenth floor. As she walked along the corridor, she re-
hearsed the words she would use to tell him that he was a
liar and that she was leaving for good. She repeated her best
lines over and over, but knew in her heart that when the
time came for her to use them, her mind would go blank
and she would shout and cry like a child.

She unlocked the door and entered the room, found her
backpack, and began stuffing her clothes into it. The new
clothes, the dresses Osborne had bought her, she left on the
bed; they had made her look silly, anyway. She packed her
t-shirts and skirts and underwear. She fastened the backpack and sat on it in the middle of the room, so that he
would see her as soon as he entered, and know that something was wrong; know, she hoped, that she had seen him
with the girl. She hoped that he would not be wearing his
pin when he entered the room, so that she would have time
to tell him what she thought of him and get away—before
he had the chance to read her and see that, alongside the
hate she felt toward him, she felt love also, and the need to
be loved in return.

She sat there, defiant, for ten minutes, twenty. She got
up, wandered around the suite. She stopped in the middle
of the lounge, considering. Soon she would be on her own
in a strange place, with only her savings, the dollars
Osborne had given her, and Vaughan's gift of a hundred
baht to keep her going. On the drinks cabinet, beside the
bottle of bourbon he had brought with him, was a pile of

259

Station currency, baht and rupees, along with over a hundred American dollars. She scooped the notes from the cabinet and stuffed them into the pockets of her shorts. She would be out of here before he noticed it missing. And, anyway, he was rich and would not miss the money.

She moved to the window and peered out. She would wait another five minutes, and if he had not returned by then she would just walk out. She returned to her backpack, sat down, and counted off the minutes on her watch.

At exactly five minutes she stood and returned to the window, looking down at the extensive grounds. She was about to move off, shoulder her pack and leave, when she saw him. Her stomach lurched sickeningly. He was striding through the grounds toward the entrance. She hurried over to her pack, hauled it onto her shoulder, and stood facing the door, waiting for what seemed like hours.

At last she heard the handle turn, watched the door swing open. Osborne stepped inside. He stopped when he saw her, displaying his easy smile.

At the sight of him, she knew that she could not leave. The feel of his arms about her, his lips hot on the top of her head, returned to her; she recalled his promises, that they would be together forever, and she began to weep.

She let her pack slip from her shoulder and stared at him through her tears. "You lie!" she wailed. "You betray me! I saw you today, I saw you with girl! You go to hotel!"

For a second Osborne was speechless, then: "Su . . . Su—she was no one. She doesn't matter to me. Su, you're the only—"

"You fuck girl, not me. You think I'm ugly. You lie! You betray me." She was sobbing now, her words hardly coherent. She gestured to her pack. "So I come back, pack up. I leave you."

Osborne looked stricken: his eyes widened in panic and he rushed toward her, took her in his arms, and hugged her to him. She tried to resist his embrace, tried not to find solace in the strength of his arms. "No! Christ, please, no— you don't understand. The other girls . . . they don't matter, only you . . ."

She slumped against him and sobbed. "I no understand! I want to leave, I want to stay—I want to understand!"

He fumbled in the pocket of his suit, and she knew he was looking for his pin. He found the case, opened it clumsily, and drove the pin into the back of his head.

She knew with a sudden, burning shame that all her thoughts, her very identity, was now open to him. She hated his knowing how vulnerable and afraid she was.

He just stared at her, an expression of amazement crossing his face. His reaction to scanning her anger, pain, and sense of betrayal, shocked her. He laughed in disbelief at something he had found in her head.

Then he grabbed her shoulders and shook her. "Where is he now?" he yelled. It was as if, upon using his augmentation-pin, he had become someone else.

"Where is who—?" She stared at this suddenly transformed Osborne.

"The man you call Vaughan! Where?" And he slapped her across the face, backhanded, knocking her to the floor. He knelt beside her, grabbed her chin, and turned her face to his.

She gagged, shocked and sickened.

He stared into her eyes, into her mind, found what he wanted, and pushed her away. He rushed into the connecting bedroom. From her position on the floor, Sukara saw him pull a case from beneath the bed, open it, and take things out, slip them into his jacket. Then he closed the case and returned it beneath the bed and came back into the lounge.

He knelt beside her again, and she flinched at the expectation of further blows. Instead, he reached out and thumbed the tears from her cheeks. "Su . . . I'm sorry, I'm so sorry. I'll explain, okay? I'll come back and explain, and then we'll be together, just the two of us, no more chasing about, no more . . ." He stopped himself, stood, and hurried from the room.

Sukara lay on the floor, weeping with pain and confusion. She pushed herself to her feet and stood unsteadily, ran into the bedroom, and knelt on the floor beside the bed. She reached underneath, fumbled for the case, and found it. She pulled it out, tried the catches. The case was locked. In anger and rage she grabbed the case by its handle and swung it again and again at the wall. On the sixth blow, the catches broke. She collapsed onto the floor and opened the lid.

Three hollow, gun-shaped recessions, one small pistol still in place . . . Then she saw, in a pocket in the lid of the case, the graphic and a news-fax sheet. She pulled out the graphic. Vaughan . . . but a younger Vaughan, standing beside a younger version of Osborne. Sukara stared at the image of Vaughan, smart and handsome, and tried to reconcile this vision with the man she had seen at Nazruddin's . . . Then her eyes strayed to the news-fax sheet. She pulled it out.

Sukara tried to scream, found her throat constricted. Blood pounded through her head, blurring her vision.

She reached for the case, pulled the pistol out, fumbled with the chamber until it snapped open. The gun was loaded with a dozen bullets. She was about to close the case when she saw something else: a golden pendant, identical to the one that Osborne was never without—a spare mind-shield?

Quickly she looped it around her neck. If she were to follow him, then she would have to be shielded . . . The thought of what she was about to do filled her with terror.

Sobbing, she pushed herself to her feet and ran through into the lounge. She grabbed a jacket, struggled into it, and concealed the pistol in the pocket.

The news-fax had shown the pictures of the eight young white girls murdered in Bangkok. Beneath each pix, fixed into place with a strip of tape, was a curl of blonde hair.

She ran to the window and stared out. Osborne was a tiny shape, striding through the grounds of the hotel toward the taxi-flier rank.

Sukara ran from the room and down the corridor to the elevator, barging into people and walls in panic and desperation.

She reached the flier rank just as the vehicle carrying Osborne screamed off along the street, climbing. She hauled open the door of the next flier in line and commanded the pilot to follow the flier in front.

Clutching the pistol beneath her jacket, Sukara wept quietly to herself.

NINETEEN

Vaughan left Nazruddin's as the sun was setting and the lights were coming on down Chandi Road. From a hardware store opposite the restaurant he bought a hammer-gun and slipped it into his backpack beside the grenades. He left the store and turned right, toward the train station, then right again along the road leading to the spaceport. When he came to the back alley, he slipped from the crowd and hurried past containers overflowing with rubbish and restaurant scraps, his progress through the twilight scattering rats ahead of him.

He came to a door in a windowless polycarbon building, familiar from Commander Sinton's memory. He tried the handle; not surprisingly, it was locked. He removed the hammer-gun from the case and applied it to the lock. When a flier roared overhead, covering any sound he might make, he pulled the trigger. The gun beat at the door with a quick, percussive blast. He kicked it open and stepped inside. He hurried down a long corridor, his way illuminated by a skylight high overhead. When he came to the first door on the left, he opened it and passed into a cavernous, empty warehouse; the photon tubes from the street outside washed the chamber in splashes of garish red and blue.

Vaughan crossed to an empty packing crate and pushed it aside, knelt, and hauled up the inspection cover. The worn rungs of a metal ladder fell away in the gloomy perspective of the narrow shaft, illuminated every five metres by an orange light of low wattage. He sat on the edge of the shaft, lowered himself into the confines, and began the long descent.

The repetitive, mechanical motion of stepping down time after time, of watching his hands move from rung to rung, was both physically and mentally tiring. Every ten minutes he stopped to rest, peering down beyond his heels at the seemingly never-ending drop. He moved slowly past the levels, the mind-hum of the inhabitants waxing and waning as he went.

The muscles of his calves and thighs spasmed with pain. He stopped suddenly, peering up into the receding shaft: he thought he'd heard something high overhead, but dismissed the idea.

He flexed his legs, took a breath, and began his descent once more, increasing his pace. He wanted to get the job over with, wanted to get back to the upper-deck and resume something resembling a normal life.

He considered the Vaith. He recalled Essex's memory of it: a shelled thing with tentacles and pincers, like some kind of monster squid or crustacean. Yet to Commander Sinton the Vaith had appeared as a shimmering force of energy, a bold and upright biped sheathed in a coruscating armature of electric blue and silver highlights . . . Vaughan wondered how it might manifest itself to him.

He looked down beyond his heels and was surprised to see, in the dwindling distance, a pool of light that marked the end of the shaft. He reached it within minutes and found himself on a narrow catwalk between two great curving sheets of riveted steel, like the interior of some impossibly narrow and ludicrously long submarine. At fifty-meter intervals, glow-tubes provided meager illumination. He paused beneath the mouth of the shaft, listening. He thought he'd heard, again, a sound from up above, but

when he peered back up the shaft he saw nothing but the
ladder and the lights receding into the blur of the distant,
circular vanishing point. He slipped his augmentation-pin
into his skull console and scanned, but caught nothing. He
told himself that he was being paranoid; if he listened carefully he could make out all manner of creakings and
twangings as the metal of the Station expanded and con-
tracted.

He checked Sinton's memory of the route, then began
walking east. After the strain of taking the weight of his
body on his ankles and wrists, this stretch of the trek was a
relief. He judged that he was in the vicinity of level 14, with
just two more levels to go before he reached level 12b, the
narrow, interstitial deck which years ago had been the
upper-deck. He considered the bustling activity that had
once swarmed across the long built-over deck, now deserted
and dusty like some forgotten ghost town. It was an appropriate place of concealment for the human-eating alien.

At intervals along the catwalk, sturdy columns passed
through the curved iron plate on Vaughan's right. He
counted ten of these, came to the column daubed innocently
enough with a splash of red paint, marking the next point of
descent. In the column was a rectangular hatch. He opened
it and was about to step inside when a sound—a footfall?—
echoed along the corridor. He stopped, one leg inside the
column, and stared back along the way he had come. It was
deserted, quiet. He scanned again. The mind-noise from the
citizens of the tenth level filled his head, but there was no
single mind-signature in the immediate vicinity. He waited a
minute, but heard, saw, and sensed nothing. He climbed
into the column and resumed the descent.

In the depths of Sinton's dying mind he had accessed
memories of where the other Vaith were located. Sinton had

not known their specific whereabouts, but Vaughan had read that one was in New York and the other in Madrid. Sinton and his cell on the Station had organized the transportation of the Vaith from Verkerk's World to Bengal Station, and their through-passage to Europe and America. After that, Disciples in Madrid and New York had taken responsibility for the concealment of their gods. The other three, each on a far-flung colony world, Sinton had known nothing about.

Vaughan considered his course of action once he had eliminated this Vaith. He had no will to continue the pursuit of the creatures himself; he hoped that there would be enough specific evidence to convince the authorities of the threat posed by the aliens and their Disciples.

The column ended and gave onto another enclosed catwalk. He was almost there. He walked along the corridor for fifty metres and paused, looking for the inspection cover in the grid-metal before him. He found it, indistinct in the shadows between the irregular lighting. He knelt and hauled open the trap door. A ladder dropped into a dark pit he knew to be the interstice between levels 13 and 12. He lowered himself down the ladder, then paused and looked around. The only illumination came from above, a hazy cone of light picking him out like a theatre spotlight, and from a tiny arc-light in the far distance.

Using the arc-light as a reference point, like a sailor in ancient times navigating by the pole star, Vaughan headed toward a point five degrees to the right of the light. The air this deep in the Station was saturated with humidity, a barely breathable mix of grease and dust. Aware that his every step echoed in the cavernous chamber, he made his way across the uneven deck, stepping over raised flanges in the deck, once or twice almost tripping. The arc-light was deceptively distant; he had been walking for five minutes and still it seemed no nearer.

As he approached his destination, it occurred to him for the first time what failure here might mean, not only to himself, but to the innocent victims of the Vaith both on the Station and elsewhere. He was the only person aware of the truth of what was happening with the aliens and their Disciples. Perhaps he should have left notification of his findings with someone in authority before setting out, or perhaps personally told someone in power what was going on . . . But the fact was that he could not bring himself to trust anyone in power: he knew, through Sinton, the identities of the other Disciples in Sinton's cell—but what if more than one cell existed on the Station? He told himself that what he was doing was the only course of action.

According to what Sinton knew, the chamber containing the Vaith was fashioned to be undetectable, cleverly constructed between bulkheads like some optical illusion made physical, and sealed with a concealed combination lock. To this point he had not given much thought to the possibility that the Vaith might possess the means to defend itself, or to attack. He had thought of it as an inert, indolent beast, reliant upon the work of its mind-drugged human Disciples to ensure its continued existence. He did not even know what the creature really looked like.

Only now, as he approached the arc-light, did he begin to doubt himself.

Ahead, he made out the bulkhead, apparently marking the extent of the chamber. Only when he approached the base flange of the wall did he see the evidence of the black paint daubed over the rivets to disguise their recent installation. The entire wall of metal had been erected ten metres in front of the original bulkhead, creating a cavity behind which the creature lay.

Vaughan scanned, and instantly the distant minds above and below sprang into his awareness. He did his best to edit them from his consciousness. He concentrated, scanning beyond the bulkhead for the signature of any Disciple left to guard the Vaith. He sensed nothing.

He was aware, however, of the presence of the alien being. It was a low-level emanation up ahead, very much like the nebulous consciousness of an animal, though so utterly alien that his mind had difficulty grasping it.

He opened his backpack and pulled out the grenades one by one and slipped them into his pockets.

He approached the bulkhead. He could see no entrance hatch. He looked into Sinton's memories again and made out a seam of metal that ran down the bulkhead from top to bottom; halfway down, the case of an old fire alarm concealed the lock. He stepped forward and pushed the case aside to reveal a key pad of numerals. He typed in the combination and stood back.

A rectangular section of the wall, edged in what looked like rust to conceal the join, swung back into the chamber. He stepped into the darkness, reached to his left, and found the switch on the inside of the wall. Electric blue light filled the chamber, dazzling him.

He stooped, peered through the hatch. He knew what to expect from Sinton's memory, but the reality was even more impressive. He made out what appeared to be the nave of a cathedral.

Wiping the sweat from his palms, and using his jacket to dry the grenade he carried, he moved further into the chamber. He stared about him in wonder at the transformation from the darkness outside to this light-filled place of worship.

It was laid out in the archetype of classic ecclesiastical

design; pews were ranked on either side of a central aisle, and on each flanking wall was a series of imitation stained-glass windows showing scenes of Verkerk's World: on one side, views of the mountains, the falls, the sea; and on the other, interior scenes of the Geiger Caves.

Ahead, above the altar, was the most impressive graphic of all. Vaughan found himself walking down the aisle like a supplicant. The icon, an idealized representation of Elly Jenson, the Chosen One, stared down at him with the wide and innocent eyes of a martyr, her full lips parted as if in benediction.

Only then did Vaughan remember why he was here. He turned his attention to what stood beneath the graphic of the Chosen One. Behind the altar was the container, twenty metres long, four wide, and four again high—a great oval etched in a pattern of whorls and curlicues.

He was hit then by the force of the alien mind, no longer shielded. He felt the rush of euphoria, realised that the Vaith was using his psi-ability to contact him. He experienced the desire to join the One that he had first experienced in the Holosseum, the overwhelming urge, both physically and mentally, to rush forward and become united with that which he knew he had been seeking all his life.

He stepped forward, and it was as if by doing so he had impelled his movement with momentum, so that he could not stop now, but must continue to advance, seeking union with the force that called.

At the same time, he was aware of the danger. He knew that in an instant he could stop himself from being dragged to his death: all he had to do was remove the pin from his console and the call would cease . . . and yet he did not do so because he was curious, fascinated by the nature of the beast that was drawing him ever closer.

He stopped himself, bracing his arms against a pew, staring at the etched, oval casing that contained the Vaith, and he sent out a probe, scanning.

He felt himself diving through the bizarre layers of consciousness in the mind of the Vaith. He encountered emotions that had no equivalent, and others that did, a strange and piquant joy—a combination of the celebration of life and at the same time the knowledge that all life must end— a rage, an anger so fierce that he was repulsed, stunned. He came upon memories, visual images of a hundred, a thousand, differing landscapes—the Geiger Caves among them—and tried to understand the importance of these myriad landscapes to the Vaith, but failed.

And then the alien spoke to him, or rather did not speak but utilized his mind in such a way as to organize thoughts and images to make it seem to Vaughan that it was speaking.

>>>*You do not believe, and yet you of the many who have come to me, you in the very core of your soul, wish to believe.*

Vaughan responded with thoughts of his own, screaming: *No! That's not true! I know the truth, and the truth is oblivion, not the false promise you would wish us to accept.*

>>>*Come, come . . . Your life is one of torment, Vaughan—or should that be Lepage? You are torn asunder within, riven by the tragedy of past events, so that even you do not know your true identity . . .*

He thought: *I am Vaughan! Lepage is dead, no more, gone!*

>>>*You wish him gone. You cannot live with the thought of his deeds. You have been trying to atone for them ever since—*

He thought-screamed at the alien: *I will kill you!*

The Vaith responded with something very much like a good-humored chuckle. >>>*But you cannot do that, Vaughan-Lepage. You cannot kill us. We are indestructible . . .*

Vaughan thought: *What are you?*

>>>I am but one of a much greater whole.

You are a monster, a devouring, evil—

>>>Because we take sustenance from those we consider inferior to ourselves? But Vaughan-Lepage, do you not do the same? Humanity devours lower life-forms without a qualm. We Vaith do the very same . . . and give you much, much more in return.

You could restrict yourself to the animals you once lured on Verkerk's World, without resorting to devouring intelligent beings—

>>>Vaughan-Lepage, we do not merely take humans for the physical sustenance that they provide. We are an inquisitive species. We absorb the pure food of the mind, we feed on knowledge. *Why else do you think we came to Earth? Your culture fascinates us; we sampled something of it on Verkerk's World, but the inhabitants there were a simple and unsophisticated people; we craved a greater understanding of your race.*

You are immoral!

>>>What is immoral? We merely follow the demands of our biology, of our thirsting need for knowledge. Over the millennia we have absorbed the knowledge of thousands of races more advanced than yourselves.

Vaughan thought: *And they let you? Not one of them protested and put an end to your games?*

>>>Vaughan-Lepage . . . You fail to understand. For their knowledge, the physical knowledge they possessed of their world and sciences and cultures, we traded the ultimate knowledge, the knowledge of the

*truth that underlies this physical reality, the knowl-
edge of what awaits us when we pass from the physical to the non-physical. We are an ancient race. For
billions of your years we have meditated upon the secrets of the universe, both the physical and the spiri-
tual. We have come to understand the nature of what
underlies the physical world, we have come to commune with God, and at the same time find the physical
world a constant source of wonder and marvel . . .*

Vaughan responded: *I do not believe in your ultimate truth!
I have seen what happens when we die! I have experienced the
oblivion that awaits . . .*

>>>Vaughan-Lepage, the Vaith thought with something like great pity, *what you experienced with your
minuscule, paltry human psi-ability was no more
than the mechanical dysfunction of the human brain
as the machine of the body closed down and died . . .
What you could not experience with your ability is the
human soul as it takes wing and departs to the One.*

Vaughan experienced at once rage and a terrible doubt:
No! No, I cannot believe that!

*>>>Over the millennia, many races—the more en-
lightened at any rate—were willing to believe, and to
trade with us—others, more materialistic or primitive, rebelled and destroyed members of our species,
just as you intend to do . . .*

Intend? Vaughan could not keep the angry humor from
his thoughts. *Intend? I* will *kill you—*

*>>>But you cannot. Oh, you might kill the creature
with which you now communicate, but I am but one of
a greater unit—*

Vaughan thought: *I will kill you, and then we will find the
Vaith in America and Europe and on the colony planets and we*

will eradicate them also. It might take time, but we will defeat you!

>>>Have you been listening to nothing I have told you, Vaughan-Lepage? The Vaith replied with patient sadness: *We are part of a much greater whole. We number in our thousands, flung far and wide across the galaxy, on planets yet to be discovered by human-kind. The knowledge taken in by myself and my colleagues on Earth becomes shared knowledge among all of us, just as their knowledge of alien ways and means becomes mine. You might destroy me, you might destroy the Vaith on Earth and on your colonies, but by then our work will be complete, we will have knowledge of you . . . and in return we would dearly like to grant you the truth, but it seems that as a race you are too young and ignorant . . .*

And the Vaith seemed to open its mind, then, to flood Vaughan with some intimation of the rapture that awaited him, the soul-opening unity into which, if the alien was to be believed, all creatures conjoined . . .

Vaughan gasped in awe and wonder, at once wanting to believe and yet not allowing himself the luxury. He fell to his knees, reaching for his augmentation-pin, his movements impossibly slow and prolonged.

Then he saw, staring down at him, the martyred face of the Chosen One, and in his mind she became Holly, and he was taken back twenty years to Ottawa, and this time in the seconds before her death she spoke to him: "Believe the Vaith, for it is true; I am alive and One . . ."

He tried to raise his hand to his head, but it was as if it were being held. He felt himself drawn forward on his knees, dragged toward the lair of the Vaith. As he watched, its near surface folded upwards to reveal the content of the case, and suddenly he could see the Vaith, calling him . . .

It was a writhing mass of pink torsos, each one a young blonde girl, each one with the perfect features and piercing blue eyes of Holly, and they were beckoning him, gesturing with alluring smiles and waves for him to join them.

>>>*Do not torture yourself for what happened all those years ago, Vaughan-Lepage. The past is over and dead. Only the truth remains, the One of which we are part. Absolve yourself and join us in the One . . .*

And a part of him, that part of him which had hated himself for so many years, had used the guilt like a sword on which to throw himself, now that part of him could not accede to the demands of the hydra-Holly.

He knew, then, that to kill himself in atonement for his guilt would be too easy; he knew that he had to suffer.

>>>*Come to me, Vaughan-Lepage. Come, join the One . . .*

With incredible effort he plunged the primer on the grenade in his hand, and did the same with a second and third. Then he pressed the red button on the first grenade and tossed it into the writhing mass of the illusion. He threw the second and the third grenades and dived for cover behind the nearest pew.

The explosion deafened him, rocked the chamber, and swept the pews across the church like so much matchwood. Vaughan tumbled with the wave of the blast as if caught in a typhoon of heat. He came to rest and looked up, and the silver container was an empty, shattered shell, and all around the chamber were the remains—the bloody strips of tegument, shards of claw and chitin—of the god the church had been built to worship.

As he lay in the tumble of broken pews, battered and bloody, Vaughan wondered if he would have gone ahead and destroyed the Vaith if he had not known that out there, scattered across the galaxy, were yet more of the mighty creatures.

He lay very still in the silent aftermath of the explosion, afraid to move in case he increased the pain that wracked his body. At last, the weight of the pew that crushed his legs becoming too much, he reached out carefully and pushed it away. The noise of the falling wreckage crashed like a blasphemy in the silence of the church. He flexed his leg; it appeared undamaged. He took stock of his injuries—flesh wounds and a lot of blood, but apparently no broken bones. Cautiously he sat up, climbed to his feet.

Only then did he see the tall figure standing just inside the entrance of the church.

Osborne wore his long black coat, the same one he had worn all those years ago, with the collar turned up in a manner both cool and Mephistophelean. He was smiling his lazy smile at Vaughan's shock.

As he stared, Osborne reached into his coat and pulled something from around his neck. He tugged, and the chain snapped. He held the golden oval in his hand, smiling at Vaughan.

"Osborne?" Vaughan began.

"It's my shield," he said, smiling. "I want you to read my pain, Vaughan!"

He tossed the shield away from him, and Vaughan could not help but scan the man's tortured mind. He saw images of Holly, read Osborne's twisted grief—and accessed other images, too: grisly images of Holly-lookalikes—

Almost shouting out in pain, Vaughan pulled the pin from his skull and dropped it, and instantly the assassin's feverish mind-noise became bearable.

Osborne pushed himself from the jamb of the entrance and took a step or two forward. "It's been a long time,

Lepage—or should that be . . . Vaughan?"

"How did you find me?"

"I always find my quarry, Vaughan. You should know that. I haven't failed yet. And do you know something else? I rather think that you wanted me to find you."

The sight of Osborne took him back to their last mission. He was in the Air America office, the building deserted but for Osborne and himself. They were posing as customers, awaiting the arrival of the terrorists they knew had planned to hold up the office, take hostages. Vaughan had not been augmented that day; Osborne, in command, wore the pin and gave the orders. For the first time in years, detail returned to him: the thick crimson carpet, the smell of pine disinfectant in the air, the snow falling outside on the crisp winter's day.

A file of schoolchildren had paraded past the building . . .

Vaughan stared across the ruined church at Osborne, into the killer's black eyes.

Osborne said, "Why did you kill my daughter? Why did you kill Holly?"

Vaughan tried to shut out the memory, but it played nevertheless in his mind, would not be stopped.

They had been tense, nervous on that final mission all those years ago. The terrorist cell had killed before, ruthlessly and without mercy. Osborne's team was under instructions to kill first and ask questions later. The press and news media might kick up an outcry, but the government would stand by them.

Vaughan recalled the feel of the pulse-gun in his hand.

Someone had burst in through the plate glass door, running across the crimson carpet, shouting . . . Only later, a *second* too late, did he hear the cry: "Daddy! Daddy!"

Vaughan had swung round at the sound of the door crashing open, was firing before he could stop himself.

The pulse caught the little girl on the side of the head, ripping away half of her face and igniting her mass of golden hair in a brief, incandescent halo.

"Why did you kill my daughter?" Osborne repeated. "Why did you kill Holly?"

Vaughan reached out, almost pleading. "It was a terrible mistake, Osborne. You know that. Don't you think I've suffered?"

"*You* suffered? You don't know the meaning of the word. I have suffered hell over the years, Lepage. Hell . . ."

"The official report stated it was an accident. Don't you think I regretted what I did?"

"Don't talk to me about regret!"

He had been close to Osborne, then, and close to Osborne's daughter, Holly, too. The purity of her young mind had countered the cynicism and hatred he read every day in the minds of his fellow men. He had sought salvation from the innocence of the girl.

One month after the shooting, unable to go on, Vaughan had staged his disappearance, dropped out, knowing that Osborne would soon be on his trail, knowing that, sooner or later, Osborne would find him.

And years later Vaughan had found Tiger, whose purity of mind had matched that of Holly's . . .

He stared at Osborne, saw again the images of the children Osborne had killed for reasons too psychologically twisted to understand. He wept. His accidental shooting of Holly had set in motion a terrible cascade of tragedy, and he could not but help feel the weight of responsibility.

"The children . . ." he cried.

Osborne smiled. "They were how I came to terms with what you did," he said. "How could they live, when my daughter was dead?"

Vaughan knew then that Osborne had somewhere down the line slipped over the edge of sanity.

Osborne stepped forward. "I want to read you," the assassin replied. "I want to read your regret, your suffering. I want to know that you too went through hell."

"That's impossible," Vaughan said, his voice almost cracking. "Impossible. You know that . . ." Built into Vaughan's skull console was a shield, ensuring that the contents of his mind were unreadable.

Osborne smiled a terrible smile. "Is it?" he said.

"No . . ." Vaughan shook his head, disbelieving. "No, you can't!"

The assassin laughed. "Oh, but I can. I'm going to rip out your console and read you, Vaughan. And if that doesn't kill you . . ." Osborne smiled, "then when I've read you I'll take great delight in executing you. Now turn around!"

Vaughan considered running, but there was nowhere to go. This was the end, then—the end he had expected for so long.

He turned, as ordered. There was something almost fitting in meeting his end here, beneath the impassive gaze of the Chosen One. As he stared up at her, he saw that the explosion had ripped a hole in the graphic beneath the girl's right eye.

She seemed to be weeping tears of absolution for him.

Vaughan sensed Osborne behind him, and closed his eyes. He felt pain in the back of his head, a cleansing pain, and then nothing.

TWENTY

Sukara lowered herself from the ladder and stood in the half-darkness of the narrow corridor. Her pulse hammered in her ears. She was unable to control her shaking limbs. She clutched the smooth butt of the pistol in the pocket of her jacket, wondering if she would be able to summon the courage to use it. She knew she was consumed by a rage that would only be satisfied when she had shot Osborne dead, but she realised too that the desire to carry out the action and the ability to do so were two different things. She thought of his betrayal, what he had done to those eight— no, nine now—little girls, and convinced herself that whatever happened, she *had* to stop Osborne.

The burden of responsibility upon her was almost too much.

She leaned forward, listening. From up ahead she heard the faint ticking of footsteps. She began walking. Every five metres she paused, head cocked. When she failed to hear the footsteps, her heart set up a fearful pounding. She imagined that he had stopped, concealed himself, and was waiting until she caught up with him. What then? Would he think twice about shooting her?

Then she heard the tapping of the steps again, released a breath, and continued cautiously along the dusty corridor. Not for the first time she wondered what Vaughan was doing down here.

Coming in on the flier, she had seen Vaughan leave Nazruddin's. He had crossed the road and entered a shop, emerging minutes later. Then, Osborne had shown himself, stepping from concealment in the entrance of a store across the road. He had followed Vaughan at a distance. Sukara had frantically called to the driver to let her out, thrown a bundle of dollar notes at him, and jumped from the vehicle before it had touched down on the rank. She had dashed through the crowd, trying to keep Osborne in sight, then followed him down an alley and into a big, deserted building. From there she had tracked him by following the tiny, echoing sounds as he descended into the depths of the Station.

Now, in the distance, she made out an open trapdoor in the floor. She could no longer hear his footsteps. She approached the hinged, circular hatch cautiously, expecting him to jump out and shoot her. She crept up to the opening, peered down into an abyss of darkness. She listened. She could just make out, on the threshold of audibility, the distant sound of footsteps.

She sat on the rim of the opening and lowered herself through it. Her arms extended, supporting all her weight, she waved her legs and tried to reach the floor. Her feet encountered nothing. She wondered whether to let herself drop, wondered how far she might fall . . . The decision was made for her. Her fingers could no longer sustain her weight and she fell, giving a little cry of alarm.

She had fallen less than a meter, but even so she hit the deck hard and fell, rolling across the ground. She oriented herself, crouched, and peered into the gloom.

In the distance, a wedge of blue light spilled out into the blackness. As she watched, she made out the unmistakable shape of Osborne silhouetted against the light. She followed.

She judged that she had cut the distance between him and her by half when she was deafened by the ear-splitting detonation. The explosion thundered in the confined space, echoing on and on for what seemed like ages. She crouched, clamping her palms to her ears. Up ahead, beside the rectangular hatch in the bulkhead wall, Osborne was doing the same. Through the hatch, Sukara made out flying debris, heard the shrapnel pattering down in the quiet aftermath of the explosion.

Osborne approached the hatch. He stood there for a long time, peering in.

Sukara concealed herself behind a pillar and watched him. She pulled the pistol from her jacket and told herself that now was the time to use it. She should run up to him, while his attention was diverted, ram the pistol into his back, and pull the trigger. She touched the golden pendant around her neck, praying that it was working, shielding her thoughts from his mind.

Osborne deserved to die, she told herself, for what he did to all those innocent girls . . . Then she recalled the way he had held her the other night, the love he had professed he had felt for her, and the feeling his acceptance had nourished in her. How could she kill the first man who had ever loved her?

And then she was consumed by anger at his betrayal. All his words, his promises, his affection . . . all this had been so many lies. And he had taken her in, used and betrayed her . . .

Sukara moved from her place of concealment behind the pillar.

As she did so, Osborne chose that second to enter the chamber. She paused, her resolve drained by his sudden disappearance. She realised that she was trembling uncontrollably, and wondered what to do next. She knew she had to approach the source of the light, but was reluctant to let Osborne see her.

Then she heard the sound of conversation from within the chamber. She tried to make out the words, but all she could hear was the low rumble of male voices. Steeling herself, she crept across the deck to the hatch, and stopped.

The first thing she saw as she stared through the opening was the massive graphic of a girl, then a tumble of benches. It looked like a church, a church that had been bombed. Over everything she noticed a film of some oily substance, chunks of what looked like pale meat, shards of what might have been the chitinous casing of some great creature . . .

And then she saw Osborne and Vaughan.

They stood beneath the pix of the girl, facing each other. Vaughan was obviously injured, his clothing ripped and bloody. The aspect of the two men could not have been any more different: Osborne sophisticated in his long black coat, smug and confident, Vaughan defeated, the expression on his face that of a condemned man.

As Sukara watched, frozen, Vaughan turned his back to Osborne, as if acceding with all his soul to the *coup de grâce*.

Quickly, before she could act, Osborne stepped up to Vaughan. He lifted something, applied it to the base of Vaughan skull, and pulled the trigger.

Vaughan dropped, felled like a slaughtered ox.

As Sukara watched, Osborne knelt, reached out, and placed a hand on Vaughan's head. Then he pulled, hard, and something erupted with a gout of blood from the back of the dead man's skull.

Sukara screamed, rushed at Osborne. He turned, his expression turning from one of satisfaction to surprise. On his knees, staring up at her, he gathered himself. He saw the pendant hanging around her neck, and smiled.

Sukara held the pistol in both hands at arms length, determined that she would not miss.

"Su—you don't understand. Let me explain."

The pain in her was too much—and his words served only to strengthen her determination.

The first shot ripped through his shoulder, sending him spinning backwards across the floor. He fetched up on his back, staring up at her with such a look of injury and pain on his handsome face that she could only fire again, to wipe it out.

The second shot hit him in the stomach, opening a hole the size of her fist. His expression became one of agony. He raised the weapon he had used to kill Vaughan, aimed at her . . . then he looked at the gun and—a strange reaction that she came to understand only later—laughed. He threw it aside.

He smiled at her, that old, lopsided smile that had melted her heart just a day ago.

Sukara fired again, and again, closing her eyes with each shot and with each shot screaming out loud in pain.

Ten bullets, one each for the murdered girls, and one for Vaughan.

The pistol jammed, or she had used up all the bullets. She opened her eyes. Many of her shots had missed, but enough had hit the target.

Osborne lay on his back, his arm held out, stilled now, in what might have been a futile gesture of entreaty.

Sukara dropped the pistol. In a daze she moved across the deck to Vaughan. He lay face down, a gaping hole in the base of his skull. She made out a bloody mess of wires and miniaturized machinery hanging from the wound like some excised organ.

Sukara knelt beside him, weeping for Vaughan and for herself, and reached out to touch his body.

EPILOGUE

Silence absolute . . .

He tried to scan, but nothing came. He tried to send out a probe, but all around him was silence. He sensed it as a vast and endless plain, white with frost. In his confusion he thought he was on Verkerk's World again, north of Vanderlaan where he had first experienced the blessed balm of mind-silence. He relaxed, reveled in the calm and placid medium of the ineffable quiet that surrounded him: no mind-hum, no background noise at all. Just silence.

Then he recalled what had happened in the lair of the Vaith, the confrontation with the alien creature, and then with Osborne. He had faced the fact of his death with equanimity, with a certain sense that it was fitting he should go like this . . . He had had no complaints. He was quite prepared to die.

And yet he was alive.

Time passed. He thought perhaps that days had elapsed, but he was unable to tell. He phased in and out of consciousness. He was aware of people around him, doctors, nurses. They seemed distant, slowed down and blurred, as if viewed through some aqueous medium. He felt as though he were viewing the world through fathoms of ocean. At one point he was aware of a face staring down at him, a brown face, staring down at him in silence.

And then, all of a sudden, he awoke and knew that the days of semi-consciousness were over, that he would date his recovery from this morning. He was in a spartan hospital room, lying in bed, monitors attached to his body. Sunlight streamed through the open window.

The face was there again, staring at him.

"Jeff . . . don't be alarmed."

Patel . . . What was his first name? The 'port telepath, anyway, who had worked alternate shifts with Vaughan.

"What . . . what the hell?" There were so many questions that he did not know where to begin.

"It's okay, Jeff. Don't worry. You're okay now."

He thought of his confrontation with Osborne in the chamber. He had been quite prepared for death then, self-ishly . . . Who would have warned the world about the Vaith, if he had died?

"It's okay, Jeff. I've alerted the authorities. They've in-vestigated the Church of the Adoration, sent teams to the colony worlds where the Vaith were transported."

"Are they going to . . . ?"

"No," Patel replied, even before Vaughan had finished the question. "They've assembled a team of experts. They're going to study the Vaith, try to learn the truth of their claims."

"And New York, Madrid . . . ?"

"All sorted, Vaughan. Don't worry."

Vaughan nodded. He considered the Vaith, the human Disciples like Dolores Yandoah and Sinton. How wonderful it would be to have faith, to believe that there was more to existence than mere life and death. He thought of Holly and Tiger . . .

But he had seen the oblivion toward which the dead travelled. How could he put aside what he knew to be true, merely because to believe in something would ease his con-science, heal his pain?

"How . . . how did I get here?"

Patel shook his head. "We don't know. You were found unconscious in casualty. We assumed at first that you'd brought yourself in, but the extent of your injuries . . ."

Patel went on, responding to some inquiry nascent in Vaughan's mind: "Your occipital console was removed by Osborne. There was some damage to your cerebellum. With luck you should make a full recovery."

He thought of Osborne. The man had torn out his console-shield, so that he might read Vaughan's remorse, his guilt at what he had done all those years ago. And, having read how truly sorry Vaughan was, had Osborne stayed the execution, shown uncharacteristic compassion and delivered him to the hospital?

Patel was shaking his head. "No, Jeff. We found Osborne's body in the secreted chamber, after I read you. He'd been shot dead."

"Then . . . then who brought me here? Who shot Osborne and brought me here?"

Patel could not answer that, and soon Vaughan relapsed into unconsciousness.

Days passed.

Vaughan regained control of his limbs. He was aware of the pain in his head, the wound where his console had been removed. But it was a tolerable pain compared to that of the mind-noise he had endured for years, and the surgeons and physiotherapists assured him that in time it would abate.

He was sitting up in bed, staring through the window at the hospital gardens and enjoying the silence, when a nurse peered round the door. "Are you up to seeing a visitor, Mr. Vaughan?"

A visitor? He wondered who might wish to visit him.

The nurse disappeared, to be replaced by the small figure of a shy young girl. He recognised Tiger's sister, but he could not remember her name.

He recalled their first meeting at Nazruddin's, and how the music of her mind had caused him both pleasure and pain. Now, without his ability to assess people by the emanations of their minds, he was like a man bereft of a sense he had relied upon all his life.

She hovered near the door, almost as if she might hurry away if he said the wrong thing.

She wore a short skirt, and a red t-shirt, and the very vocabulary of her body language, the way she tipped her head forward, held her right hand nervously to her lips, declared that she felt ashamed of the scar that bisected her face.

He wondered if he should speak, or smile. He smiled.

She responded like a flower opening to the sun. She smiled herself, and took courage, and entered the room. In almost a whisper she said, "Hello."

He found it hard to know what to say, to know what she wanted him to say. Without his ability, he realised, he had no way of judging her mood, no way of even guessing what she might be thinking.

He recalled her name. "Sukara," he said. "It's good to see you."

She smiled again quickly, shyly.

"Sit down," he said.

Obediently, she sat.

They faced each other like actors in a play, bereft of script. The silence stretched awkwardly.

Then she said, in a voice so small that he could hardly hear her: "I wonder if you okay. I come see you."

"I'm fine, Sukara. Who told you I was here?"

She frowned, a gesture that made her face quite pretty.

"No one told me. I bring you here."

He stared at her. "You?" he said.

She frowned again, struggling to summon the words to describe what had happened. "I . . . I find out Osborne evil man, do bad things. He want to kill you. I follow him, under Station. I hear explosion. I see you. I see him shoot you here, in head. I think you dead. I shoot Osborne, for all he did . . ."

"Hey, hey—slow down. Start again, slowly, from the beginning. You said you knew Osborne . . . ?"

She nodded. "I knew him—"

"How? How did you meet him?"

"In Bangkok. In Siren Bar, where I worked. He come, take me away . . ."

Vaughan listened to her story, stopping her from time to time to clarify a point, ask questions. He listened, attempting to see past her words and gestures to the person behind those words.

Sukara fell silent. She sat staring at her fingers entwined in her lap, unable to look up at him.

From the pocket of her shorts she pulled a scrap of paper, and with a much-chewed stylus she wrote an address in big, childish handwriting.

"I stay in Chandi Road now. Try to find work. Maybe sometime we meet for coffee, beer, yes?" She looked up at him, her eyes large, almost imploring.

He took the address, but could not bring himself to agree.

As if at his lack of response, she said, "Okay . . . I go now."

And before he could stop her she sprang to her feet, almost knocking over the chair in her haste, and hurried from the room.

Vaughan lay in bed and stared after her, going over their

meeting, and thinking about the future.

He recovered slowly over the course of the next few days. The pain in his head diminished and he sat for hours in a chair beside the window, staring out at the sunlit greensward that fell away to the edge of the Station.

Life would be different from now on. He had been granted the balm of mind-silence—he was no longer beset by the clamorous din of the minds of those around him . . . but it had come at a cost.

He had never really realised how much he had used his ability to judge people—he had taken it for granted. Now people came to him, nurses and doctors and officials from the police, and he had no way of assessing the essence of these people, their goodness or otherwise.

It came to him that if he wished to function in society, then he would have to learn how to read people anew in the same way as did normal, non-telepathic human beings . . . and to do that, of course, he would have to socialize.

He considered his past, Holly and Tiger. He considered the children Osborne had killed, because of him.

It came to him, quite suddenly and with something of a shock, that he needed to talk to someone about what he had done.

He remembered the address Sukara had given him. He sat in the sunlight for a long time, staring at her big, loopy handwriting.

He knew he should, for his own sake, contact her. But something stopped him, some awareness that every other relationship he had ever experienced had ended in failure.

He sat and listened to the silence.

How could he live in a world of total silence, without contact of any kind?

He raised his handset and tapped out the code of the cheap hotel where she was staying.

Minutes later Sukara stared up at him from the tiny screen.

"Hello," she said, shyly.

"Hello," Vaughan said.

The sunlight felt warm on his face.

ABOUT THE AUTHOR

ERIC BROWN, born in 1960, is the author of sixteen books, including science fiction novels, collections, and books for children. His first book was *The Time-Lapsed Man and Other Stories* (1990), and his first novel *Meridian Days* (1992). He has published over seventy-five short stories in magazines and anthologies in England and America, and has twice won the BSFA best short story of the year award. His latest novels are *New York Nights* and *New York Blues*, the first two volumes in the Virex Trilogy. *New York Dreams*, the concluding book, is due out in the UK later this year. He is married to the writer and medievalist Finn Sinclair and they live in Haworth, West Yorkshire, England. His website is: ericbrownsf.port5.com.